GROUND ME

TRAVIS D LYNCH

First edition 2025
ISBN: 979-8-218-61302-0

GROUND ME

A Novel by Travis D Lynch

Chapter One

"Welcome to the morning strut. I'm your host, Tom Timbers, with the news. It's a gorgeous morning out today with temps in the thirties and climbing through the day with a high of forty-three degrees Fahrenheit. So, the commute should be a little more tolerable than last week. First up on the report: Meta-human incidents are down 12% from last year. It shows much improvement as meta crimes have dwindled to almost non-existent levels compared to two years back. Terrorism became the leading cause of death next to heart disease that year. With Congress's involvement in curbing the meta epidemic, we can feel a little safer knowing that Apex Operatives are actively making a stand. For those who missed the proceedings, Apex was enforced as a task force dedicated to seeking and detaining meta-human anomalies." A montage of video recorded feats flash across the screen. Apex operators displaying super-human feats as they capture their targets. One particular operative takes the majority of the screen time is Trailblazer, a speedster meta-human imbued with the element of fire. Other operatives like Northstar, levitate to survey from the sky. Each one of them were trained

specifically to detain targets in inaccessible environments, land, and air. Tom Timbers continues, " If it wasn't for the brave meta-humans from Apex, the Chicagoland area would still be a warzone."

The television hums as a commercial played.

"When are you going to get a job?" Grandma asked as she spooned her gravy thoroughly. She didn't make eye contact as she did. I tapped the table with the hilt of my fork. Considering she mush be tired seeing me home all the time. We sat at the dining table, like every morning as we enjoy the light coming through the window and breakfast spread. Biscuits and Gravy, eggs, sausage and black coffee.

I looked up to answer, "When the job agency calls, I'm sure they'll have something good for me." I gave her a mournful eyeful and said, "Do you want me to go out there and run into a meta-human? I remember the neighbor boy!" I sat pondering the name, "Tony! He ran into a meta and lost his eyes for his trouble. Turned a corner at the pharmacy downtown, and ran right into one."

Grandma starred grieffully, "I never heard of anything like that here. You think a town this small that everyone wouldn't know if one of *them* were hanging around."

Meta-humans caused a lot of trouble two years back when regular folk started showing up with strange abilities. It was happening all over the world. like a light switch the flicked on, and all of a sudden, meta-humans existed. Granted, In this little town there was nothing. There wasn't a single meta sighting in this town. With a stern look, she stared into my eyes.

"It's been a year, Charlie, you heard the news—There's nothing out there to worry about. The Good Lord will see to that." She spun her fork as she smashed her hard-boiled egg onto toast, then looked to the window next to us. "We'll make it. Like always. But that doesn't give you an excuse to sit upstairs for the rest of your life."

"It's still going to take a long while before everything goes back to normal. I mean, the ordinances are still in place around town—They still check for metas everyday in the stores, and a few job sites. There's got to be a good reason for it." I leaned in closer over the table. "I still can't believe that just because they get some sort of strange abil-ity, they immediately go on a rampage and start killing. I mean, do they get rabies?"

"The world is just going crazy, if you ask me. The Bible said this would happen. Nostradamus too." She pointed her fork at me and gave another stern look. "I might not be around when it all happens... But *you*! You'll see it. Then all the people will know."

I rolled my eyes. "Grandma, you know what they say in the Bible isn't *all*..." I paused because a growing strain in my vocal cords kept me from saying the words. "What... What I'm trying to say is, there are so many versions of that book, and don't forget the different translations. Who's to say what's real or not?" I said, shoveling a gravy-covered piece of biscuit into my mouth.

Grandma dropped her fork into her plate and started at me with her finger waggin' my direction. "I served the Lord ever since I was a little girl. I know for a fact that God was there in my life when I needed him." She stood up and swiped her plate from the table, then shuffled toward the kitchen sink with heavy steps. "You got to *believe*, Charlie. You don't see him, but he's all around us."

While scrapping my plate of leftover gravy, I said, "There's nothing wrong with believing in what you don't see, but everything we see is what matters... I can't ask God questions and expect an answer."

"Not true, he answers me every night. You're just not open to him... All you do is stay in your room, you barely go outside. Except to run. Half the time, I barely know you're here!" She dropped the plate in the sink and it made a loud, clanking noise. "So yes, you need a job! Get you out of the house and doin' somin'."

I sat silent for just a moment, lacking the energy to complain to her, "Well... Like I said, I have been calling for temp work, I'm hoping they get back to me any day now."

She nodded. "Well, I hope they call you soon. Your last job at that warehouse was a good one. I don't know why you didn't keep it."

I rubbed my hand along the side of my face and said, "It wasn't the right one for me... Didn't fit in."

"Pfft!" The old lady rolled her eyes. "It's a job, it's not supposed to be fun or anything."

"I know, Grandma, I know. I've always had trouble with... ya know."

"When I was working in the shoe factory, it was very hard on me. Dealing with people and my boss, but I had to support my family, and I didn't have a choice in the matter."

I let her trail on. She'd told me this story twice this week. It's gotten worse as she got older. Her doctor had her on nine different medications, some of which are just to counteract the effects of the stronger meds she takes.

"Charlie! Are you listening to me?"

"Yes, Grandma. They still didn't give you enough for your pension and it was a major court case that your husband took too far.

"He was always so angry, just waiting for an excuse to go off on someone all the time."

"I know."

After a bit, I decided to leave the table. I placed my dishes in the sink and cleaned them off, then heaved myself up the loud, creaking stairs to my bedroom. Moved my feet with minimal effort as my thoughts wandered about the task. The moment doesn't usually take this much brain-power to grasp, not usually. With one hand I grasped my stomach, and a queasy throb came from my bowels. I breached the top of the stairs with subtle relief. With one foot on the top floor, I muttered to myself, "I ate way too much..."

Inside my bedroom, I heard laughter and play. It had been more common lately since the country's state of emergency had slowly been lifting. I peeked out the window. There was a school bus down the block that was picking up children. Parents were gathered around to let their kids go for the day. It was a mandate to accompany minors at any gathering. Used to need a police escort to oversee a single bus stop even if children were being picked up in mass. That was years ago, and the police escort had since vanished after the meta epidemic had declined. Even parents who accompanied their children had come in less frequently.

I continued to watch as the yellow metal tube pulled away and the folks who gathered left one after another, leaving only a man with a walking stick that stood on the corner. He wore a long coat and straw hat. For some reason... He was staring straight at me. It was hard to tell because he was so far away, but I felt it.

"Charlie! Get down here and take out the trash!" my grandmother yelled with a guttural thrall.

I snapped back to the current moment, and quickly said out loud, "Let me clean up and I'll do it before noon!"

With that said, I urged my body to the bathroom across the hallway, dragging my bare feet enough to hitch my heels on the doorway's lip. The doorknob shocked my hand as I reached for it. I recoiled and shook my hand vigorously to ward off the buzz in my fingers. In the bathroom, I slapped cold water on my greasy face. In the mirror, I noticed my brown hair had grown longer than I liked it. My stubble had gotten a little out of control and the paleness of my skin had started to match the wallpaper. My round brown eyes held bags from a few sleepless nights.

I'd usually take short peeks at myself in the mirror, but I never looked closely at my reflection. I opted to stare at myself this time. Just really looked. I could see odd distortions. They started to rearrange my facial features. Some weird trick of the mind. My eyes started to look blended and empty, as if my eyes were missing entirely. Shadows permeated around my face, thinning it out, making the person in the mirror seem less... less human. I forced myself to blink to reestablish my tired face to what it was. The muscles in the corners of my mouth resisted as I tried to grin to check my teeth. They were as crooked as always... I really should have screamed for braces in grade school. After a quick look inside my mouth, I went downstairs.

I walked into the kitchen where my grandmother prowled. With a fly swatter in one hand, she moved slowly and waited for one of the little buggers to land.

Then *smack*! We had a storm door at the main entrance that didn't shut around the bottom edge, but we wanted to let in more light. So we would bear having flies in the house. I walked into the kitchen, and she turned to me. Her mouth hung open and she dropped the fly swatter. The look on her face was something I hadn't seen in a while. Her eyes got wide. The wrinkles on her forehead scrunched.

"Charlie! Your nose!"

Caught off guard by her volume, I jumped a little from the urgency. Looking down at my body, I was very surprised to see my shirt nearly soaked through with blood.

A deep red stained down my chest and it was all coming from my face. Granny hurried to get a towel. She picked it up and dabbed it against my face.

"I have never seen you have a nosebleed in your life. Did something happen?"

"No. I didn't know till you pointed it out." I felt numb to the experience. It felt weird though.

"Well, whatever happened, be more careful. Don't want you to bleed out on me." She rang out the towel and ran cold water over it.

"There's still a lot of work to be done today—There's laundry, these dang-burn flies, the flowers need watering outside..."

"It's October, Grandma."

"Oh, I better check the weather."

She hobbled out of the kitchen. For as long as I could remember, she'd always had a hard time relaxing, settling in. She needed something to worry about, always—but in her own little way, she *accepted* the way things were. She didn't complain, and she truly smiled at the little things: the first snow of the season, the look on someone's face when they enjoyed her cooking.

No matter how terrible things were outside the house, Whatever the news would say, when something *actually* did happen, she'd be the one to reassure you everything would be fine. It was like the worst part for her wasn't the bad thing itself, but the *waiting*—the lead-up, the dread. The actual event never hit her as hard as the anticipation. Except for meta-humans, of course. '*They'll be in the house any day now,'* she'd say. But over the last two years, we waited—and worried—and waited some more. To her surprise, it never came. And for the first time, I believe she stopped worrying about it. She was ready to move on.

Needless to say for her. But I saw something different. I never considered meta-humans a threat, *per se*—just a passing phase until we, as a people, could adjust. Sure, it was the most interesting thing that had ever happened to the human race. I mean, how could all this happens, why did it happen? But honestly, I just didn't care that much. Of course I'd pay attention, I would read about it through countless articles, watch news stations and check police reports. To actually go out and see them for myself... No, There was nothing out there I wanted to see. It was actually a relief that I had an excuse not to leave the house.

I opened the fridge door; I just wanted to feel the cool presence of the icebox and look around for something. Our sweet tea container had a cup full left but I didn't want to take the last bit, thinking Grandma might want it with her meds later. She always poured too much sugar into it, anyway. So, I turned the stove to boiling water in a kettle to make more.

I stacked away the dishes sitting on the drying rack and needed to go into the cabinets. Lunged my hand for the metal handle of one of the high cabinets and *zap!* An arc of electricity strung from my fingertips to the handle. It hurt—It hurt a lot! I recoiled and stuck the tips of my fingers in my mouth to dull the pain. I'd never seen static electricity flash that brightly. My hand was a good distance away as well. I *focused* this time as I stretched my hand out to shock the handle again. I went slow; there would be no way it would happen twice. With intent, I rippled electricity in between my fingers. I didn't connect with the metal counter handle this time, and it hurt less for the moment.

It was amazing. I stared at its wondrous blue light. It made my fingers glow blue and the electricity would zap quickly and then settle. A second later it would zap again. It felt tingly on the tips. It was hard manifesting it at first, but it became a lot easier to maintain after I got it going. I was so enthralled about what was happening that I didn't notice the burning smell. A stream of smoke filled the air like a lit cigarette. When I noticed the singe of burning skin, it hit hard, and I tucked my hand into my stomach and held it with the other. I shocked myself.

My mind started to race frantically because right then I knew... I didn't understand why or how this had happened. Most metas had appeared around two years ago. At least so I thought. It's what the news said. To think that I... I couldn't bring myself to say it! The heat from my face started to rise and droplets fell from the point of my chin. If anyone found out about this, I'd be dead for sure.

The government would capture me and who knows what will happen? I'm not like those in Apex. They'll just chop me up and burn me. That's what happened in Utah. Memories of the news report flashed in my head, some small town who'd gathered all the metas and burned them in a big woodpile. Everyone from middle-aged men to small, helpless children. All screamed inside this fenced-in woodpile. They didn't even have dangerous abilities either, or so I thought, anyway. It just took a handful of armed civilians and a local sheriff to do it.

With time, I was able to calm myself. I just had to hide. For the rest of my life… Meaning I couldn't get a job without somebody finding out. I couldn't do anything outside this house without someone finding out. Whether it was a doctor's appointment, a public outing, or school, someone would find out. They always checked you for meta signatures. Everywhere you go, they do it. I paced the kitchen floor in front of the sink, anything to help me think.

I have to keep it a secret. I can still do odd jobs for cash and go to the grocery store without getting checked. Moisture permeated my forehead. Yeah, I'm sure I can do that much. I stared down into the palms of my hands. I looked intently for differences in my skin, something that could give me away. Some metas end up looking different in some way. Some take on animal attributes or just a change in skin color. I checked my body for anything out of place. Under my shirt, up my arms, and back. Even took off my shoes to see if I had webbed toes. I at the very least appeared human. I brought my hands up one more time to check my fingerprints and the back of my hands. Now if I could just understand what my abilities are, I could work to control them, hide them. No one would ever know.

I walked to turn off the light switch next to the patio door in the kitchen and sparks flew from the fixture as I touched it. I pulled my hand away, but a string of electricity was continually arcing to the switch. After a moment, the lights dimmed and flickered before the kitchen ceiling light went out. I stood there in the dark, my thought process switching from being a hopeful degenerate to thinking I'm probably screwed after that outburst. I hadn't even tried to do it that time.

The lights turned on in the kitchen. It startled me and I hid my hands like I was hiding an adult magazine. My grandmother stood there in the doorway. Her mouth hinged open, and her eyes didn't blink. We stood there and stared at each other. Was she waiting for me to say something? What could I say? I know she knew; she had to.

"Please tell me you were just playing with the light socket!" she said with a timid tone in her voice. The kind of tone where she wanted me to lie to her.

"Granny... I, no."

"Then it was your weird electronic toys or that lamp you like so much." I shook my head as I stared down at the linoleum floor. I tightened my jaw and the muscles in my throat swelled.

"I think I'm one of them..." I eked out as I darted my gaze to meet hers.

My grandmother's eyes glazed over; the air in the room felt a few degrees colder. Her chin started to shake as she tried to mouth a word.

"No, no..." she said with shortness of breath. She stepped backward into the living room away from the kitchen, avoiding eye contact with me as I stepped closer.

she whispered to herself, "Not my baby boy."

I walked toward her with my hand out. "It's okay," I stammered.

"*No, it's not!*" she raised her voice. "Do you know what the gov'ment does to... *them?*" She whispered 'them' under her breath.

"But this could be the start of something new, i mean good! After finding out what I can do... Maybe I can help someone—"

"You'll help yourself to an early grave! That's what you'll do!" She had trouble catching her breath. I walked over to try to help her.

"Get away!!" she yelled.

I stepped back as the pressure in my eyes welled up. "I'm still Charlie... The same little boy you raised all these years ago." I raised my hands with my palms facing her. "You know, I'm not going to go crazy. No, Not like them. This isn't like what we see on the news."

Grandma struggled to catch her balance, and she jerked and swayed as she tried to stand in place. Her ankles were always a bother to her and didn't get much better in her eighties. She finally looked at me; even when doing so, glassy streams ran from her cheekbones. She shook her head as she spoke.

"You have to run now."

A tear breached the corner of my mouth.

Grandma darted her eyes toward the kitchen, then looked at me with her eyebrows perked in concern. "Do you smell that?"

I didn't notice, but she was right, there was a smell, something of methane - GAS! It had filled the kitchen from the tea I'd been making on the stove. I'd gotten so distracted that I hadn't noticed the pilot light going out. I turned quickly and walked over to the seeping appliance, then reached my hand out to shut off the knob when suddenly a light blue string sparked from my finger. I yelled out, "Get back!" but it happened too quickly. From the very spark ignited a blinding flare that enveloped half the kitchen.

My senses were overwhelmed for half a second and then I felt lighter than air. Suspended in limbo for some time. I couldn't form a thought that was entirely my own.

Pain gave way as my back hit the wall that separated the kitchen and dining room. Having crashed and sunk to the linoleum floor, the ringing in my head started along with a searing pain that throbbed beneath the skin. When I tried to move, I winced and yelled out instead. A jerk reaction to the pain I never felt before. If I didn't think about that old woman, I might have gone into shock. Slowly, I was able to deal with it. With one foot firmly on the ground, I yelled:

"GRANDMA!!"

My vision consisted of red pulses and blurred darkness. Felt my hands along the wall that I'd crashed into and used it to guide me into the doorway. I made my way toward the living room and stumbled on large pieces of debris. It all felt so hot, I couldn't taste anything but chalk in the air. The heat stroked my back as I fell to my hands and knees in the living room. The carpet was riddled with glass bits and hot particles that pierced my fingertips.

Again, I yelled out, "Where are you!?"

I reached forward and found a foot! She lay flat on the ground and wasn't moving. My eyes managed to focus enough to see blurred constructs of color. I made it to her head and tried to feel her breath on my hand, but my fingers were too numb to tell the difference. The blast had knocked her out and I couldn't tell if she'd broken something. She bled enough for it to seep into the carpet, leaving a dirty burgundy color as it pooled. I tried gently shaking her awake, but to no avail. Thoughts ran rampant in my head. Things that I forced myself not to think about.

"She's not dead!!" I screamed to the heavens as if there was someone there to argue back. I tried hard to convince myself.

My vision sharpened just a bit more as my senses started to fissile back. The kitchen was intact, but pieces of the ceiling were falling in. All the windows were blown out, allowing more and more air to filter in. The house was burning down and all I could do was shake my unconscious granny. I couldn't sit here like a stump, waiting for something to just happen, so I buried my hands under her body to try and lift her up. The old lady was all of ninety pounds, yet it was a struggle to get her off the ground. My knees popped and my back spasmed as I did, but I fought through it. The smoke was thick as I carried her to the front door of our long-time home. With one subtle push against the screen door, I managed to get her outside and away from the inferno.

From the porch, I slowly managed to carry her down the concrete stairs and lay her in the grass. Adrenaline was helping a lot. My heartbeat thumped in my ears as I didn't notice the neighbors running over. Four or five grouped up on the lawn. Some I didn't recognize, while a few others were longtime friends of the old woman. I looked at them with dire eyes and asked them, "Call someone! We need an ambulance. Come on, Grandma? Grandma!?" I spoke in between short breaths. "Edna! It's me, Charlie!" I yelled her name, but still no response.

Her body was still. Pale, not cold though. The blood from her head soaked into her hair and those eyes remained closed. Her leg looked disjointed... It might be out of place. She was badly hurt. One of the neighbor friends knelt next to me, placed her arm on my back, and brushed the fabric of my shirt. There might have been embers on me.

"Don't worry, Chuck! We have folks on the way," she said.

Soon two others came up with a bag of ice and wash-cloths. They sat down next to me and propped a towel under Grandma's feet. "She's bleeding on the back of her head." I snagged another towel and gently placed it under her head.

More people came gathering around. From a distance, I could hear the sirens. As I sat on my knees, I leaned back on my heels to look around and behind me. The fire had grown to swallow the back end of the roof and the people started to back away from the yard. I felt the heat lathering on my back. I didn't want to move her any more than I had to. I just hoped the paramedics would get here soon.

A spark flung from my eye and stretched a good yard in front of me. Like a twitching office light, it sparked on and wasn't letting up. The folks who'd helped me aid Edna yelped and dove away from me. Quickly, I covered my right eye with the palm of my hand, but it was too late. The crowd of people had seen it.

I looked at everyone and it was like reliving that moment with Grandma in the kitchen. It was deathly silent. No one around here ever thought they would encounter this sort of thing. I could see in their eyes that no one knew what to do. The uneasy crowd murmured, and it was like they'd forgotten all about the house burning behind me and the lifeless woman in the grass. People walked away and immediately dialed their phones. A voice screamed at me to get away from Edna, my grandmother. They dared not to come too close. The neighbors who'd previously sat next to me gravitated to the crowd with unease.

Tension ran up the back of my neck. My hands started to shake. I felt it—They looked at me like a monster.

"Pfft, I... This!" I tried to speak but couldn't get my thoughts straight. I looked one more time at the still body of my grandmother lying in the grass. "It's not my fault." I eked out. The sirens blared even closer, and it was all I could do to keep my electrical outburst in check. It was hard... I didn't know how I could hold it in, so I held my breath and tensed my body. For a few seconds, I felt like it was working but it didn't. Jolts of electricity kept radiating from my body. I couldn't stop it. The crowd stared silently with adverse reactions; I couldn't stand it.

"It's not my fault!!" I screamed out. "Just please help my grandma! PLEASE!"

The police cars arrived and there were two of them coming in my direction. They pushed through some of the frightened people and took in the sight of our house burning and the two of us sitting in the grass. Another assortment of bolts strung out from my body and made the cops jump back.

"Woah! My god," one officer said. He was tall with blonde hair, possibly in his forties.

As quick as their training permitted, they drew police-issued firearms with sloppy haste and pointed them at me. My heart thumped hard against my ribs as I raised my hands.

"Easy! Easy! I know what it looks like. She's hurt, bleeding from her head, and her leg might be out of place," I said clearly. I had to convey quickly or things could escalate.

"Step away from the woman and put your hands behind your head!" the blonde officer said sternly.

I did what the cop said. There was blood painted on my hands when I carried her out. I skirted off to the side of the front lawn and nudged my head toward her body. "Okay, please check her." My face was wet, and I could taste the blend of iron and salt in my mouth. "Hurry,"

"What happened here?" the second officer asked.

"There was a gas leak in the kitchen. Just boiling a pot of tea and... yeah."

The same officer spoke on his comms, "Yeah, I need a Detaining Unit to come right away." The radio muffled the sounds of a man to the officer I didn't understand, it didn't sound assuring. "Just do what you can! If you can't get local, then call in the Urban Unit."

The second officer finally ran up to my grandmother and started checking her over. She was from the Sheriff's department, blonde hair and local to the area. She'd arrested me before for public noise disturbances and public drinking once. It was some years ago, but I remembered her all the same. I think her name was Mal... Mallory. She checked Grandma's pulse and brushed some of the debris that rested on her body, then checked the back of her head where she was bleeding. When that happened, I felt a brief release and started to let my hands down.

"Get those hands back up in the air! Right now!" the male cop approached with his handgun. Freaking out, I placed them back up.

"Don't. Move. A muscle!" The cop's hand was shaking, and I could tell he wasn't experienced in this. If I did anything that was slightly off, I would pay for it. Not a lot of metas had been seen around here, so no one knew what to do. *I* didn't know what to do. They just see a burning house and an unknown.

"This was all an accident." I pleaded.

"Don't you worry, just stand there and don't move! We're going to fix this," the guy said without blinking. From a distance, I saw the lights of the ambulance pulling around a corner. With all things considered, I was happy to see that something was finally getting done.

"The ambiance is here, Grandma! It's going to be alright!" I said in a tone louder than normal.

"Shut... Up," the male officer spat out.

"I just wanted her to hear me.."

Her body didn't move, Mallory only knelt over her and wasn't attending. She must be waiting for the ambulance, I thought.

"She's going to be okay, right, ma'am?" I asked. She didn't face me.

"Ma'am?" I persisted. She stared off toward the crowd. Like I was a ghost that shouted on deaf ears. Without thinking, I stepped towards her.

BANG!

A shot from the officer's handgun whizzed past my face. "Shut up, freak! Go on, give me a reason!"

The officer's face was beet-red, and his nostrils flared as he pierced me with his gaze. The people were startled behind him when the shot rang out and some ran. I'm sure they thought the worst was about to happen. A memory of a newscast flashed in my mind of metas taking on the law in a final shootout. It never ended well for the meta, nor for the people caught in the crossfire. With that flash of memory, my teeth clenched, and I felt cornered.

"I'm harmless, ok? I never hurt anyone on purpose." I said.

Mallory darted towards the guy and slowly laid a hand on his arm. "Dan! You don't have to prove anything here, just take a breath and wait for Apex to arrive."

"They better come now," Dan said without blinking. He sneered his lip. "It's because of their kind, Mals. It's because of assholes like this that my brother isn't around."

Mallory looked at him with a kind of remorse.

"Dan! This isn't the place," she said. She lowered her voice enough so the scattered crowd behind them wouldn't hear. "If you shoot this man in front of these people... There's just no going back from that. Our first meta encounter in this town and you want to off him after he draged his grandmother out of a burning house!" She paused.

"Listen to her, Dan. It wouldn't look good for your department," I said.

"I said shut your mouth, meta!" Dan walked two hurried steps towards me, and I stumbled a half-step back. I closed my eyes, thinking this was going to be the end. I waited for the sound of the barrel to empty a bullet in my head... But it didn't happen. Eventually, I opened half an eyelid and spied Mallory with a handhold on Dan's police-issued jacket. At the same time, the EMTs were holding distance away from us. Waiting to get my grandmother on the stretcher. I assumed they were too afraid to approach with this psycho breaching his sanity clause.

I was worried sick for her. Looking at the cops, the EMT, and my grandmother, I sputtered, "My. My..."

I couldn't help but recoil to the back of my mind, seeing myself in 3rd person. Then a voice inside my head pronounced itself loudly:

-RUN-

Visions of my grandmother standing in that archway telling me, *"You have to run"* kept replaying over and over. My lower lip quivered and I could no longer focus. But that voice in the back of my head kept telling me,

-RUN-

Sparks shot out of my body at a higher frequency than ever before. I couldn't keep it controlled anymore; it emanated on its own. The blue glow contrasted with the flames behind me as the house burned, and the cops rushed the lawn in numbers behind the two that were already there. Memories flooded my mind of all the things that made my teeth clench, and my eyes swell with heat. I just... Wanted to lash out. The memories poured heavily from the times in high school when I was bullied, and when I felt alone in my mother's house. I lurched forward and grabbed my head.

"I don't want to remember this now!!" I screamed aloud. It felt like nails were being driven into my temples. Being forced to remember. Again, my grandmother tells me to hide while she stands in the archway.

"He's going to do it! Everyone back away!" Dan the officer yelled out. "We don't have time for Apex to come, we got to take this son of a bitch down NOW!" The police were now standing over my grandmother. It was like a terrible dream.

–RUN–

My body acted on it's own the electricity increasing and my feet propelled me from the front yard. One foot in front of the other, I sped through the center of the firing squad and down the street. The sound of gunfire and the screams of people got louder.

I couldn't see a thing; it was all a blur in my eyes.

I'm fast though. Real fast!

The wind was pulling against my body and before I knew it, I was running through town. I felt a drain on my body. My knees buckled and wanted to give out. I slowed down in the park near the baseball fields on the edge of town. My eyes were able to focus again, and I took note of the oak trees and empty parking spaces. No one was there. The electricity that coursed through me started to die down, as did the speed I once had carried through the weight of my body.

Nevertheless, I couldn't garner my balance and stop at the same time. My body was going to plow right into a tree and there was nothing I could do about it. My right side hit the bark of a tree trunk first and a bite of pain shook me as my body settled on the ground. My ribs popped as I shuffled my feet in the grass, anything I could do to stop the pain. The electricity was gone and, for the first time today, I felt the stark cold air. Droplets slipped from my eyes. I balled up on the ground and tried hard to regulate my breathing.

Sirens echoed in the air. They didn't seem close enough to find me. What am I going to do now?

Chapter Two

I didn't ask for any of this. This whole situation just fell into my lap, and now I have to keep going. I'd been happy in my little bubble, happy to look out the window and see a world I had no interest in. Honestly, who would want to. I see now my biology had other plans... I don't know how I aligned with such an infliction, but its thoroughly destroyed my life in no less than an hour.

I stumbled over tree roots as I ran through the woods, trying not to stumble into sticky clumps of brush. I'd already spent four minutes trying to reboot my cell phone. It was lucky that it had survived the blast at all. The screen was now fractured, with small particles of ash filling some of the cracks. The only thing showing was the 'low battery' icon. Vaporous static still misted off my arms. I should have thought of that as I smacked the device with my palm, fizzling out the motherboard. I tossed the phone into a deep pocket of a nearby creek. Better than burning another hole in my pocket.

Light glimmered through the treetops. Oaks lifted into the sky as leaves fell from their branches on this cold morning. It was slightly wet, but the encroaching day was burning off the moisture quickly. A path lay barren in front of me. A hiking trail maybe? No, just a treaded path. Birds sounded out as I passed, chirping and whistling from their boughs. It had been a trek making my way from Gibbins Park; I should be plenty far from town at this point. Still, I couldn't help but stare blankly in the distance—anything to stop myself from thinking. Still covered in soot and blood, my tennis shoes and jeans were a mess. I'd changed into them to take the trash out earlier. Numbing shivers invaded my shoulders, only bearing a charred tank top. There hadn't been many options before getting out of there.

The news reporter had said it was thirty degrees Fahrenheit—Just thinking of it made me sneeze. At the very least, I had the sun on my back. My hands shuffled into my pockets to keep warm. I had a few five-dollar bills... There must be a place I could hide out. The Sheriff's department would have likely reported this by now. They'd even gone as far as Apex to detain me. Thoughts of my grandmother echoed through my mind. I can't believe I'd just left her there.

"She has to be alright," I mouthed quietly to myself.

I couldn't judge how big the blast had been in the kitchen, but I'd been in the center of it and i made it out okay. At least I'd gotten her out of there before it all burned down. Her potential for bleeding out was a real possibility... Hopefully the paramedics were in time.

I climbed over a hill where the trees were sparse. On the other side, I could see the residence of a farmer: a two-story house with a gravel patch leading out to the bend of a county road. On the far side of the house from me sat two silos with a bit of rust that corroded the roof. The field around the property had recently been harvested and burned. I could see the black mass of mulch with broken, prickly stems, stretching throughout the fields and all the way to the tree line. This was the Mayfield property.

I used to go to school with Ted Mayfield—eldest son. We didn't associate much, but everyone knew the Mayfields. Ted himself left for the city after high school. I remember being envious when I heard. I also remembered him bragging about 'having a place to himself' in school. Which was just a detached guest house on his parents' property. Looking now, I could even see it: a mid-sized guest house that sat behind the big one. Had a separate gravel patch that spilled out in front of the entrance and conjoined with the gravel in front of the main house. I didn't see anyone around, but I could only assume that the guest house was still Ted's room. If I could get inside and find something, at least a jacket, it would help.

Slowly, I nudged along the tree line and ventured onto the property. The brush from the path I walked wasn't more than ten or so feet from the mowed grass. The guest house had red brick walls with a dark roof that barely had a pitch. It had clearly been modeled after the bigger house. I pressed my back against the brick wall and inched myself to the corner nearest the front door. A few cars drove by on the road. Every time one did, the hairs on my neck would stand on end. Through the window near the front door, I could see a bit of the bedroom. It looked spotless inside, with no signs of anyone staying here. Pictures of Ted and his friends hung on the walls, while various trophies lay atop a long industrial cabinet that ran along the far side of the bed. The trophies were for tennis and other banal sports that Ted had played in high school. The window itself had a storm grate covering the frame. The Mayfields lived pretty far from town. I can't imagine they worried about anyone coming and going out here.

I kept myself low as I ran up to the front door, then fiddled with the doorknob for half a second before realizing it was locked.

"Shit."

I frantically looked about the yard. Anyone who wanted to see me could from any angle, especially from the house. My knees started to shake and tension soared through my neck. I felt it spreading through my body. I'd never thought about breaking into someone's house before. I bit my lip and took a deep breath, then applied pressure on the doorknob with both hands. My arms strained enough for the veins on my forearms to pop out.

"Come on... Break!"

BANG!

The distant noise startled me so bad, electricity sprung from my arms. I heard something snap inside the knob mechanism and I fell through the doorway. My feet scrambled to maintain my balance as I hurried near one of the windows. If I didn't see anything, I'd proceed to the next one to peek through. If anyone was coming, I needed to know. In the bathroom, there was a round porthole window that sat next to the shower stall. The moment I checked it, I saw them: out in the field, two people with orange vests wrapped around their bulky camo jackets. One held a rifle while the other bent over to pick up a bird. Its wings spawned out lifelessly as he held it by its feet. The one holding the bird seemed to be the father and the other holding the rifle was a boy. They smiled at each other, the boy seeming to want to jump in excitement. He didn't, though.

My heartbeat regulated to a steady crawl, then I closed any window blinds that remained open and made sure the guest house door was firmly shut. I couldn't un-break the lock, but I hoped that no one would be able to notice. When I felt secure, I found my way to the shower and washed all the blood and soot covering my body. The water pressure felt amazing, and I'm surprised they kept the hot water heater running out here.

After cleaning off with a fresh towel, I rummaged through the closet and found a thick, fleece hoodie with red sleeves and a dark navy blue jersey pattern on the front. I slipped it on, then helped myself to an all-black skull cap that sat on a shelf in the closet as well as gloves, a folding knife, and some thicker socks. The pocketknife was an especially good find. I held the sucker closer to my eye line to analyze—Wooden handle with a steel emblem on its side. It was sharp, with no jagged edge on the blade. For some reason, it hurts when I touch metal objects. Electricity would zap from my body, conducting to them. Out of curiosity, I wanted to try something. I held my breath and took my index finger and slowly ran it along the point of the blade, piercing my finger with just a bit of blood to blot the skin. With a slow exhale, I folded the blade and placed it in my pocket.

"Doesn't happen every time, I guess," I said in a mild whisper to myself.

Through the window, I noticed the orange-clad pair were still there in the field. I'd heard a few more shots ring out while I was cleaning up in the bathroom, but I hadn't paid them any mind. They were sitting on the ground with their game. Probably teaching the little one to clean it. With those two still out there, I wasn't going to risk leaving. In hindsight, I was surprised they hadn't spotted me before I broke in. It had to be a few hours now since the incident at Grandmother's house. By now, the tri-state area would know, even Apex… I envied those guys when the meta outbreak happened. No one could make heads or tails on how to regulate people who'd gained strange abilities. A measure of force had to be implemented.

My back landed on the bed as I fidget with my hands. Just a bit longer. The chances of me sneaking out clean were slim. They were just sitting outside and might be messing around until lunch. I needed something to take the edge off. Take my mind off of things until I could move freely. There was a smaller flat-screen TV on the corner counter next to the closet. It was pointed towards the bed. The more I looked at that TV, the more I wanted to turn it on. The news would be on around this time. My eyes

glared at the clock above the bathroom door. It was almost
II a.m.

My feet dangled off the foot of the bed and bumped into
the bedpost, making a hollow metal sound. The little muscles on the back of my neck tensed up every time I looked
at the TV, almost to the point of my shoulders shaking. I
so badly wanted to keep my mind occupied.

I flung my feet above my head and swung them to the
floor, then practically attacked the TV with my index finger, tapping the power button multiple times like it was
going to boot up faster if I did. Finally, it lit up.

"Welcome back for Rockford local news at noon. Today,
Bernt Hollow has a bit of excitement as Apex's very own
Trailblazer has run all the way from Chicago to visit the
Children's Hospital. Bob Joselyn is live on the scene. You
there, Bob?"

The news showed Trailblazer, the head honcho from the
inner city. Trailblazer was an advanced martial officer
who Apex employed to hunt and detain meta-humans
while also being a meta himself. At the moment, he was
hanging Halloween decorations up in a long hall populated with jumpy children. There were boxes in the background with jack o' lantern baskets of candy. The children
lined up one after another to get their goodies from local
law enforcement and nurses. A short, balding man with a
pudgy nose was holding a microphone in the frame. He'd
positioned himself next to the towering, armored meta,
then waited a second before making his statement to the
camera.

"We're here live with The Trailblazer! The children are ecstatic to see the super-human in person. As everyone knows, Trailblazer was one of the key figures who helped eradicate the meta presence in the Chicagoland area and has done well to help the people in need."

Bob Joselyn waved Trailblazer into the frame and lifted the microphone above his head to reach the meta's chin. The meta almost couldn't fit in the frame, so the camera-man had to take a step back to have him visible from head to waist. Like always, the man is clad in his signature red jumpsuit with sponsor logos plastered on both sleeves, his shoulder pads thinly layered into his carbon-fiber chest piece. On his chest, the APEX logo is chiseled in a yellow font, making him look like the cross between a football player and a Nascar driver. His red helmet fits slim with a black visor. Couldn't see the facial features of this guy. Come to think of it, I don't think they've ever shown his face. Trailblazer gripped the microphone.

"*Thank* yo-ou..." He looked down at the reporter to help him with his name.

"Bob! Bob Joselyn, sir, and thank *you* for coming to our humble little town and showing goodwill to these chil-dren. Is there anything you'd like to say to the people?"

Trailblazer locked on to the camera. "Well, ya know, Bob, I love our humble small-town neighbors and find it necessary to check in and give back to these communities. Apex and I thought we could ring in the fall season by showing some of these kids that we *are* here for them. My team spent so much time in the urban precincts curbing the meta population that we sometimes forget that we can do more. And today we have done exactly that!"

Bob pulled the microphone to his own face, "How do you mean?"

"Well Bob, for starters, Apex will be donating fifty-thousand dollars to this hospital."

"That's amazing, Trailblazer!"

"Now, I know this town *of...?*"

"Bernt Hollow, sir," said Bob.

"Yes!" Trailblazer looked closer into the camera. "I know the town of Bernt Hollow doesn't suffer from meta corruption like other areas, but let it be known! Apex will be here—Evil cannot run faster than the Man in Red!" He gestured toward someone off-screen and whispered, "Clip that last bit, will ya?"

Trailblazer whipped his body in dramatic grandeur towards the children. They were frantically digging through their baskets of Halloween candy. He picked up a sickly looking six-year-old boy with dark rings under his eyes and rested him on his forearm.

"Just remember! You're *safe* in our hands. Isn't that right, kids?!"

The children shouted in unison. It went on for a few seconds till the camera tightened onto Bob again.

"There you have it! From the words of Apex's Trailblazer himself, they are here to protect us! I tell ya, I feel safer already."

A sickly feeling convulsed in my stomach; it almost made me sick. Trailblazer was in the area. For the first time ever in this town. And I felt pretty sure he wasn't just here to hand out candy. Granted, he had the perfect outfit for it. All I knew was that I needed to get out of this town, and *fast*.

There was only one place I could think of going, and that was in Chicago, where my sisters lived. She and my niece had lived there for years, since even before the Outbreak. I haven't seen them in such a long time. I didn't want to risk anymore family getting involved with me. If they got caught harboring me, it could be bad. Granted, I had nowhere else to go. No one else to call on for help. If anything, she might know someone who could help me. She wouldn't have to get *that* involved; I don't even have to stay the night...

I'll do that then. Maybe she can help. At least I would be away from here.

The other thing that bothered me was that it seemed the police were keeping my meta-status quiet. By now, I should have seen something in the news. Those warnings usually hit fast for every media outlet. I wished I had my phone so I could check. Sirens would be heard, even from here. Perhaps they didn't want to cause a panic? That would have to be the reason. No matter, it gave me enough space to move around at least.

I fell back on the bed and sprawled my arms out. My attention fixed on the popcorn ceiling as my mind explored the possibilities. Maybe they didn't care about finding me? I mean, it certainly didn't seem like they were trying that hard. Suddenly, the memory of my grandma standing in the archway popped into my head. She was there right before the blast. Just a faint look at her face. She looked sad. Her eyes pierced me, almost like I was a stranger to her.

–RUN–

I shook the daze off. "No, no! I can't think that way. Of course, they're looking for me. Every step I take must be a cautious one."

I strolled up to the television to turn it off. As I extended my hand toward the console, a sudden jolt of electricity arced from my index finger to the TV screen. A sharp twinge of pain shot through my fingers just as the TV began to spark, followed by smoke billowing from its back. Instinctively, I curled my fingers into my palm and hissed through clenched teeth.

"There's no getting used to this," I whispered.

Just then, I heard a distinct click coming from just outside my field of vision. When I turned, I saw the little boy wearing an orange vest. He had his hands gripping that rifle, its barrel pointing vaguely in my direction—though not directly at me. His wide, owl-like eyes were tense, and his lower jaw trembled uncontrollably.

His hair spilled out wildly from under his oversized trucker's cap, which he wore backward with the fitted clips adjusted to the very last hole. The look was almost comical, especially with his big ears poking out amidst the mass of bushy hair. But I wasn't laughing.

Despite the lingering pain in my fingers from the earlier shock, I swiftly raised my hands into the air.

"Woah... Take it easy, kid. I'm not here to hurt anyone."

The little boy stood there and didn't say anything. His lower jaw still trembled.

"I just walked in to get out of the cold. Don't go all trigger-happy on me."

"Did... Didn't you blast that TV?" The kid finally muscled out a few words.

"Ahh..." I gestured nervously. "You saw that, did you? Sorry bud, was it yours?"

The kid shifted his eyebrows my way, indicating his curiosity. His shoulders went from being stiff and hunched to relaxed as he pulled them back. Straightening his whole body, he looked like he could be eight years old.

"Sooo... You're one of *them*?" the child asked with his head slightly lunged forward.

"You could say that. I don't really have the hang of how all this works yet, but don't be afraid! I'm not here to cause you or any of your—"

"Could you do it again?" the kid asked with intrigue, the kind that can only come from a child. His reaction caught me off-guard, every person up till now who'd learned about my powers had met me with open disdain. He stood there waiting with a slight smile scrunched on one side of his face. The rifle he held tightly began to loosen from his grasp. Feeling more relaxed myself, I lowered my hands and perched them on my waist.

"What's your name, kid?"

"Deon... My name is Deon."

"Well, *Deon.* I don't know how to do it again. I've only been able to light stoves. Not to mention, it could be very dangerous. Don't you watch the news?"

Deon lowered his gaze slightly. With a timid swivel on the balls of his tennis shoes, he said, "Mom and Dad don't let us watch TV. They say it's not good for us."

I glanced at my fingers that still felt numb from the shock of the television set. "I would be inclined to believe your parents."

"Could ya give it a try?! I never seen a meta before."

"I think you would have more fun meeting that fire guy, he's in town right now. And again, all this is way too dangerous. Normally, you're not supposed to walk up to strangers and ask them to do party tricks."

"Normally, *you* don't break into people's rooms and bust their TVs up..." Deon pointed out, then took a quick half-step forward and extended his finger. "*I* won't tell anyone you're here if you try. Promise!"

"Kid... Deon—" I paused in mid-sentence. It would be a benefit to me if no one knew where I was. If I had to entertain this snot for a second, I would. "Fine. I'll give it a shot."

Deon smiled big and hopped in the air one time before awkwardly resuming his previous composure.

"Now, I have a few conditions," I said with a single finger pointed at the popcorn ceiling.

Deon smiled.

"You need to stand in that doorway," I said, pointing toward the bathroom. "There aren't any electronics near it. I'll stay over here—" I gestured toward the far side of the room. "If things start to look dangerous, I want you to dive into the bathtub. Got it?"

"This is going to be sooo cool!" Deon leaned the rifle next to a cabinet where the TV was, then shuffled toward the bathroom and stood intently in the doorway.

"Just to be safe, stand inside the bathroom. If something happens, I don't want you to have to step back and *then* aim for the tub. Got it?"

Deon eagerly complied with a frantic head shake and stepped back into the bathroom.

"Perfect!" I said.

A quiet moment passed before I shut the bathroom door with Deon trapped inside, then took a nearby wooden chair and braced it under the doorknob to hold it in place.

"Hey!" Deon pushed on the door and the doorknob turned profusely, but it wouldn't budge.

"Nothing personal, Bud. Take care of yourself."

I ran toward the front door and peeked at the rifle leaning on the cabinet for half a second. It looked to be stainless steel... I considered taking it, but my experiences with metal so far hadn't been great. I wouldn't want to channel electricity through a loaded weapon and have it fire on its own. I left the rifle where it leaned and quietly pushed myself out the front door. Finding a way to my sister's is my number one priority. I wasn't sure how Little Gracie would feel about all this, but I had to try.

The moment I stepped outside, I heard the heavy voice of an older fella bellowing in my left ear. I had to turn my head to get a good look at him because of the blindness in my left eye.

"My my, if it isn't ol' Charlie Con'way," he spoke in a heavy Southern drawl.

It was Mr. Mayfield. His hair was graying, and he had a bullish nose that garnered a jet-black mustache. He had a narrow pointed chin and a enormous forehead with aged lines that resembled freshly folded towels. A tall man bearing the same orange vest as the kids, he wore overalls underneath his denim jacket. Hadn't changed a bit since I last saw him back in high school at his sons football games.

I quickly raised my hands to make them visible—his double-barrel shotgun was just three inches from my nose.

"Hey there, Mr. Mayfield!" I never knew his first name. I'd always referred to him as Ted's dad.

"You've been all over my radio, young man. Funny that I'd find *you* here. Stealing from Teddy's room." He pressed the gun barrel against my temple. I had to turn my head so the cold steel wouldn't lean against the more sensitive areas on my face.

"Deon! You alright in there, boah?!"

"I'm okay, Pop! I'm stuck in the shitter!"

"What I tell ya about that language!?"

"...Sorry!" Deon said, sounding annoyed.

Mr. Mayfield turned his attention back on me. He spat once on the ground and said, "Doesn't surprise me one bit. Looking to get out of here I reckon."

"If you know that much, then just let me go."

"Heh! You'd like that, aye? To be honest, I'd liked nothing more than to put you down."

Mr. Mayfield's double barrel pressed more firmly on my temple. "Sad about what happened to your sister back then. Anybody that knew, felt for ya. Although, I knew diff'rent! I knew what kinda person you'd be."

"And what kind of person is that?"

He leaned in close to my ear as he pulled the gun away: "A coward."

The tension in my neck stiffened and I felt the heat from my eyes grow. He replanted the shotgun against my temple.

"You don't know a damn thing about me!"

"Oh, but I do. It might be hard for others to see, but I see it!"

He coughed into the fold of his arm and hawked a secretion from his mouth onto my left tennis shoe. My teeth clenched as my lower jawline shook. From one of the second-story windows of the big brick house, a panel flung open. Mrs. Cynthia Mayfield's voice rang out:

"They'll be here in a bit, hon! Where's my little boy?!" she said,

"He's fine, Cindy! Lock all the doors till all this is over!" Then his voice grew deeper. "Don't try any funny stuff! We'll wait right here all nice and cozy, like." He pulled away the barrel of the gun and swung the wooden stock into my kidney.

"OOF!"

I felt the strain of tendons spasm in my side as numbness ran down my leg. I dropped to a knee and held myself below my ribs as my forehead almost touched the gravel. The heavy thud of his steel-toed boot skidded off my face. Mr. Mayfield's breath gushed heavily. He planted his gun in the ground to steady himself.

Just then, an abrupt collision sounded out from Ted's room. Mr. Mayfield flinched! I grabbed the shotgun by the muzzle and held it in place so I could lift my shoulder into his solar plexus. It winded him enough to let go of his weapon. He stumbled backwards like his feet were doing Salsa lessons for the first time. He was hard-pressed to keep his balance, but gravity had other plans. I nudged him with the stock of his weapon and he went down, landing awkwardly on his back.

Before I could gather my thoughts, a loud, awkward noise jolted my attention—it was coming from inside the guest house. Turning toward the sound, I saw little Deon had moved the chair away from the bathroom door. Through the storm door, our eyes met.

Not wanting to scare him any further, I quickly emptied the barrels of the shotgun and flung it toward the edge of the forest. Meanwhile, Mr. Mayfield, completely out of breath, was still struggling to stand. I glanced back at Deon once more and a pang of guilt washed over me—he was just a kid; he didn't know any better.

"I'm sorry, kid," I said empathetically.

Suddenly, blast of scalding wind tore through the air, searing the back of my neck and sending a shockwave of heat through my body. Flames and ash roared behind me, an overwhelming presence that froze me in place. Deon let out a piercing scream, before bolting into his brother's bathroom and slamming the door shut.

I couldn't move. My jeans burned through to the skin, and my knees buckled under the sheer force pressing down on me. The sensation was unlike anything I'd ever experienced—it was paralyzing.

Then, from the chaos behind me, a voice emerged. Heavy and all too familiar. The heat lapped at my neck as the acrid smell of burning oil filled the air.

"Charles Matthews Conway."

The name hit me like a hammer. I didn't want to recognize the voice. I prayed—desperately—that it wasn't who I feared. But then his head leaned over my shoulder, the fibers of his helmet brushing against my skin, confirming my worst nightmare.

"You have the right to remain silent. Anything you say can and will be used against you."

My heart sank. Please, God, don't let it be him.

"Everything will be used against you, for the only right of a meta is compliance with humane processing."

Apex was here.

"Do you understand your rights... meta?"

Mr. Mayfield was frozen as well. I could only imagine if there was a phone call that could open Pandora's box of demonic horror, this was it. I was too scared to turn around, so I watched Mr. Mayfield instead.

"Trail... Blazer," the farmer stammered, his eyes stretched wide, and I saw the glint of yellow reflected in his pupils. Then all at once the fire, the heat, and all signs of a furnace out of control seemed to stop. Vacuumed back in the carrying body it expelled from.

"I heard you were fast, meta," Trailblazer's voice hissed through his helmet, close enough to send a chill down my spine. His gloved hand clamped down on my shoulder like a vice. Without warning, he spun me around, my feet stumbling to keep up with the force of his movements. Before I could react, I was slammed against the brick wall of the guest house, the rough surface scraping against my back. His massive hand pinned me.

Trailblazer loomed over me, a hulking figure in armored gear that seemed to swallow the sunlight.

"Speak up, boy! I don't have all day. Are you fast or not?!" he barked, his voice sharp and commanding.

"I... guess. I was?" My words wavered, trailing off weakly, every syllable exposing my hesitation. As if talking to another meta wasn't nerve-wracking enough, it had to be *him.*

Trailblazer's sharp, judgmental glare cut through me. "I didn't come all the way out to this podunk hellhole for 'I guess,'" he sneered, his tone dripping with disdain. He released his grip, but the sense of confinement didn't lift. His fingers moved to his helmet, tracing its edge as a crimson glow ignited in his visor. His head tilted slightly, and I could feel his eyes analyzing me, dissecting me.

"My information checks out," he said flatly. "Height, likeness, location. My sensors confirm a meta signature deep inside you. Resonating under your ribs."

At his words, a surge of panic clawed through my chest. Instinctively, I dragged my hand across the area he'd described, as though the very idea of a tumor-like meta energy lodged there might make it tangible.

Trailblazer shifted his gaze, turning toward Mr. Mayfield, who was still struggling to stand nearby. "Thank you for your compliance, sir," Trailblazer said, his tone icy but polite. "Contact your local law enforcement about compensation for your civil duties. I'll handle the rest."

Mr. Mayfield, brushing off dirt and smoothing the wrinkles in his reflective yellow vest, responded with a nauseating cheerfulness. "Thank ya, Mr. Blazer. Ya know, catching metas is a passion of mine. I strive to carry this town on my back—"

"Thank you, citizen! That will be all," Trailblazer cut him off abruptly, silencing him with a curt, faintly menacing tone. Mayfield froze for a beat, then collected himself and started walking toward his house, his steps practically buoyant with satisfaction.

"I hope you rip this one apart!" Mayfield called out without looking back.

"Run," said the enormous meta.

"What did you say?" I looked at him in astonishment.

"I said *run*, meta." Trailblazer tightened the Velcro on his gloves. "I want to see it."

Not able to fully grasp his request, I hesitated. What was he playing at?

"I don't know how they work. These abilities, I mean." I gestured my hands outward, like I had nothing to give.

"That's quite alright—run anyway." Trailblazer's voice carried a mocking edge just moments before the back of his palm cracked against my face. The force of the blow sent me sprawling onto the gravel. Pain exploded in my jaw, leaving it numb, while my head spun, dazed and rattled.

"Now then, since we have a mutual understanding," he sneered, gesturing toward the east side of the property, "try running to that tree line on the far side of the silos. If you can make it... Let's say grab a first full of leaves, i'll let you go." His gloved hand pointed, the tree line standing at least a third of a mile away.

I pushed myself halfway up, one knee digging into the gravel, the sole of my shoe pressing against the ground. I hesitated to rise any further, resisting in the only way I dared.

My gaze dropped to Trailblazer's boots—a sleek, blood-red armor that stopped just below the knee. They gleamed with an unsettling, machinal quality, vents covering the soles like tiny industrial engines. Steam hissed and filtered from the vents in slow, deliberate bursts

Trailblazer was a speedster meta, enhanced with rapidly increased body heat that expels from his feet when running. And right now, the iron cast of his feet started to glow red.

"It's not going to be any easier if you don't do what I say," he said with mild frustration.

"So," I spoke as I coughed. "You're the real deal then?"

"I'm the *only* fucking deal... Now. Do. It!"

So, I ran. My legs lurched into motion, the first few steps awkward and unsteady. Pain flared in my side, a fiery reminder of the kidney shot from earlier, but I forced it to the back of my mind. Gritting my teeth, I drove myself forward, foot after foot pounding the earth beneath me. The grazed field was just ahead—a beacon of desperate hope.

But before I could reach it, a sudden, brutal force struck the upper part of my back. The impact stole my breath, and my legs buckled instantly. My body crumpled across the grass. I landed sprawled at the edge of the field.

Gasping, I turned my head, the sting of the blow still radiating through my spine. Trailblazer loomed above me, his colossal frame blotting out the sun. He stood un-moving, his presence almost otherworldly. Steam hissed and rippled around him, distorting the air and warping his silhouette like some malevolent mirage—a dark aura mocking an eclipse.

"I think we had a misunderstanding. I want you to *run!* Like your life depended on *it!*" The armored meta cracked his neck. His breath vented out of the front of his helmet and a string of red horizontal LED lights resonated from the center of his visor. Without a thought, something in my body jerked and jarred itself, almost akin to the feeling of getting out of bed when you're supposed to be at work in five minutes. I scrambled to my feet and took off as fast as I could over that field. The adrenaline kicked in hard, and my body felt invigorated with drive. A purpose to do something beyond merely existing. I welcomed it.

Almost to the tree line. I hopped through harvested stems and crumbled ash while only looking forward. The moment I would have looked back, I knew that *he* would be there. A few meters from the tree line, I lunged one hand towards a low-hanging bush. Bonk!

It happened again... I hit the ground. The field's remnants pricked my face. A swelling started developing along my shoulder near my neck. I attempted to stand, but Trailblazer's boot sank into my back, pushing me down into the dirt.

I yelped loudly. It would've been louder had the air not been knocked out of me. The heat from his horseshoe-plated foot sizzled a layer of skin where it rested.

"Why?! Why are you doing this?!" I roared, my voice cracking with fury and disbelief. My hand shot up, shoving his boot off my back as I twisted onto my side. Sparks of electricity burst from my eye, crackling across the ground and snaking toward Trailblazer's feet.

"Aren't you supposed to take me in? Arrest me? Rehabilitate me?!" The words tore out of me, raw and trembling with rage. My temples throbbed, the pressure building like a storm, and a violent twitch jerked at the corner of my eye. Every nerve in my body screamed for answers, for justice, for anything but this.

Trailblazer braced himself for a moment, then rested his body with a lean on his hip. "Don't tell me you believe everything you see in the media?" The meta folded his arms. "Things change rapidly when the higher-ups find out they can't '*harness* the power' for their own gain. So, tell me—What did you think was going to happen?"

"I-I don't know." I tried to catch my breath. "Make use of my abilities, chop me up, and study my meta remains? Hook me to a machine to draw out my power source? The glass is half-full here."

"You're useless!" Trailblazer's voice boomed, each word dripping with venom. "You offer nothing—no skill, no value, no contribution worth a damn to society. The only thing you're good for is making me look even better." His words carved into me.

Before I could react, Trailblazer seized me by the neck, his massive hand clamping down like steel. His thumb pressed mercilessly into my trachea, choking the air from my lungs. Pressure surged in my skull, a suffocating agony that threatened to overwhelm me.

But in that moment, something snapped inside me. A burst of energy pulsed through my body, and the numbing jolt of electricity surged down my leg. Without hesitation, I thrust my knee hard into his ribs. The impact echoed with a dull thud against his kevlar armor, but it was enough. His grip loosened—just enough for me to break free.

I dropped to the ground, gasping for breath. My eyes locked onto the tree line ahead, It all lead to the reserve, I could possibly lose him in among the tress, in that moment it was the only thing I could act on—my beacon of escape. My chest burned, my muscles ached, and I sprang toward the horizon.I wasn't useless—I *wasn't* done.

So, I ran. With a thunderous vigor, I ran.

Lightning crackled behind me as I darted between the trees, weaving desperately from side to side. The forest was my only chance, the only sanctuary in sight. I had pushed an eighth of a mile down the line when it happened—a bone-crushing right hook smashed into my jaw. The impact detonated through my skull, and before I even registered the pain, my body was airborne.

I hurtled backward, crashing down toward the burnt fields like a rag doll tossed by a giant. The charred earth became my playground of agony as I skipped across it—once, twice—like a stone skimming water, each bounce igniting fresh shockwaves of pain. My body finally tumbled into the mulch, sliding through the scorched remnants of land until my momentum surrendered to stillness. Dust erupted in my wake, clinging to the air as if the ground itself resented my intrusion.

Flat on my back, all I could do was stare up at the sky, watching soot drift lazily into the atmosphere. In that moment, just that fleeting, unbearable moment—I wanted to die.

A shrill ringing pierced my ears, drowning out any hope of coherence. I gasped, barely dragging air through one nostril. My fingers twitched. Then, something sharp stung my palm—a foreign sensation amidst the numbness. My gaze shifted, and there, clenched in my trembling hand, was a fistful of mangled leaves.

"Heh."

A dry laugh escaped me, bitter and delirious. I must've grabbed them when Trailblazer hit me—before I was ripped from the tree line. Somehow, impossibly, it felt like a victory. I'd made it to the forest.

Tears blurred my vision as laughter bubbled up. Broken, possibly paralyzed—I laughed. The clouds above seemed to relish geometry with their shapes, bizarrely resembling boxes or skyscrapers. Wet from the morning dew, my eyes wandered, unfocused.

My hand tightened instinctively, crumbling the leaves into fragments. The wind swept them away, scattering them into nothingness.

But the reprieve was short-lived. A sudden wave of heat poured over my body like a furnace opening its maw. My lips cracked and peeled under the dry, suffocating draft. I ran my tongue along the ruined skin, the metallic taste a bitter reminder of my condition.

Slowly, I tilted my head, and there he was—Trailblazer. Towering over me like a reaper with grim patience. He flexed his fingers, popping each knuckle with deliberate ease, the sound a cruel rhythm in the silence. Shaking out his hand, he stretched his fingers before placing his other hand on the side of his helmet.

"Don't call in backup for this one. It's a Mets fan civvy with no scratch." He walked a circle around me while he spoke to someone on his comms. "Yes, yes. I can take him in. Maybe the Golf can..." He cocked his head to listen for a moment. I could tell by his mannerisms that he wasn't pleased. "You know I hate working with that thespian prick! Have North Star make the dea—" Trailblazer lamented childishly as he leaned backward and expelled a long sigh.

"Fine! Fine. Ya know, it's not enough for me to play good-natured gimp to a bunch of runts, I gotta be your delivery boy too!"

The Trailblazer rattled on and on, seeming totally unconcerned regarding whether I was going to do something. His guard was completely down. By now, my cheek had started to swell up. I was surprised I still had a jaw after that hit.

I turned my head and my gaze fell upon the wreckage of a life—a bird, shredded and strewn across the ground like a discarded memory. Not a duck—no, it was a quail. Or what was left of it. The once-whole creature now existed only as a tuft of feathers, a patchwork of brown and white blending hopelessly into the sticks and dirt. Its head lay separate, unnervingly close, while the severed feet were scattered like forgotten pieces of a puzzle, never to be reassembled.

The eyes—the eyes stopped me cold. Glossy black orbs, holding no light, no warmth. Lifeless yet staring, as if condemning everything around them. I hated it. Hated the sight.

The ground moved beneath me with a solid tug on my ankle. I discovered the source was still arguing on his comms. I phased out his voice as he carted me toward the highway with only his thumb and index finger pinching the cuff of my jeans. Lumps of small rocks and hardened dirt skimmed my back. It pulled my fleece up near my underarms. At the very least I felt pain again. The transition onto the Mayfield's lawn was a welcomed comfort. My fingers started to bend more, and I worked movement back into my wrist. My body started to regain minimal functionality. I even felt my heartbeat pulsing in my ears as the ringing faded.

This was all very strange because any other person would rightfully be dead right now. Yet for whatever reason, perhaps it was my abilities, I remained conscious and still on this earthly plan. I remember metas becoming more durable in some respects, the police reports I've read can attest to that. Though I flew into the air after getting hit in the face... I landed hard and skipped like a rock. Yet I'm still here.

Close to the guest house, Trailblazer had cut across the yard. He turned a corner toward the front entrance of Ted's guesthouse and, POWP!!

Trailblazer's head jilted off to the left and he immediately dropped my ankle. A bullet ricocheted off his helmet. He caught himself from falling, shook his head, and reacted with an ignited flare bustling from his suit. Flames focused out from the vented areas of his boots and shoulder blades. He eyed the source of his immediate discomfort, and his hands shook as he clutched them.

"What. In. The. Hell!!" He bellowed from his diaphragm. From behind the corner I couldn't see, but the whimpering voice of a child I *definitely* heard.

"You little shit!" Trailblazer roared, "Do you know who I am! Your daddy just lets you run around with guns in the yard!?"

The whimpering escalated to a dull buckle of Deon's voice. "I'm sorray" he sniffed. "I did'n know it was you! And—"

Trailblazer's gauntlet turned red like it had been pulled straight out of a forge. "And now, I think you need a reminder. A daily reminder of what you did today." He spoke with vile undertones in his voice.

"No, I'm sorray. I didn't mean ta," Deon frantically pleaded as the meta approached him. I couldn't believe my eyes. This government enlisted diva was going to... With a frail heave, I said:

"Leave the kid alone!" I tried to sit up, but my body didn't want to. Trailblazer disappeared around the corner, and I knew the kid was freezing up. He's just a sitting duck. If I could only get my body to move...

"Ju–just move. Just freaking MOVE!!" I screamed.

I thrust my legs off the ground and rocked them about. The tingle of magnetic embers started to rise around me. Static bolts bled into the air. Deon's cries continued and I heard the struggle ensue a few feet out of my line of sight.

Just then, Mr. Mayfield and Cynthia burst from the back porch in a frantic haste.

My eyelids flew open, and in a surge of adrenaline, I rolled off my back and onto my feet in an instant. The air around me felt heavy, charged. Dirt and debris floated as though gravity itself had faltered.

I rounded the corner and saw him—Trailblazer, gripping Deon by the collar of his jacket. The boy's face was streaked with tears, his cheek pressed against the glowing red gauntlet that threatened to sear his skin.

My teeth clenched, and without hesitation, I reached for Ted's knife. My grip tightened as I closed the distance, and with a single, deliberate motion, I drove the blade into Trailblazer's side. As I plunged the tip, I relayed a surge of electricity into his body.

The meta let out a guttural sound, his body seizing from the shock. His grip on Deon faltered, and the boy dropped to the ground.

He turned, grabbing me and throwing me across the side yard near the gravel road. My body rolled in the grass before I managed to balance on my feet again. But I'd certainly gotten his attention; for now, Deon was safe. The Apex officer clambered towards me, still staving off the voltage coursing through his body.

By now, the Mayfields had made it to Deon's side; that kid was going to have a time at school telling everyone how he got that scar.

I felt so full of energy. Electricity still flowed through my body. As the Apex officer closed in, my feet carried me towards the highway. The taste of iron flooded my mouth, the smell of blood and cow manure grew stronger with every step. I kept running, and running...

My vision grew hazy, and I felt the stark fringes of heat on my heels.

'You have to run now.' That old lady's voice echoed in my mind. 'Run. And. Hide.'

Suddenly, an explosive pop of air ignited all around me. The skin on my face pulled hard as it tried to stretch around my ears. The light of the sun elongated like a fine needle in the sky. I knew to follow the yellow line at my feet as arcs of blue sinews paraded out from my heels. Suddenly, A blurred fluff emerged in front of me. Barely noticeable to the eyes, but enough to alter my path.

I leaped!

In mid–air, a hand caught my ankle. For the moment, I could tell that there was a Chevy pickup truck crossing the road from field to field. Trailblazer collided with the vehicle. He was tall enough that the truck catapulted him over the back end, causing him to tumble on the road. I hit the concrete hard but missed the truck completely. Using the momentum I still had, I rolled upright and kept running.

My feet carried me far but not as fast. Every time I looked back, he wasn't there. Nevertheless, I made as many turns as possible, down gravel roads and up county blacktop, anything I could do to lose Trailblazer. By now, my heartbeat had slowed to a crawl, making it painful to breathe. The moment I stopped, my legs wanted to collapse along with the rest of me.

Lucky for me, I wasn't far from a gas station. It was off Interstate 90 and far from other commercial buildings. I knew I had to get out and fast, so I hurried out of the weeds and onto the gravel. I weaved through the semi truck on the darker side of the lot. From afar, I noticed a blue and yellow bus letting off travelers. It was a mix of older couples and the like. On its LED display read the words 'CHICAGO'. I waited for the bus driver to leave last and to my fortune, he left the doors open. I hurried inside clamping my hands on each seat headboard before lying down in the very back.

It was warm here on the leather seats. Now that I could relax, all the aches and pains from my morning started to settle in. My jaw grew numb, my ribs popped back into place. The shift in my body to heal itself was the oddest sensation. In any case it made me tired. It'd been so long since I'd talked to Little Gracie. Would she know about what had happened to Grandma? Would she know what had happened to me?

Chapter Three

With a dry taste of dust and salt in my mouth, I woke to find that I had fallen asleep against the bus's cold window. Fog blotched the area around my mouth, The bus dipped into an suspecting pothole which smudged my face across the window. It had been much warmer when I'd first drifted off, so I tightened my hoodie around my chest.

After a moment, I warmed up a bit, then curiosity gave way to the world outside the foggy bus windows as I planted my hand on the glass, wiping away the condensation. Then I saw it—all of it. The tall, ridged silhouettes shadowed from a distance. The populated roadways packed bumper to bumper. Distant horns sounded off as exits began to appear. The sun was going down, and we were in the middle of rush hour. So much was different here than where I was from—If only I'd felt allowed, I could have come sooner.

The bus shifted as we took the off-ramp heading downtown from Interstate 9o. My eyes darted to every conceivable corner, taking in the atmosphere. I couldn't help but be excited to be someplace new, even if I was wanted and hunted. Nervously, I used my thumb and forefingers to play with the few five-dollar bills in my pocket. The texture was comforting. Threaded memories wove to the forefront of my mind again: Trailblazer knocking me across the field, Grandma lying in the grass... I hope Gracie can help me. I need to get my barings strait.

There was a summer when Gracie and I played in a yard bordered by trees, with a little blue house perched at the corner of a quiet crossroad. It wasn't our yard, but it didn't seem to matter. Our parents were busy inside that house, leaving us to roam, free and untethered by time. I couldn't have been older than five, and Gracie was barely three.

A bonfire burned at the center of the yard, its heat twisting the air, its light dancing on our faces. We circled it endlessly at first, daring its warmth like it held secrets we wanted to unravel. Eventually, we slowed, entranced. A metal rod stuck out of the fire—one end glowing brilliant orange, the other still cool to touch. I picked it up, captivated by its molten beauty, holding it like a scepter of some imagined kingdom.

For reasons that only make sense in the wild, impulsive logic of childhood, I raised the rod and drew it back. Gracie stood next to me, small and oblivious, her wide eyes fixed on the fire. She wore nothing but a t-shirt and a diaper, her tiny frame outlined by the glow. Time seemed to hold its breath in that moment.

And then...

The bus slammed to a stop, and I almost hit my head on the seat before me. I was hoisted back into the current moment only to realize that my trip was over. Riders spilled out into the center aisle as quickly as the bus had halted, gathering their heavy luggage and other curious things from the overhead compartments. There was no need to rush and fumble about with the other people. I didn't want to take any chances of my abilities accidentally shocking someone. Lucky for me, I've been able to keep a leash on my outbursts. I waited to double-check my seat and make sure everything was with me, then shifted towards the back of the line and found myself behind a mother with a small child draped over her shoulder. The infant stared at me, eyes blinking as if trying to get a better look; it was kind of uncomfortable, so I turned away.

The line inched forward, until eventually I reached the front of the bus and exited into the brisk air. The breeze hit me, and I tightened up my hoodie's drawstrings and fitted my skull cap just over my eyeline, taking in the busy surroundings of people working and hurrying along. In the near distance, a train rambled along a track that was one-story off the ground! I missed this feeling, like any-thing could happen. Shivering, I took off in one direction and matched the pace of other pedestrians.

I walked down the street, and avoided people who would get too close. I remembered Grace's place was around here somewhere. I'd helped her move several years ago and have the information tucked away as a faded memory. I remember her being excited back then. I was happy for her, if not a little jealous. She was a bit of a brat, I couldn't get her away from me when we were kids, but once we finally grew up, we never saw each other much... Not till we were teens.

"Yo, kid, c'mere,"

The voice drifted from the sidewalk. An older man sat behind a small folding table, his presence commanding yet subdued. The three bent playing cards before him seemed worn. He wore a straw-like fedora, and an aged brown coat that kissed his knees. His wiry beard ran streaked with silver, and his eyes were shadows barely glimpsed beneath the brim. Beat-up kicks with peeling sides barely hid the dirt-stained slacks beneath.

"You tryna keep movin', or you got a minute for an old man?" His smile was crooked, almost knowing.

"I'm kinda in a hurry," I replied, feet hesitant to continue moving.

"Rush ain't goin' nowhere fast, my friend. Whateva you're lookin' for, I can help ya find it—guaranteed," he said, dragging out the last word like it carried weight.

His words wove through the air, catching me mid-stride. Against my better judgment, I paused, my curiosity a tether. "Why not?" The scent of rum hung in the atmosphere.

"Just a game. Let's warm up, eh?" he said

He placed a marble on the table—a peculiar, pale green orb swirling with orange trapped within. It shimmered in the sunlight, almost alive, before he covered it with cards creased. His hands moved swiftly, deftly shuffling the cards in smooth, hypnotic arcs. When he stopped, his fingers hovered.

"Pick."

I pointed to the left card, and with a flick, he revealed the marble exactly where I had chosen. The sunlight glared off its surface in hues that seemed to shift with the angle.

"Not bad, not bad. Wanna go again?" he asked, already shuffling faster. His movements blurred, the cards whipping in a figure eight as he spoke again. "So, what's got you runnin', huh?"

"What makes you think I'm running?" I said.

He chuckled, his laugh deep and earthy, like roots tangled in soil. "Ya keep looking behind you mor'in what's in front of ya."

When the shuffling ended, I pointed to the left card again. He flipped it to reveal the marble, but now its orange had deepened into a fierce, radiant glow, with veins of blue crisscrossing its surface. I picked it up, startled by its coldness. When I placed it back, it rolled to its original spot with eerie precision.

"Woah," I murmured, peeking beneath the table but finding nothing to explain its behavior.

He gestured toward a mason jar at the table's edge—a jar I hadn't noticed until then. I pulled a five-dollar bill from my pocket and slipped it inside.

"Bless you," he said with a cryptic grin. "One more round."

"I really gotta get going..."

Ignoring my protest, his hands moved faster this time—so fast they blurred. When he stopped, I chose the middle card. But instead of the marble, he revealed a cigar—a fine roll bound by a gold band etched with the word *Bohekio* and a tribal mask. I sneered at first, confused by the offering.

"I don't smoke."

"Don't matter," he replied, his grin turning soft, almost fatherly. "Keep it. Might come in handy."

I hesitated, feeling the weight of the cigar as I turned it over in my fingers. Its scent was sweet and sharp. I tucked it into my pocket.

The man touched the brim of his hat, tilting it back slightly to reveal eyes that burned with something strange. "Good luck, kid. Take care of ya feet at the cross-roads."

As I turned to leave, a strange warmth swept over my back, like sunlight breaking through clouds. His voice stopped me one last time: "Take a left, kid. That's the way you wanna go."

I nodded and quickly walked off in the direction he'd in-dicated. I'd never had a street merchant give me anything before. I kept walking, mostly keeping my eyes to myself. After crossing the street, I recognized the building I'd seen with a glance. It was all brick with a bell tower perched on top, and above the doorway was a mantle with some-thing written across it. The words 'SKOLA' were carved into stone. I walked up to the door and looked at all the numbers and buttons for each unit, trying to remember Grace's suite number.

"303," I said out loud, not meaning to utter my mind at work.

I pushed the 303-intercom button and waited for a response.

A familiar voice immediately shouted from behind me: "It's 313, you moron."

I turned to notice my sister, Grace, holding a paper sack full of groceries.

"You're going to get nothing but an old Russian woman with a bad ear on that buzzer. Lucky for you, I guess," Grace said.

The expression she held was one of bored disdain. With a slender face and button nose, she cocked her head to the side. She had her brown hair tied up in a bun with a few loose strands.

I noticed someone wiggling around behind her legs—A little person trying to hide as best as she could. Then my niece, Amari, jumped out from behind her and yelled: "BOO!"

She stood a bit over waist-high to Gracie and sported a pair of puffy pigtails tied toward the back. Her eyes were huge and brown with a button nose just like her mother's. Her cheeks were puffy and she wore a white shirt with a cartoon bumblebee on the front that had the words 'Bee Cool' written under it. She jumped around in a circle in her pink shorts and white tennis shoes. The clothes contrasted with her mocha skin.

"My god... Is that little Amari?!" I exclaimed in a hesitant gasp. "I haven't seen you since you were in diapers."

I knelt from the stairs and Amari approached me from the bottom. She was hesitant to climb the stairs but held an inquisitive curiosity as she looked me over.

"Mommy, who's that?" she said and then pointed.

"Ha! This *homeless guy* is your Uncle Charlie... Unfortunately," Gracie said.

"What the... Fudge, Grace."

She proceeded to roll her eyes and direct her attention down the street. Granted, her words weren't false. I looked like I'd been dragged through a field.

"How old are ya, Amari?" I asked.

She wasn't sure what to make of me as she stared at me some more. Then she whipped her hand up with three fingers.

"I'm this many." She smiled.

"Haha, w-wait a minute, you can't be that old yet. How old is she, Grace?"

Grace turned her attention to the sign above my head, then lowered her sight to me and said, "She's almost four, Charlie."

My smile dropped.

"Hahaaa... Where has the time gone?" I said nervously.

"What are you doing here, Charlie?" Grace asked.

"It's kind of a long story, can we go inside first? The walk around the block has winded me."

Graces tilted her head and gave me not-so-trusting eyes. They peered into my soul like thin blinders on a window. Amari ran up to her and pulled at her arm.

"Mommy, you said I can have juice when we got home."

Grace didn't get the chance to respond. A blaring siren erupted from a bullhorn mounted on a telephone post across the street, slicing through the moment like a blade. The world was swallowed in an oppressive, saturated red as the streetlights flared to life, their intensity forcing me to squint and shield my eyes. The air buzzed with static, and then the bullhorn crackled, unleashing a robotic, deafening announcement:

"ALL CITIZENS—PLEASE LEAVE THE RED ZONE. ALL CITIZENS—PLEASE LEAVE THE RED ZONE."

"What the hell is this?!" I shouted, my hands began to shake uncontrollably, every nerve in my body screaming for an explanation.

–RUN–

The word echoed in my mind like a gut-punch. My breathing hitched. "They're coming, aren't they? I–I never should've come here," I stammered, my words stumbling over each other in fear.

The siren wailed again, shrill and unrelenting, drilling into my skull. Instinctively, I cupped my ears. I dragged myself toward the stairs to escape, but Grace's firm grip clamped around my arm. She shoved her bag of groceries into my hands, her movements quick and sharp.

"Hurry inside, you big baby," she snapped, her voice tense as she fumbled with her keys. She unlocked the front door to the apartment building and waved Amari and me inside with an urgency.

As the door swung shut behind us, I caught a glimpse that made my blood run cold. A black van crawled down the street, its engine a low, ominous growl. Stamped boldly on its side was a single word: APEX.

The driver's gaze locked onto mine as he passed. My stomach twisted into knots. He knew. They always knew.

"I said get your ass in here!" Grace yelled.

"Mommy, you said a bad word."

"I know, Sweetie... Let's head upstairs."

The inside of my sister's place looked very... post-modern. Everything was square-like and painted in this off-white color. The walls were off-white, the furniture, the little inconsequential art statues, every-thing—Off-white. The only things that weren't off-white were the curtains, the kitchen counters, and the fancy backsplash.

There were also little stains in the shag carpet where Grace must have worked vigorously to clean. I assumed Amari was the culprit; being just three years old, it wasn't hard to imagine her spilling something. Meanwhile, Grace poured orange juice for Amari at the dining room table. Amari naturally interrupted, lifting her little rainbow cup so that I could see it. The fact that it wasn't off-white made me smile. I then proceeded to tell her how cool it was.

"What was that all about outside? The red lights? The sirens?" I asked.

"Well... I guess I shouldn't expect you to know very much outside your little bubble." Ouch... "That system has been in place for the last year here."

"We have nothing like that back home. So, I'm guessing it's meta related?"

"Bingo, big bro. It reacts when nearby metas have been identified and fed into the system. The police can't track down meta-humans like bloodhounds, so they have this system in place to light up a city block of the last positive ID, and then they'll have Apex to search the area."

"Wouldn't that scare off the metas within the red areas to move away from them?"

"The system isn't for metas, per se. It's for the people to buckle down in their homes and lock the doors. Makes it easier for Apex to navigate on their search. And if there is a positive ID, the authorities already know who they're looking for with a DNA scan and face match."

"It really is a jungle out there," I said.

"It's a jungle gym!" Amari threw in while raising her juice above her head.

"Only if you happen to be the poor meta found by Trailblazer or something."

"...Right. So, do you think we can talk—in private?" I gestured my eyes toward the little girl blowing bubbles in her orange juice.

My sis directed her eyes at her daughter and paused. She sucked on her teeth before nodding. Grace told Amari to go to her room while we talked. The little one did so with her lower lip puckered out and sad eyes like she was about to cry. It was close to her bedtime, after all.

Both Gracie and I walked into her living room, and I sat across from her on the opposite side of the coffee table in one of the off-white chairs. She handed me a cup of hot tea. It was a mug with fairytale characters printed on it, flying pixies, and such. She leaned into her cough and just stared at me. It was so silent we could hear Amari kicking her feet on the bed in the other room. I tilted my head down to break eye contact. Took one deep breath and exhaled.

"I need your help," I said.

My sister folded her arms across her chest and leaned back into the flat cushions of her uncomfortable-looking couch.

"Really! Do you mean like therapy? Because I can rec-ommend someone."

"No, nothing like that." I took my left hand and rubbed it along my right elbow. "You're the only person I can come to."

Grace leaned forward, propping her elbows onto her knees. She weaved her fingers interlocking her hands so she could rest her chin. A bit of a curl in her lip started to form. "You just don't change, do you? I mean, what is it this time? Did you run off from Grandma again? Trying to make it on your own I bet and let me guess! You want me to help you with a place for a while?" Grace tossed her hands.

I stood up and pointed my finger—I didn't know why any of this had to be brought up, but I was on edge. Maybe it was the lack of sleep or having the shit kicked out of me earlier, but I was not in the mood.

"That was different! You knew I hated that job and they did everything they could to get me out of there. Not to mention this was, what, eight years ago?!"

Grace stood up to meet my eye level. She was never the type to be talked down to. "Seven years ago, actually! And so far, I haven't seen any change! Still coming out of nowhere to ask for help! Without a word of warning, I might add—No phone call, no nothing! You just show up like a poor little stray and force yourself onto others!"

I could feel my teeth clench and the heat in my eyes simmer at my sister's words. "Again! Not like last time. You're not even giving me a chance to explain!" I stretched out my arms. "This situation is dire, and you're the only person I know to come to. I don't want to sleep on your couch, I don't want to eat your food, in fact... Take back your crappy herbal tea!"

I slid the ceramic mug across the coffee table toward Grace; it spilled just a bit as it stopped. She hurried to place the mug on a coaster designed like the Ace of Diamonds.

"Ooh, you petty son-of-a-bitch! Every time with you. You want to know why I'm the only person you can come to?"

"Gracie, none of that matters right now—"

"It's because you drive everyone else away with your selfish bullshit and excuses!!" Gracie raised her voice an octave higher. I could see the red swelling up in her face. "You never listen to *anyone* for *anything* if it doesn't have anything to do with *you!*"

I looked around the room with my mouth hanging open as if there was an audience. "That's just not true! It's not!" I said as I firmly shook my finger at her. "I done plenty of things to help people—Hell, I helped grandma when she had no one else. And, *and...* I helped you move anytime you asked."

"Living with Grandma wasn't by choice, Charlie, and you know it."

"It was to help Grandma! H–E–L–P, *Heelllpp.*"

"Whatever, because every time a person meets you and gets just a taste of what kind of person you are, they quickly realize that you're just some overgrown child. That's why you're here right now, whether you admit it or not!"

I stepped out from the enclosed furnished area and turned towards my sister. "Fuck you, Grace! That's not even fair."

"Just grow the fuck up, Charlie! And you know what?" She pointed toward the front door of her condo. "Get out—"

Knock–Knock–Knock

Her stabbing words were interrupted by a knock at her door. Most likely a neighbor who'd heard us arguing.

–RUN–

"Excuse me, Mrs. Johnson!?" A woman spoke from the other side of the door. Gracie sneered a bit from the voice; I could tell she didn't recognize it.

"Who is it? Give me just a minute!" Grace spoke loud enough to be heard clearly from the apartment hallway.

"I'm Detective Schulz of the CPD. I want to ask you a few questions."

My legs got a bit shaky, and I bolted in front of Gracie and crossed my finger over my mouth. Grace looked at me with wide eyes and bewilderment.

After a pause of her trying to understand my poor attempt at sign language, she waved me off silently like a fly buzzing around her ear.

"Mrs. Johnson?!" the detective cried out again.

"Coming!" said Grace.

I ran back into the hallway next to the kitchen and placed my back against a closet around the corner. It was just out of sight of the front living space. It could be nothing, the detective could be doing a routine red district check... Or maybe that guy in the van had recognized me... A wanted meta could never be too careful. The thought of Gracie turning me in played through my head. An unwanted thought that caused me to breathe a bit harder than was necessary. With that, I clasped my mouth with both hands and sunk my back against the closet door.

Knock–Knock–Knock

"Mrs. Johnson?" the detective persisted.

Grace fiddled with a total of three locks before she swung the door open.

"That's Ms. Johnson... detective," Grace said, correcting the detective in a posh way.

"...Ohh, my apologies," the detective said. "Can I come in and ask a few questions?"

"*You* may... Come in."

"Ahh yes."

From my hiding place, I heard the pair of them settling in upon Grace's uncomfortable couches. I fought to keep my senses focused on them. For some reason, a song popped into my head and I couldn't get rid of it. Every time I tried killing it, the song only got louder. Come *on*. Focus! I screamed internally at myself.

"Does this visit have anything to do with the Awning Protocol?" Grace asked.

"No ma'am, that was some incident with a blob meta at the local dinner."

"Wait, you mean the one with the gold and black ceramic tiles on West Polk?" She said with curious venture.

"Yes. It had tried to make its way in through the window seal of the place. Certainly strange."

"I... *love* that place. It wasn't destroyed or anything, right?

"No, it's intact."

"Thank the Buddha because that place is to *diiie* for," Grace said with more enthusiasm than I'd ever heard in my life.

"Ha hah! Yes ma'am... But, back to why I'm here, there is a personal matter with, I believe it's your grandmother."

"Edna?!" I could hear Grace shifting around at the mere mention of her.

"Yes, she's in the hospital right now."

"What!! Wha–at, how? What happened!?" Grace blurted out.

"Take a breath... She's in critical condition. There was an explosion at her house but she's hanging in there.

"Ooh, no no no... I can't believe that could happen!" said Grace. "And I thought she was under such good care..." she added with fuming anger.

"That's the other thing. Your brother—" Here it comes— "is the primary suspect and remains at-large."

"My brother? Well, that can't be. He wouldn't do it on purpose, I'm sure."

"We would like to straighten this issue out and find him. We're checking in with all the locations he could possibly—"

The Detective talked at her. Grace sat quietly taking it all in. There was no telling what she might be thinking. In the dark hallway, I heard a muttering just out of my eye line. The little squeaks of a little girl meandered down the hallway. She wobbled in step with a tired look in her eye. She dragged a little purple blanket behind her.

"Whatcha doin?" she said loudly.

I signaled quietly with my hands and placed a finger over my lips.

"Shhhhhhh!" I signaled.

The front room went silent for a moment. Amari didn't know what to do, so she just stood there in the hallway in front of me. It was so quiet I could hear my heart beating out of my chest.

"Is there someone else in the house?" the Detective asked.

"Heh, yeah! It's just my daughter... Honey? Are you okay in there?" Grace yelled out with a hint of worry.

I shook my head vigorously and pointed both of my index fingers towards my chest. I felt horrible asking a little girl to lie, but I was in a panic. Amari hesitated; I could tell she didn't know what to do. I took a deep breath, leaned over towards her ear and said, "It will be okay."

With that, Amari took a breath as well and shook her head in a mini spret of action.

"I'm okay, Momma, just going to the *potty*!!" she said.

Amari opened the door to my right and turned on the light to the restroom. To my surprise, she closed the door and continued standing in front of me. We both sat silently, listening in on Grace's conversation. I wished she would have just gone back to her room. Everything going on right now was something a little girl shouldn't hear about her uncle. I was going to be verbally crucified. Possibly literally, after this night was done.

"So... Is there anything else, detective?" Grace continued.

"Yes, you see, ma'am, your brother Charlie *may* have been identified—as a meta-human."

The air in the house grew cold, for that silent moment after the detectives' words left the air still. At once, I regretted ever coming here. If she lies about me now, she'll be involved, '*aiding and abetting a meta*'. She could suffer consequences because of me... I looked up at Amari. Her eyes fixated and not understanding all that well, but she read the moment. My thoughts funneled into the worst things that could happen from here. I pulled my knees in tight and buried my face in my arms. I thought about what could happen to Amari—She would be lost in the system… an orphan! Again, it would be all my fault.

"Ma'am, I know that's a lot to take in, but be assured I'm here to help. Have you heard from your brother lately?" asked the detective.

"I never hear from my brother," Grace said as neutrally as possible. Amari clinched her teeth to express a 'yikes' gesture. I clasped my nose with my palms in a prayer gesture.

"Mind you, Ms. Johnson, I'm here to help. If your brother gets a hold of you, make sure to call me." I heard the detective flap a card on the surface of the coffee table. "He could be very dangerous as his abilities seem unstable from the reports I've read. Keep a distance if you can."

"Like if moving here wasn't far enough…" Grace lamented.

"I'll show myself out, and it was a pleasure speaking with you Ms.–"

"Just Grace, Grace is fine." She spoke with short and abrupt tones. "I'll let you know if anything is amiss. I wouldn't want to put my child in any sort of danger, Detective Shultz?"

"Schulz, Mallory Schulz… Ma'am."

At last, the detective left and Gracie locked the door with haste. Amari ran out into the front room. My little sister didn't say anything. I was almost scared to move from my dark little spot in the hallway, but I knew I must. I followed my niece into the living space and saw Amari with her arms wrapped around her mother's waist. Gracie looked down at her and swayed her gently as she hugged her back. I didn't interrupt, just quietly sat down at the kitchen counter.

I sat there for a time while Gracie put Amari to bed. She read her a story about a princess in a high tower that was guarded by a dragon, and a knight who tries to save her. The story went in a direction I didn't expect it to. One of those new-age methods of storytelling. The knight was shunned after he tried to fight the dragon. Turned out the dragon was a friend and protector of the Princess, and she was already living *her* happily ever after.

At last, I saw the lights go out in the hallway and Gracie walked into the kitchen without saying a word. She has an oriental sort of housecoat on with fuzzy pink cuffs. She cleaned the counter and picked up the plates and cups and placed them in the dishwasher. Finally, I couldn't take the bothersome atmosphere any longer.

"She's right, you know," My voice pierced the air. "I found out just this morning after breakfast."

Grace continued to clean the counters with her back turned towards me.

"Grandma walked in on me when my... issue started acting up in her kitchen. To say she wasn't thrilled would be underselling it a bit. The explosion was gas from the stove, and my issue ignited it. It wiped out Grandma pretty bad."

Grace slammed the pantry door hard. She continued to clean with her back turned to me.

"I tried to get her help, which she did get! But I was manifesting in front of the entire neighborhood and there was–was nothing I could do." A solitary tear rolled down my cheek. "So I ran, I ran fast, Grace, faster than anyone could possibly go. The whole town saw it, including Grandma's neighbors."

"Apex?" Grace interjected.

"Yes... Apex too."

I stood up and started pacing the floor in the dining space.

"So that's why I'm here," I said. "You're the only person in the world, Gracie. The only one I knew with absolute certainty wouldn't turn me away... Or so I thought. To be honest, right now I wouldn't blame you if you called that number the detective gave you."

Grace allowed her forehead to fall on the refrigerator door. She took a deep breath and pushed herself away from the fridge before finally facing me. Her eyes were dark and whelped from stress.

"You know what, yeah. I could just do that," Grace said. "I–I really could. There's a part of me that would love to smile and wave as they tossed you in a van to whatever hell this city has for metas. I can see why you would come here, and I know you don't have anyone else. I can understand all that."

She quickly ran up to me and placed her hands on my cheeks, cupping my face. She looked into my eyes.

"But, Charles—" She swallowed a lump in her throat. "With Amari being here and you being... Unpredictable, you know I can't help you."

I broke free from her grasp and walked toward the living space.

"Gracie! I can control this!" I flopped my palms out, facing toward the ceiling. "This won't get out of hand, I'm learning now, and I didn't have an incident on the way here."

"You destroyed Grandma's house like a day ago... You're *really* going to stroll up in my apartment building, with tons of neighbors by the way, and tell me you got this?!"

I was silent, my hands falling flat along my sides. I looked for the words to prove myself capable, but the words never came. So badly I wanted to say the right thing in the moment, to force Grace to think twice about me and accept me. But blood wasn't enough to make this happen, and I couldn't pretend she wasn't right.

"I know... I thought maybe, if at all, you could point me in the right direction." I turned towards her, and my eyes were worn red. "Things are feeling a little dark right now, and I'm not sure I can handle it."

Grace approached me and placed her hand on my chest. She wiped a single tear from my eye and said, "I promise to go check on Grandma, sit with her. She can see her grandbaby, it's well overdue, of course."

I smiled and sniffed. A particular weight was lifted.

"Thank you" I eked out before my vocal cords tightened becoming harder to speak. "I don't know where—""I'll find out," she said. "There's only one hospital back home, where else are they going to take her?"

I used my hoodie sleeve to wipe away my shame.

"I wish there was something I could do, Gracie."

"You know, I've heard of weird chatter from around that there's a refuge for people like you. I've heard it more than once. I hear all kinds of things, of course. The world *is* going mad. Maybe you can find something out there."

"Sis... You can't expect me to go out and just find some other metas. It's not like there's a social media group for it."

Grace wrapped one arm over my shoulder and the other arm under my lat. She closed in and squeezed me tight. I mounted my chin on her shoulder and wrapped both my arms around her. I couldn't remember the last time we'd been like that.

I needed it.

Just then, a little patter of footies came shuffling into the room. Amari rounded the corner from the hallway with a piece of paper.

"Look, Uncle Chuck, I made you a pic'sure."

I resisted the urge to break away from my sister's hug but only for a moment. I turned towards that adorable face and smiled. She handed me a piece of paper with crayon markings of three stick figures in the left corner. On the other side was a rectangle with jagged edges scribbled on top. "See! This is me, this is mommy, and in da middle is you!" Amari said gleefully.

I ran my thumb across the drawing. *Did she draw this for me?* I thought.

"Cool, what's this purple square around the person in the middle?"

"That's Uncle Chuck—It's your supaaa hero cape!" She exclaimed, then put one hand on her hip while the other pointed up towards the ceiling. "You are saving me and mommy from a burning building!"

Grace then coughed in her hand to interrupt Amari's little presentation. "Okay then, Mari, baby, I think we should cut down on your tablet for a while. Burning buildings is a bit much for mommy to hear right now."

I placed my hand on top of little Amari's head.

"I love it, sweetheart!"

I folded the picture up and placed it in my back pocket while kneeling to hug her. "You'll be a great artist someday if you keep practicing."

"Yeah, it's always an awesome thing being *poor* and *talented* in this city..." Grace interjected under her breath. She then turned to her daughter, "Sweetie, we have to let Uncle Charlie go for right now. Kay, baby?"

Amari's smile widened. "Bye, Uncle Chuck!" She gave a loose-wristed wave. With her arms outstretched, Amari ran back into the hallway like some airplane.

Grace then gave me a look, the kind of look that said it was time for me to go. She gestured her hand toward the front door.

"Kicking me out so soon, sis? I half-expected to freshen up a bit before leaving. Like a shower, maybe?"

With a breath of intense energy in her voice, Grace said, "This place isn't going to be easy on you, the metas around here show up on the news a lot. Plus I can't risk any more surprise visits from local law enforcement.

"Do me a favor, though," she went on. "Don't become one of *them*." I was taken aback by her anger. "I don't want my daughter to live in a world where anything can hurt her... And Charlie, call me, okay?"

Tiredness fogged over Grace's eyes; she walked over to the kitchen cabinets and pulled out an amalgam of tupperware containers. She lazily dumped them on the counter and started filling each one with food from the shelves, the fridge, and the pantry.

"You're lucky I needed to get rid of this stuff—the pediatrician told me Mari has a gluten allergy. Can't have half this crap in arm's reach anymore."

I walked into the hallway with a bag full of food and a few extra dollars in my pocket. She gave me her phone number on a scrap of paper since I'd practically lost everything before coming here. I turned toward Grace as she stood in the doorway. She tightened the skull cap over my eyes and lifted my hood over my head to better hide my face.

"Charlie, whatever you do, don't go feral out there," she said.

Then she closed the door and I was left to stand in the hallway alone. For some reason, I waited. Maybe for her to change her mind, or just to think about what I was going to do next. Even so—I noticed she didn't lock her doors.

I can't say I'd expected a warm reception, but I was going to have to look after myself. It's honestly all I ever wanted, but not like this.

Chapter Four

The evening traffic volleyed by like brightly colored beads on a rope. The sound of atmospheric runoff trailed dully as I descended the steps of the apartment building. The night was cold, but it didn't bother me. I looked back at the wooden entrance way with a line of metal buttons on the side. A part of me wanted to lash out and press every single one of them, just to annoy everyone in the building for just a moment before running out of sight. Instead I tucked my hands into my pockets and continued down the sidewalk.

I understand, I thought to myself. A stern, flinching blood vessel percolated the upper reaches of my hairline. I understand that she had to do what's best for her and Amari. It would be reckless to harbor your own brother due to things outside our control. My fist clenched and my arms tensed as I picked up the pace towards an intersection. *How could she just let me go like that...? We we're suppose to be family. We were suppose to have each others back.*

I kicked over a metal trash, the kind with welded fixtures that bolt directly into the concrete. Knocked it right out of the sidewalk and launched it into the intersection.

I felt the shock from my abilities carry through my foot and into the steel, launching it from the ground like it was mere styrofoam. Traffic honked and chatter from a nearby parcel driver attacked me in a language I couldn't understand. I startled myself and spun my head haplessly to see who else was looking. My shoulders sank as I stepped backward around a corner and off toward the darker reaches of the block.

A part of me wanted to sprint ahead, but I was reluctant to make myself stick out so much from the other commuters, so I decided to take a brisk, speedy walk—like I had to be somewhere, but my life wouldn't depend on it. A sedan drove by me with a child in the back seat. The child poked its head out the window and screamed "Neeeerd!" as it passed.

A darker inlet of an old brick building caught my eye and I rushed to lean within the space for a breather. The space was perhaps three feet deep with a curved brick overhang and was cluttered with trash, crates, and a chronic stench of piss. My teeth grit and my hands began to shake. I was going mad and, no matter what I did, someone was always bound to be watching me. For a few minutes, I cursed myself for ever coming to Chicago in the first place.

"Why did I think this was ever a good idea?!" I punched the wall. The brickwork caved in around my fist. "Stupid! Stupid man."

I paced frantically around the inlet. I wanted to cry, but I also wanted to take a metal pipe to some parked cars.

"Where am I going to go?" I clawed at my hair. Grace could have at least let me shower, stay the night, anything! But no, no, no, no. It's always about my, "Negative bullshit!"

She always has to kick me, "Right in the balls!"

A group of strangers passed by and overheard my yelling, startling both them *and* myself. We stood there staring at each other for but a moment until I nodded sheepishly and apologized. They walked away, but they kept on staring... I nodded aggressively at their departing forms.

"Yeah! Sure! Get a good look!" I yelled, prompting them to whisper among themselves. I continued down the walkway, not looking where I was going. As I turned my head to break eye contact with the group, I immediately bumped into someone else.

"Gawd, damn it!" I growled firmly.

Upon looking up to give this new stranger a piece of my mind, I recoiled and stumbled a half-step back. My throat quickly dried up and my eyes grew wide upon finding myself face-to-face with two police officers wearing black overcoats and uniform-issued caps. One approached with his hand venturing out in front of him.

"Are you doin al'ight, buddy?"

"Yeah! Yeah... I'm, uhh," I searched desperately for an excuse. They didn't seem to know... I shifted my eyes to the right and the officers glanced at each other.

"You startled me... *buddy?*" I said awkwardly, waiting for them to fall for some lie that wasn't so much of a lie. Grace gave me pie, didn't she?

The officer in the back caught feedback from the ra-dio hanging from his belt, then turned around and spoke some indecipherable jargon into the receiver. The other cop locked eyes with me, flexing his upper lip as he took a deep breath and spat out a laundry list of questions:

"What got you so angry?" He flipped a small flashlight into my eyes, causing me to wince. "Easy, I just want to check on your state of mind."

I answered back with a deep breath and said, "My... stupid lady kicked me out. I'm just, ya know, venting."

"Got any ID on ya?"

"Sadly, I don't, which is part of why I'm angry."

"Name?"

"...Chandler."

"Odd name." He stepped closer to check my eyes. I could only imagine what they looked like. "You been smoking any ice?"

"What?! No!" I said defensively and stood taller as I answered. "It's been a rough day, ya know?"

"Can't say I do, why don't you tell me?"

I had no idea what to tell this guy. A freaking meta punched me across a field and my own sister pushed me out into the cold. I haven't showered or eaten since this morning. My nose flared as I sneezed into the nook of my elbow. As I looked myself up and down, something started to click in my head.

"Okay, guy," the cop initiated. "If you head two blocks thad a'way, you'll see a big red building. Go in and they'll get you a hot meal and blankets to sleep." The officer pointed behind me and in the opposite direction of Gracie's apartment. Just as I thought, he thinks I'm homeless, thank god for that.

A subtle smile crept in and quickly faded as I changed my stature to seem hungrier than I was, weaker than I was, and a bit more off. It honestly wasn't that much of a stretch. The police officer curled his lip and shifted his eyes at my best impression of what I thought a hobo would act like. I couldn't tell if I was doing it right or bombing my performance. Either way, he looked extremely uncomfortable. His mouth hung open with a sneer that flashed on his face.

"God bless, I din'it know where I could go from here. Thank ya," I said.

"Hey, hey now. Protect and serve is what we do. Now get out of here." He reached over and brushed my shoulders off, simultaneously attempting to straighten my posture, but in so doing my body zapped his hands and he pulled them away.

"Woah! You got some weird static thing going on!" He flung his hands and even sucked on them to ease the sting.

I approached the man with concern. I'd nearly had an emotional breakdown a minute ago, so my abilities could be reacting to touch. "Yeah, sorry about that," I said. No sooner had the words left my mouth that I turned to head toward the shelter.

"Wait! Wait a minute there!" The other police officer approached me and pulled out a pen-like device with a glowing yellow tip. "The shelter requires a scan for meta genomes. We can give you a stamped pass to save on testing and paperwork." He waved the device in front of me. The glow was hypnotizing and made a beeping sound.

My eyes went wide.

Without a thought, I smacked the pen from the officer's hand; it clinked on the concrete just to roll into the gutter. We traded glares and sat in a stew of silence. The officer didn't break eye contact as he made a play toward his belt. I shifted my weight with my feet slowly inching behind me. The officer tightened his jaw and thinned his peepers as his face was illuminated by the glow of my flickering eye, almost akin to a bug zapper activating from my right eye.

–RUN–

With haste, he drew his firearm, and the officer behind him immediately started yelling a code into his radio. I stretched my hand out to shield myself, but in doing so a thin bolt of electricity struck the officer's firearm. The gun flung from his grasp and, before it could touch the concrete, I had turned and begun to sprint away. Their voices screamed for me to halt, but I kept going. Loud pops sounded out and one bullet whipped past my ears. With that, a jolt in my spine seemed to activate as strings of light blue electricity spread throughout my body. As it surged, so did I. In an instant, I was running till my surroundings blurred and a bellow of air exploded in my wake. It didn't last very long, however, until the electricity grounded out and the energy faded along with my speed.

The world came back into focus, and I nearly ran into a white delivery van.

I fumbled my footing to avoid the vehicle and tripped. This was bad because the speed carried through me as I tumbled in the street and onto a patch of grass that stretched a few acres. Fortunately, I managed to tumble into a thin, swamp white oak tree. The bark connected with a floating rib on my right side, and I immediately curled up in a ball after the impact. The pain from my rib numbed my right side and my entire body felt like it was on fire from multiple jellyfish stings. Quickly, I covered my mouth not to scream as the pain ran its course. With numbed fingers and toes, I was able to stand upright with the help of the tree I'd hit. I coughed up blood as I looked around, finding myself in one of the parks near the lake, I couldn't tell which. They all looked the same to me right now.

I'd managed to get away for the moment, but I had no idea how much distance I'd covered since that exchange with the cops. I allowed my breathing to settle, giving myself time to recuperate before moving again, maybe too much time. The silence felt comforting at the moment. Alone to think about what happens next... I missed my bed.

Before I could think more of home, the entire block around the park became engrossed in red lights, beaming lamps of ember weeping down the streets. Of all the lighting choices to catch metas, this was surely the gaudiest.

The sirens erupted on each corner around me with the familiar automated warning:

"ALL CITIZENS—PLEASE LEAVE THE RED ZONE—ALL CITIZENS—PLEASE LEAVE THE RED ZONE"

I trotted off through the sparsely layered trees that failed to provide adequate cover. Nursing the side of my body, I slowly regained feeling in the tips of my toes. The back of my head pulsed as I scanned my surroundings for a place to hide. The only luck I could muster was a dark alley on the other side of the street. It wasn't tarnished in red light, and no one was around. I could tuck away in the darkness before the police showed up.

Exhaling, I placed one foot on the concrete of the red-lit street. The alley was dark as night and feelings of safety washed over me as I hobbled closer. I was in the middle of the street when a bright, roving light spotted me from above.

It was fast!

The high-pitched whine of an engine cut through the air, sharp and sudden. My head snapped up, but it was already too late—a KTM 450 dirt bike came crashing down on me, slamming me flat on my back. The impact knocked the wind out of me, and all I could see were its thick, treaded tires and the gleaming white frame I'd admired so many times before. I'd always wanted to ride one of those. Now, it was pinning me to the ground.

The rider was draped head to toe in sleek white protective gear—pads, a helmet, and a dark gray fiber jumpsuit underneath. Under the harsh red glow of the lights around us, her entire figure burned crimson, but even then, I knew who she was. I'd seen her on the news. Apex's infamous lookout. The rider of the skyline.

With a deliberate motion, the kickstand clunked onto the pavement, and she swung herself off the bike. The moment she removed her helmet, long blonde hair spilled free, framing her slender face and sharp triangle nose. Her presence was magnetic and chilling all at once.

"North... Star," I slurred.

Her fit was similar to Trailblazer, except she only had one sponsor sewn onto her jumper. She hovered a thin, cylindrical device with a beeping sound over me, same as the cop from before. The light at the end of the device flashed until it grew solid yellow and sounded out with a long, drawn-out beep.

"Hi Mets fan," she said with a smile.

"I don't even like the Mets." I coughed and continued nursing my side.

The overhead floodlights turned off and the streets reverted to their normal levels of dark and dreariness. Northstar grabbed both my hands and dragged me out from under her bike. Her boot jammed into my injured rib, causing me to flip over on my stomach.

"You have the right to remain silent!"

Next, she fastened a pair of thick, blocky handcuffs around my wrists. The steel on them was freezing.

"Anything you say can and will be used against you. For the only right of a meta is—"

"Compliance with *humane* processing. I know!"

"Fine then, smart ass."

Northstar proceeded to push my head into the concrete. As she held my head down, she called out on her comms:

"Northstar to Marker One, Northstar to Marker One. Come in, Marker One. I believe I have the perp who was speeding via foot, downtown. Send evac."

Clonk!

A sharp, metallic thud rang out, cutting through the chaos. The hollow pipe collided with Northstar's temple, and her grip on my skull loosened instantly. Her body crumpled forward, hitting the ground hard, and her unmoving form confirmed she was out cold.

Before I could fully process what had happened, hurried footsteps echoed nearby, closing in fast. A strong hand yanked me by the scruff of my hoodie and my handcuffs in one swift motion, nearly wrenching my shoulder out of its socket.

"Hey! Hey, watch it!" I spat, the pain forcing the complaint out of me as my feet stumbled awkwardly.

I barely had time to turn toward my aggressor before I was shoved into the shadows of a narrow alley. I turned to face him.

There he stood: taller than me, though not by much, with an undeniable presence that commanded attention. His long, matted hair was tied into a rough bun, streaked with wear and neglect. A thin, scruffy goatee framed his face, complementing his sharp features. His skin had a mild brown hue.

But it was his attire that caught my eye—the faded brown jacket hanging loosely on his shoulders, heavy boots worn, and blue jeans that looked like they'd seen more winters than I could count.

Despite everything—his scruffy appearance and abrupt actions—there was an intensity in his expression that hinted at purpose. This wasn't random, and this wasn't coincidence. Whoever he was, I wasn't sure whether to feel relief or dread.

"Easy, comrade. De cavalry has arrived." I was surprised by his blend of Southern drawl and French-like accent. "We need to move now, before dey swarm."

"I'm not going anywhere! Who even *are* you?!"

"I'm de man saving ya life. I can not explain now, but I am in need of your services." He grabbed me and tried to push me further into the alley, but I resisted by pulling myself toward the road.

"Try explaining anyway!" I yelled. He took my cuffs and plunged a knife into them, causing them to spark. He then attempted to pry them off but wasn't able to. "Get away from me, man."

"I am trying to release you," the stranger said.

A fluorescent bead of red could be seen in the distance. A marble of flame that grew in size the closer it got.

"Damn! We got no time!" he said.

Within the struggle, the stranger decked me in the jaw and slung my body over his shoulder, then ran through a wooden door. He dropped me on the concrete as he started blocking the doorway. I stood up to realize that we were inside a garage. A stack of microwaves was piled on the far corner of the room and dust and dander misted around us due to our intrusion.

"Be quiet. Don't breathe, don't move. Not *anyt'ing*," he whispered urgently.

He proceeded to push near a dirty window seal and sat next to me peeping through the glass. I started ruminating about this guy. Who comes out of nowhere and starts barking orders at strangers? So, what if he saved me from Apex? It's not like I'm indebted to him.

"Who the hell do you think you are?!" I screamed.

The moment I said it, a streak of flame flashed as Trailblazer appeared. Any further words I wanted to expel fell deaf in my throat and a familiar shiver ran up my spine. My body sank lower to the ground and any way I could limit my noise output, I did. The Apex officer strolled in a circle around Northstar and scanned the area. I could tell he was surveying by the vertical LEDs flashing on his visor. He kicked Northstar in the leg on one passing.

"Wake up, Tasha. I know you're not dead. Your vitals are stable."

Before long, Chicago Police squad cars pulled around the corner on both sides of the meta couple and Trailblazer held his hands out to stop them short. Finally, the young lady on the ground started to stir and prop herself up one arm at a time. She rubbed the back of her head.

"What happened? Where's speedy?" Trailblazer said.

"I... I don't know. One moment I'm apprehending the subject, the next I'm lying here with a blistering headache. Someone must have gotten the jump on me."

"You got to be joking. No one's stupid enough to try that. Meta or human."

Northstar shrugged. I looked over at the culprit and noticed a generous smile on his face. We were able to observe from the window under the cover of darkness.

"That's *great*, ju–ust perfect. Did you atleast get the tracker on him?"

Northstar managed to stand, brushing herself off.

"Yes, sir! He's cuffed. Should be an easy matter."

My eyes widened as I watched through the minimalist of peepholes through the glass. I rubbed my fingers along the shackles that were fastened behind my back. Trailblazer knelt on his haunches and gazed aimlessly at the ground. The police lights continued to flash, creating a melodic silhouette of the speedster meta. I didn't know what he was doing. Possibly reading something in his visor.

"Tasha?"

"Sir?"

"I don't see him. Are you sure he was cuffed before you went down?"

"...I-I'm certain. Yes. Perhaps the tracker isn't online."

Trailblazer hung his head low and sighed.

"Lucky prick. You know what?! Fine... Spread out and keep searching. He couldn't have gotten far."

From his kneeling position, he launched forward in a trail of scorching flames, vanishing into the distance like a living inferno. Meanwhile, Northstar swung herself onto her KTM 450 dirt bike with a practiced ease that spoke of raw precision. She gripped the throttle tightly, revving the engine with an intensity that seemed to shake the air around her. The bike roared like a feral beast as she aimed it at the towering building beside her.

With a sudden burst of power, the front tire struck the brick façade. The entire bike surged upward, defying gravity as it clung to the skyscraper's vertical surface. Painting streaks of light against the night as she scaled the wall like a predator chasing the sky.

It was impossible to look away. Watching Northstar ride was like witnessing the impossible brought to life—a blend of grace and brutality that left me awestruck. Or, at least, I would've been if I wasn't still fuming about the fact that she'd hit me with her damn bike.

Time crawled to a standstill as I crouched in the shadows. The cops lingered, their flashlights casting long, searching beams over the area. One of them ventured dangerously close, the light grazing my hiding spot. My pulse pounded as I held my breath, every muscle frozen in place.

Eventually, they moved on, muttering amongst themselves as they retreated. My shoulders sagged in relief as the red lights from their patrol cars dimmed in the distance.

"Nonm Blan!" the stranger referred to me.

The stranger inched over and pulled me up on my feet. He pushed me out the door and deeper into the alley.

"Too dangerous to walk the streets."

"Where are we going? I appreciate you saving me and all but, like, you're practically kidnapping me."

"Meta-Gason, let's talk things out."

Through the alleys and cutting across bare streets, he strung me along. There wasn't much I could do with the cuffs still tight around my wrists, blocking any chance of using my abilities.

"So, what do you want? Also, who are you?" I asked.

"Dey call me Wick—Wick of Haiti. I'm here to find someone very important to me... and my country."

"So, what does that have to do with me?"

"You? Heh, well, you are goin' to be my way in to find her."

"*Her?*"

"Yes. Yuh see, she is a captive meta. Kinda like you. I need a way in to reach her. You will help me get inside to do that."

"Inside where?"

We ran through another alley that was thin and hard to walk through. It sat between two apartment buildings that only lent us inches of space. When we funneled out from the other end, and the spaced opened up to an interesting sight. One that made my eyes grow wide and nearly forgetting my current situation—waiting like a predator in the shadows—a 1966 Chevy Impala. But not just any Impala. This one was a masterpiece of subdued menace.

Its sleek, jet-black body gleamed under the dim light, with only the faintest accents of chrome catching a glint. The rims, painted a deep black, had dark blue piping tracing their inner edges—a touch of sophistication that whispered danger. That same blue trim accented the tailgate, grill, and the outlines of the windows, giving the car an aura of understated power. The stranger opened the passenger door of the sedan and gestured for me to take a seat. I hesitated.

"We don't have time. We've got to go now!" he said with a sliver of urgency.

"Where are you taking me, and why should I care if you find this woman?"

"Look, you are stranded in de middle of old town. Handcuffed with a meta inhibitor. the whole city looking for *you!* To do yuh harm! they will mess you up!" He took a deep breath and sighed. "And now *you*... Are standing dere like a loose asshole because you won't get in the damn car!"

I shook off his words and quietly strolled over to sit in the passenger seat of the car. He slammed the door, then sprinted around the other side and climbed into the driver's seat.

"Was dat so hard?"

"Don't patronize me," I said.

He turned the key in the ignition and the engine turned over smooth as silk. A minor pop sounded from the muffler. It was enough to make me paranoid, more than I already was.

We crept around the corner from the alley at a slow idle. Wick muted the radio despite its playing the middle chorus of Stevie Wonder's "Living in the City". The red tint of the emergency lights was close, but not close enough to illuminate the vehicle. Wick looked around suspiciously and waited for a clear window to drive out.

"It looks clear, just hurry to the other side of the street," I said.

"No! If we move, we keep movin' till we get out," Wick said. "Any moment's hesitation from here will end us."

What he said seemed like a parable from any old Chinese flick. I still didn't know why he'd saved me from the cops, especially since I was already in Apex's custody. Most people would have given up after that.

"What do you want with me?" I asked again.

Wick kept looking up and down the empty street and paused a moment when a few cop cars pulled out. I ducked in the passenger seat as they passed with their sirens blaring. After we'd lost sight of the patrolling convoy, Wick shifted into drive and pulled the Impala out on the street. He turned north towards Highway 55 and sped off under the overpass.

"You a meta. You are my ticket inside Malcolm's Warehouse," Wick said.

"Malcolm's? What is that? And why me?? Couldn't there be another meta, maybe one that's good at finding people to help you?"

"No meta is stupid enough to walk 'round in broad daylight. Too many ways to spot the mutation... Except you."

He gave me a sharp look. "Lucky for me, because I do not need someone special. Just *a* meta."

Wick turned off on a nearby frontage road and quickly went into a storage yard. The gated entrance was already open plenty wide enough to slip the Impala through. We crept through the stall of doors until we got to the back of the facility. Each stall looked dingy and rusted out, like this place hadn't seen business hours for a long time.

"Soo..." I broke the silence. "With all that being said, I'm perfectly fine just walking away from this whole situation, sounds like you're turning me in." The handcuffs knocked into the center console as I tried to shift positions.

"Not far from de truth. but if dis all goes smoothly, each of us will attain what we want."

My neck stiffened at the thought of being turned in. "What the hell do you know about what I want? I'm really fed up with what other people want."

We approached a large, yellow chain-linked fence. The car came to a stop and the engine shut off.

"You know ya need to get dem cuffs off to be free, yeah?"

"It can't be that hard to get this off. Got a key?"

"No... Dem are stainless steel Apex shackles. When that green light is on, you have no powers. Had I not disabled thee track'a, they would have you by now."

"Okay, so you don't have a key."

"Malcolm might have a way to get dem off."

"Can't you just smash it?"

"No chance. I was able to break de track'a, but if I tamper further..." Wick spread his hands out and mouthed the word 'BOOM'.

I sank deeper into the passenger seat. My ambitions were crumbling before me. If I had thought about it, I could have snagged the key off NorthStar when she was knocked out. I looked over and said, "What is Malcolm's Warehouse? How do we go about doing this?"

Wick smiled and stepped out of the car. As he walked along the yellow fence, he reached up and appeared to unhook something from the top of the frame. Gradually, then, he pulled back the fencing, just wide enough for a person to squeeze through. It was hard to see with no light, but I managed to step out of the car on my own and traverse through the open space. We walked through to view an ominous brick building looming in front of us. A commercial property that looked long abandoned.

The back door was already open as we pushed through into the darkness. That's when I saw Wick connecting two metal clamps on a car battery propped on a table. As he did, sparks shot out from the connecting points of the battery post and lights flickered and flashed brightly. The illuminated space revealed a makeshift safe room in an office. There was a single cot in the corner with loose papers scattered under it, and a single plastic table with what looked like blueprints sprawled across its surface. In a separated corner on top of a wooden desk was an array of weapons and lethal equipment displayed nicely on a cloth surface.

Lastly and most interesting was a small table propped against a wall with trinkets cobbled together to form... What I could guess was an altar. Candles sat on the ground on both sides and old faded pictures pinned on the wall around it. On the altar were scraps of metal. In the center of the table was a bowl with ash, wood debris and empty bullet casings. In front of that was a machete with a red cloth handle, almost ceremonial it seamed. Wick shut and locked the door behind us.

"Do you know who dis man is?" Wick inquired as he held a picture in front of my face.

The image was of a man with long, dirty blonde hair, dark glasses, and a thin face with a pointed nose. I squint-ed at the image and tried recalling this figure in front of me, like I was supposed to know who he was, but I couldn't. The quality of the image was terrible, like it had been clipped from a security camera.

"This is Malcolm, Malcolm Daily. He operates here as an international philanthropist. In the public eye, he's known for supporting causes and charities across de globe... All to serve his agenda."

"...Okay, doesn't look too bad to me."

"This man poses as a wealthy do-gooder, but what he really does is travel place to place, abducting meta-hu-mans and selling them to anyone who can afford the skin off their hide."

"Ohhh..."

"Now, Malcolm has taken someone who infused hope where I'm from, and I've been tracking him since he left

Haiti. From what I've gathered, he will be co-hosting a gala this week, but it is only a facade for his auction."

I stood silently as he continued.

"Wi, de target, is at an elevated risk of getting sold at the auction. I have to retrieve her before then, or she be lost." Wick lowered the photo and pointed the cuffs from behind my back. "You, my dear vagrant, will be my ticket into Malcolm's."

"Woah, wait a second... There's no way you're using me as your personal chess piece."

"Chess piece?"

"A pawn!"

"Stick to de plan, and you won't."

"Your plan is to use me as an entry fee!"

"Wi, you get in, find de target, I find you... And we all leave."

I paused to rolled my eyes, "Smell like B.S. How do I know you won't just leave me there?"

"Because Kalia would kill me if she knew I'd traded one meta life for hers."

"Kalia? Is she some religious figurehead?"

Wick nodded. "She is of Haiti. You will know when you see her." He lost me as his gaze stared off into the distance. "Eyes like a demoness, beautiful like de sun. Bright as de moon."

"Hold up, I haven't agreed to anything; there's just no way you would be interested in saving my life after I'm in."

"...You're right, vagrant, it's not like you have much to live for on the outside, but I give my word, my honor!" At this, Wick pulled a blade out from his pocket and started to slice it down his palm. "That I will not leave you behind, I will free you out of those cuffs... And, even if I wanted to, I will not leave you to die... So, take my words in good faith." Wick shoved his bloodied hand in front of me. "Do we have a deal?"

Wick's presence told a truth I could not fathom rationally. Using blood to seal my protection. I wanted not to believe him, but nothing about this man made me feel like I couldn't. A decision needed to be made. I leaned back on a nearby wall to straddle my hands under my legs, bringing my cuffs in front of me. I spat into the palm of my hand, then reached out to shake his own.

"Wait? What are you doing?" Wick said, urgently pulling his hand away.

"I'm agreeing to your terms."

"But, you spit in your palm... It's disgusting. I offer a blood oath! Which is only meant to be answered with blood."

"I mean... Mixing blood is kind of weird, isn't it? You don't have any weird blood diseases, do you?"

Wicks eyebrows shifted flat. "Make the deal with blood!!"

I jumped back from the abrupt volume of his voice. "Fine! Asshole." I reached into my pocket for the knife I'd taken from the farmhouse. Upon flicking it open, however, I lost my grip on the blade, but I picked it up quickly like it didn't happen. The edge of the blade was clean; it gleamed in the light. As best I could, I used it to slice the meat of my palm. A clean cut as beads of red seeped from the wound. Our hands conjoined. I looked into his eyes, and he glared into mine. Dark brown with shades of red overlaying the white.

"Get some sleep." He turned away. "And do not touch anyt'ing."

He picked up a chain and, before I realized it, he'd lapped over my restraints with a padlock. The chain was bolted to a girder in the corner of the office space. My jaw dropped at the sudden security measure placed on me.

"We just made a *blood* oath!"

"Nothing personal." He shrugged. "Don't get cold feet, yeah?" In his clean hand, I noticed he held the cigar that had been inside my pocket. He sniffed it once and looked me over with faded eyes. "I don't know where yuh got this, but I'll hold onto it, eh?"

"Do whatever, it's not like I smoke."

He smiled as he brought the lighter to it, inhaling the fumes and letting the smoke billow from his mouth. The aroma was rich—almost like chocolate. He took one more short drag and announced, "This'll do."

Then he set the lit cigar on the bowl at the center of his altar and lit the candles around it.

I had to ask, "What's that for? You worship the devil in here?"

Wick choked on the smoke as he wheezed out a chuckle. "That's good, Vagrant."

He picked up the machete from the table.

"This—this is my guardian spirit. My protector from harm."

He flipped it once in his hand. "And my answer when things get dark. It's all I need. No devil can defile me as long as I hold it."

Wick gazed studiously as his sharpened trinket, he said, "It would due you greatly to find a spirit... One of courage perhaps." He said as he placed the blade back where it originally sat.

I rolled my eyes, *"Yeah, well, spirits don't do much for me. Courage or otherwise."*

I leaned on the wall and nodded toward the blade. *"That thing ever pay your rent? Keep your lights on?"*

"In many ways," Wick nodded.

I gave him a look—not mocking, exactly, just... tired. *"You call it a guardian. I call it a security blanket with an edge. Like anything else, it doesn't need my belief for it to serve its purpose."*

Wick smiled, "Everyone needs a foundation, somet'ing that keeps us grounded. How else do we face the atrocities in our way?"

"Easy, you just walk away from them."

Wick paused a moment, "May you never have to face yourself den, Vagrant."

The lights turned off and Wick turned over onto the edge of the cot until his body flattened against it. It wasn't but a few moments until I heard the Haitian churning rhythmically in an unconscious slumber. I stood alone in this small space. Found a corner to sit in and watched the rim of the door as hints of light pierced through it, the lights of the city making sure it was never completely dark. I felt comfortable, though. Out of the freezing cold, at least. I stared blankly and thought about Grace, how she'd pushed me out. I thought about Grandma standing in the archway with the look of shock on her face. I hoped sis was able to make it to her. I should call tomorrow... If I can.

A slow realization crept upon me: I was going to be sold to a merchant of meta-humans. An illegal operation. For what? So this guy can rescue his girlfriend? My hands ached from the shackles as I lifted them: Apex-branded gene inhibitors. Why couldn't we just wear these as bracelets if everyone was so scared? Let the people who didn't choose this burden live their lives like everyone else.

Before I knew it, my eyes grew heavy and I slipped into an unconscious fervor. Rested my head on my shoulder and let the sounds and the sights dim into oblivion.

I felt the crisp air nudge me as I got out of the Impala, we were in a part of town that was littered with foreclosed properties and condemned warehouses. I believe it was somewhere on the southside. I noticed blisters forming around my wrist when I woke this morning. The sooner I get these off the better. Wick approached me, his accent much thicker in the morning.

"I know there's no way you're ready for dis. Be vigilant," he nodes his head to reassure me. "And always watch yuh behind. And most importantly, keep yuh mouth shut. The more you can blend in the bett'a."

"Is there anyway I can talk you out this?"

"If dere was another way... But sadly, no."

He grabbed the base of my elbow to pull me along through a stretch courtyard. It was a mini park with overfilled trash cans and a marble installation dawning red paint. We were approaching a seedy-looking building. I diverted my eyes as the light of the sun pierced my vision. Not a lot of wandering eyes here from what I can tell. Seemed like a place where someone can disappear. My hands remained bound in front of me as we stood at the door.

"Don't say or do anyt'ing. We get in; dey take you away," Wick whispered. My chin was buried in my chest.

"Don't panic. You will be caged."

"Have you ever thought this task was too big for you? Just one person?"

"De only changes we make are the ones we believe in, my friend." I looked at Wick as he grabbed my arm to present me as his prisoner.

"Find Kalia! She will be locked away. When you do, hit the tracker I gave you."

I tongued my back right molar. "Then you'll find me?"

"Just bite down, and I will."

Wick knocked twice. We waited...

He knocked again and we waited some more. I was getting nervous as we stood there, outside the home of someone who sells meta-humans for a living—It bore repeating in my head. I looked at Wick.

"Yeah, maybe this was a bad idea..." I started to pull away from the door.

In the very next moment, someone slammed the door open. They walked through, startling me. It was a big guy with a greasy, bowl-shaped haircut wearing a suit and a gray tie.

"Who the hell are you?" the doorman said.

"I have a deal to strike with this one, new blood," Wick said.

The doorman peered closely into my eyes; I stared back wickedly. Anger started to build from my gut as the feeling of shame curdled to the surface.

"What are you looking at?" I remarked.

The doorman darted his eyebrows and grabbed me by the drawstrings of my hoodie, then pulled a scanner from his pocket and waved the mechanism in front of me until a yellow light turned solid. When he grabbed my arm to pull me through the door, Wick fought back by not letting go of my other arm.

"I want tu see Malcolm! He don't go anywhere until I get that!" Wick demanded.

The doorman stood composed and let go of my arm. "The boss is entertaining guests for much of the evening. He has no time for squirrely newcomers."

"Ego then! Tell her, and only her... that Wick has arrived with a gift."

The doorman scoffed, clearly taken aback by his request. "If this is your *present*, I'm afraid it will sour her mood more than usual."

"Just do it. She will see de value to Malcolm's cause."

The doorman stood idle for just a moment, then stepped aside to allow us to enter the building. We were in. My mind eased for reasons unbeknownst to me, but I was still stressed when I was referred to as 'being of value'.

We marched into a small waiting room with boxes and pallets thrown to the side and plastic lining covering every inch of the floor. Wick pulled me closer to whisper in my ear:

"From here on out, everyt'ing is part of de plan, and I'm sorry."

"Wait! You're sorry?"

Before I could grasp the severity of Wick's words, the doorman struck the back of my head with something solid. My world faded to black and I crumbled onto the plastic.

Chapter Five

"WAKE UP!"

I couldn't easily move, and pain streaked through my body, as did a lingering soreness. The thoughts filtered and fell away like sand through a grate, and the only thing remaining was a person.

Dark... Cold... Wick!!

"WAKE UP, BOY!"

A rough open palm grated across my face. All my senses returned in an instant and I materialized back into the current moment. In front of me was a man, tall in stature, balding and with a slight widow's peak. His crooked smile made me uncomfortable.

"You're up next, little pup. You'd better pray to whatever God twiddles your fancy because your opponent is in a foul mood."

What the hell was he talking about? The man was laughing through his teeth, making the sound of a snake whenever he exhaled. I could tell he delighted in the idea of hurting me. The man continued walking down a large, dark hallway. I was barely able to assess. I was still cuffed, but they were pinned to a wall behind me. My back was flat against the wall in a seated position and wires and tubes were hooked into my arms and chest, tracing back to a few monitors on my right that bolted into the brick wall next to me. I attempted to break free and pull the cuffs out from the wall while standing at the same time. My heart felt like it was beating out of my chest, and I could tell because one of the monitors was going haywire, showing large spikes from an EKG.

"Relax, buddy, relax!" A settling voice, retrained my focus. Panic still consumed me as my fingertips shook, but I was able to breathe through it and my heart rate returned to normal.

"This ain't doin' you no good, we all tried to get out. It won't work," the voice said.

I stopped and darted my attention to the man on my left. He was restrained with weird-looking handcuffs the same as mine. An elderly black man with a balding top with hair sticking out to the side. He was wearing a plaid button-up tucked into his blue jeans. He looked weathered, like he'd been here for a while.

"Good, if you make too much noise they'll come back and work you over again. All that panicking will get you killed... faster," he whispered.

I shook my head and drifted my eyes around the room. Even more people were being held against their will. It was then that I started to understand the severity of my situation. In this warehouse space full of crates and boxes were people walking around and armed with weapons. Big ones. AR-15's with extended clips, single-barrel shotguns with slugs mounted on their frames, even sub machine guns. Many men, women, and at least one child was being held captive. Seven from my count. Across from me, I saw a little boy stretching across the hallway, reaching for a woman's hand on the other side. A few others were balled up against the wall, huddled next to their restraints. A subtle clank of iron embellished in a distance I couldn't make out, like someone pounding a hammer it seemed. I'd never seen anything like this.

Thoughts of the man who'd turned me in came to the forefront of my mind. Immediately, I hit the tracker embedded in my back right molar. I chomped once, but nothing happened. I did so again, chewing on the area. Again, I didn't get any indication that the tracker was working. I tongued the area in my mouth and realized it was missing. My thoughts dwindled in disarray. Did they check my mouth? What else did they check? Was this all planned by Wick? Perhaps he'd turned me in for profit. Had he done the same thing to others? So many questions filled my head. I turned to the man next to me.

"Were you delivered here? Captured by Apex?" I asked, noticing that some of the restraints had the Apex logo embroidered on them.

The stranger shook his head, "I know wha' cha' thinking, but this isn't Apex. We're into something far worse."

"What do you mean?"

The man leaned in towards me and whispered, "Have you ever heard of Malcolm Daily?" The name triggered a memory, my conversation with Wick about Malcolm sank back in.

"I have, yeah." Lights flickered around us, making the hallway temporarily dark before turning back on. The stranger continued.

"He's... A collector of sorts. *I* was a part of his syndicate. Until I wasn't."

My mind funneled back to the deal I made with Wick, and my head sank down and my chin hung near my chest. Then I realized, all these people being held captive, they were all...

"You're all metas, aren't you?" I spoke with grand revelation, the stranger nodded.

A guard came strolling by. It wasn't the same one who'd smacked me before, but some short, potbellied guy armed with a flashlight and assault rifle. On passing, the fat guy kicked a little boy out of his way. The same little boy who'd been reaching for a woman, possibly his mother. The woman grew frustrated with the guard.

"You pig!" she shouted. The short guard stopped in place and directed his attention toward the lady.

"You should act like a proper lady." He walked over to her and grabbed her by the tip of her chin. "I could be your hero, sweetie. Now you make *real* nice, and maybe I won't feed that little boy to the beast."

She proceeded to sink her teeth into his greasy hand, latching on with strained jaw muscles. The guard yelled out in pain.

"Fuk'in twat, let go!"

He kicked her in the stomach, which only made her bite harder. The little boy managed to get close enough to grab the guard around his ankle, causing the short man to sink to his knee.

"You specks!" said the guard.

It was only a matter of time before the other, taller guard came running in. It was the one who'd woken me.

"Are you honestly getting your arse kicked by these two!?," the taller guard cackled, then walked over and grabbed the woman by her hair.

"How bout we take you in and put you through... another cavity search, love?"

The woman began to tear up a little, "No," she pleaded, continuing to stammer her words.

The taller guard pulled her closer to his face. "But you still have so much fight in yah, be ah damn shame to waste it." He lapped his tongue on the side of her face.

"You're better off poking a soda bottle with that twig you're holding," said another strange girl that sat across from me, her voice sharp and dry. She sat slumped like the rest of us, her wrists cuffed above her head, tethered to the ground. A bruise darkened her cheek, and dried blood matted the jet-black strands of her hair. Her accent was American, but her features hinted at South Asian roots.

"Are you out of your mind?" hissed the elderly man next to me, his voice trembling with a mix of fear and disbelief.

The guard turned toward us, his expression blank for a moment as if his brain needed time to catch up. He dropped the woman and stalked over, his eyes narrowing, lips curling into a sneer.

"Well, ain't this a treat," he mocked. "Looks like we got ourselves a volunteer."

The taller guard followed. He stopped in front of the girl, his face twisting with irritation. "You just don't know when to shut up, do you?"

She smirked, her teeth stained with dried blood. "My mom used to say the same thing. Guess it's a family trait."

The tall guard's jaw tightened. "Why don't you put that mouth to use in the cage again? You gotta run outta luck one of these days."

"Anything's better than staring at your ugly ass," she shot back, her grin widening despite the tension in the air.

From somewhere down the dimly lit corridor to my right, the roar of a crowd echoed, distant but growing louder. Armed guards moved in and out of the shadows, their faces unreadable under the flickering light.

The old man beside me leaned closer, his voice barely a whisper. "Don't do it, Cookie. You don't want no part of that again."

"Shut it, old-timer," snapped the tall guard, his tone laced with venom. "Your turn's coming. Just wait."

The old man's face fell, his eyes heavy with sorrow as he looked at the girl. "May God guide you and keep you safe," he murmured, almost to himself.

The shorter guard stepped forward, his gaze raking over Cookie like she was a piece of meat past its prime. "Yeah, you're right, Chet. This one's gonna get eaten alive."

"I bet she begs this time," Chet replied, his voice cold and detached.

The short guard grabbed Cookie by the cuffs and yanked her to her feet. She struggled, her legs kicking out as she tried to find her balance, but Chet's boot slammed into her ribs, sending her sprawling to the ground. She gasped, clutching her side, but her defiance didn't waver.

That's when it started—the ringing in my ears, faint at first, like distant laughter carried on the wind. It grew louder, rhythmic, almost hypnotic. I don't know what came over me, but before I could think, my foot shot out, hooking under Chet's ankle. He toppled forward, landing face-first with a satisfying thud.

"Hey there," growled the short guard. "You think this is funny? I saw you trip him, you little punk."

The butt of his rifle slammed into my face, and pain exploded behind my eyes. My head spun. Before I could recover, Chet grabbed my cuffs and drove his heel into my stomach, knocking the wind out of me.

"It don't matter how much power you freaks got," Chet sneered, leaning in close. "You don't know how to use it. Makes me sick. You're just like the rest of the trash here—untapped, useless."

The guards didn't wait for a response. They grabbed me and Cookie, dragging us both down the corridor toward the deafening roar of the crowd. The dim light flickered overhead, casting long, shifting shadows on the walls.

Is this it? I thought, my mind racing. One night in the city, and this is where it ends?

As we neared the open light, dread clawed at my chest. The girl beside me thrashed violently, leaving behind a smear of blood on the concrete. My silence felt heavy as metas lined the walkway, their blank stares piercing through my panic.

The tunnel ended abruptly, spilling us into the blinding arena lights. The roar of the crowd hit like thunder, chaotic and deafening. The scene ahead was surreal—everything, from the ring to the betting booths, was suspended in midair, held by cables stretching to the rafters. Below, event workers in yellow darted around, prepping the stage for the next horror.

A cage creaked as it lowered, its metallic groans punctuated by the garish voice of the loudspeaker hawking ads. Inside lay a broken man, limbs bent grotesquely, surrounded by the mess of blood-soaked mats. My stomach lurched at the sight, and a cruel smile spread across Chet's face.

"You meta trash really think you're special," he sneered, unfastening my cuffs. Relief flooded my wrists, but the sharp barrel of a rifle ensured escape was impossible. I froze, holding my hands up. Behind me, the workers hustled the corpse into a black bag, hosing the mat clean as if it would erase the madness.

When Chet shoved me toward the cage, acceptance seeped in. I wouldn't survive this. I didn't know how to use my abilities. "I can't stand you pukes," his partner grumbled, shoving the girl in after me.

We fell hard onto the mat, the air thick with blood and sweat. The girl scrambled to her feet, kicking at the locked bars. "You couldn't bother to uncuff me, you hicks?" she shouted, her fury cutting through the noise.

The guards sauntered off, their laughter cruel and distant. A creeping chill settled over me, the locks clanking shut with finality. Across the cage, I spotted another man leaning against the bars, his calm demeanor almost mocking.

"Don't piss yourself yet, kid," he said, his voice low and steady. "The real show hasn't even started."

Upon closer inspection, I noticed that he too was handcuffed, but fastened to the bars behind his back. With that fact in play, I could breathe easy just a bit longer. His face had dark rings under his eyes and a slender and pointy nose, with wrinkles that cascaded along his mouth and cheeks. His hair was a bit straggly and soaked with blood, which freaked me out. Also, he was shirtless, revealing skin covered with old scars and some brand-new ones too. He was wearing gray suit pants with expensive-looking loafers. The leather binding ruined from blood soaked into his soles. Seeing him in the ring didn't look all that natural.

The bound lady didn't waste any time; she lunged towards the guy rearing her cuffs, looking to bash his head in. I couldn't help but watch. To honestly attack another person while they were helpless seemed unthinkable. Granted, it is some crazed... Well-dressed manic against myself and a very angry meta. The girl connected with his jaw. The personnel looked on with a watchful eye and did not approach. Again, she struck, again and again and again. The man smiled and decided to strike with his foot, connecting in the woman's chest. Her feet left the ground and she landed near me. He was fast.

"Look—" The bloodied man lifted his chin to further reveal a smile. "I know you're scared and all. Heck, the only reason you're here is because you suppressed your powers."

"How would you know that?"

Our opponent laughed, "You know those people in the stands, and all the cock-knobbers at the booths? They're not here to see one man kill another. That's just what happens when *you* don't give them what they want. It's a consolation, so to speak."

"Then what the hell do they want?" I further pried.

"The last few years since the metas have been around, cooking up trouble, causing havoc. A lot of the population got scared. But... There were a few—Let's call them a sizable minority—who couldn't help but be fascinated by it all. Especially... the untapped ones, the ones who got flagged positive for having the meta gene but didn't show signs of, what did they call it?" The man pondered oddly, "Ahhh, *infection.* They wondered, what they could do?

Like a mail-in loot box. Would it be useful? Could it heal the world or maybe... heh, you get the idea."

This guy rambled like a jackass. Yet, I still preferred him talking then getting my face grated against the chain-link fence.

"That still doesn't explain what they want," I quickly replied.

The man then looked at me like I was seriously dumb. "They want to see you crack, you dolt. Whether you use your powers or not. Will you crack or will you use your magical fucking genes to live another day? I'll let you in on a secret—" He lowered his head then slowly raised it with his hair over his eyes. "The house usually wins."

My eyes widened and I looked toward the girl as she struggled to stand. I went to help her the rest of the way up, but she slapped my gesture away.

"How do we take this guy down?" I asked.

But before she could reply, the bound man spoke once more. "Granted, living another day is subjective when you're in Malcolm's Rink, but let's be hopeful, shall we?" he said with youthful enthusiasm.

After standing, she quickly hunched over to release the contents of her stomach. I went to help once more, but thought it would be better not to touch her. After she'd wiped her mouth, her hand snapped to the collar of my hoodie. She pulled my face towards hers.

"You take him while he's cuffed! Get him now!"

"But isn't he defenseless? He's bound behind his back."

Her eyes grew bewildered, and a sneer flashed under her nose.

"We're going to die..." she lamented.

The cage creaked a little and in a sudden jerk, it ascended. It swayed some, but shortly regulated itself the closer we got to the top. As the cage emerged through this entry port, I noticed all the people, the lights, and the crowd roaring with excitement. A shiver ran down my spine that quickly took over the rest of my body. They were all waiting for the next blood bath to start. All eyes were on us. Some of them took a quick look at me and immediately threw away their ticket. Other people in the stands muttered things like, *"I told you, just like the last one, a dud, ha!"*

This was not at all helping me in the confidence department. The other guy in the cage didn't seem to care much. I wasn't even sure he was a meta.

In between the stands were gated walkways that circled around the cage and led back behind the bleachers in three directions.

"Yes! Ladies and gentlemen," a voice poured over the loudspeakers that were hanging high above. From behind the stands on the steel walkway strutted the announcer. An English woman dressed in this skimpy business attire. Blazer and miniskirt with her hair tied up in a bun. She wore these square framed glasses and readily waved to the crowd as she soaked in their admiration. Glowing with pride, she shimmied her shoulders and propped the microphone to her red lips in grandiose fashion.

"After the fights tonight, you too can come to join the auction tomorrow night. Check out our finest stock. Fresh from the city streets of Chicago! I'm sure there's something for everyone. And I'll see you there!" She winked at the crowd. To be honest, I wanted to go too, and I didn't even know why.

The cage jolted to a stop, and for a moment, everything else faded. My breath caught as I took it all in. The arena was a grotesque masterpiece, a spectacle so overwhelming it almost made me forget the life-or-death stakes. The crowd roared like a living beast, their voices merging into a deafening cacophony. They weren't just spectators—they were predators, drunk on the promise of blood. Hands waved wildly, faces contorted with excitement, and the air buzzed with an electric, primal energy.

It was like stepping into the ring at a wrestling event, but I wasn't the hero. I was the heel, the one they wanted to see broken. The mat beneath me bore the evidence of countless battles—stains of blood and sweat that no amount of scrubbing could erase. The crowd's eyes bore into us, dissecting every inch. Some looked like ordinary people you'd pass on the street, but their expressions were anything but. They were here for carnage, and we were the entertainment.

Guards approached the cage, their movements methodical as they unshackled our opponent. He didn't even glance at us, his gaze distant, unfocused. He leaned against the cage wall, his posture eerily calm, as if he'd already accepted whatever was coming.

The lights above burned bright, casting harsh shadows across the cage. The air was thick with the stench of sweat, metal, and something darker—something that smelled like fear. My knees felt weak, but I forced myself to stand, to face the inevitable.

I glanced at the opponent again, his stillness unnerving. He wasn't just calm—he was resigned. And in that moment, I realized I wasn't leaving this place alive. The thought settled over me like a shroud, heavy and suffocating. The spectacle of the arena was dazzling, but it was a cruel, hollow beauty. It wasn't meant to inspire—it was meant to consume.

I turned to the girl beside me "Are you okay?" I asked, my voice barely audible over the crowd. She didn't respond, her focus locked on the opponent.

"You really took a hit there; you have a plan for getting out of here alive?" I asked.

The bound lady shrugged me off by pushing me aside. Soon after, she tripped over her feet, landing on her knee.

"Seriously, let me help you!" I followed, trying desperately to ingrain some cohesion into our situation.

She pushed me off again and peered into my eyes, her eyes shimmering hazel now.

"You want to help?! Catch him off balance! Make him bleed—And stay out of my way."

The announcer circled the cage from the steel walkway. Within the walkway were four guards equally spread out and standing by with assault rifles. This Malcolm guy kept this place well-guarded. She turned toward the crowd with a striking pose. It was difficult not to look.

"Eyes right here, folks! If you don't know, *I'm* Ego! We're back again for another round of MERC VS META!" She flung her arm into the air and waved it around, riling up the crowd. "You know the rules. Our traitorous Mercenary *Vincent!*" A mild compilation of boos sprung from the crowd. Maybe he was the heel of this gig. Ego continued when the boos had settled. "Our merc gets to stress test every dormant meta we have until one of two things happens: Either the meta uses their powers to survive... or they don't... survive, that is. He ha!"

The crowd laughed and whistled at Ego's remark. Some screamed their undying affection for her. "Either way, it's going to be a hell of a lot of fun. AM I RIGHT!!" The unanimous response filled the arena. One guy actually fell from the top of the stands and hit the concrete below.

"You all love it, I know. But next on the chopping block is a fresh one straight out of the dark alleys of CHICAGO! No idea what he can do, but the lab boys say he holds more electricity in his body than a car battery. Sooo... What can he be? A lightning rod?" Some of the more analytical spectators moved closer from the stands in excitement. "Or... Maybe he shoots thunder beams out of his hands—" Ego pretended to shoot invisible lightning from her hands, "I know you gotta like that. Or could he be good for charging your cell phone? Just a bit more than useless if that's the case."

Lab boys? Shoot lightning?! Could I actually do that? If I didn't think I was about to die, I would've been a bit more ecstatic.

"Accompanying our static charged friend is Cookie! A Chi-town local who's been with us for quite a while. No idea what her powers are. Once we tossed her in a cage and she finished things the old-fashioned way."

Wait! She's done this before?? I stared at the shackled young lady as she leaned against the cage wall. She looked off into the rafters lost in a world of her own, like she wasn't even here. I couldn't help but wonder how she'd survived the first time.

"Ladies and gents! Will we finally get a peek behind the genetic curtain??" The crowd went partially mute. "Can't fool you lot, heh? Now... ARE *YOU* READY!!" The crowd erupted. The acoustics were so bad I had to cover my ears. "Then let's get this bloodbath underway!"

The bell rang, and the match began. It was two-on-one against a mercenary, and none of us moved at first. Vincent stood with his hands in his pockets, his posture casual, almost bored. Cookie glared at him, her breaths shallow and uneven. Someone had to make the first move, and desperation surged through me. That someone would be me.

I charged at Vincent, hoping to summon my abilities like I'd seen Trailblazer do on TV—speeding up, lighting his fists on fire. I clenched my fist, holding my breath as if pressure alone could trigger something. "Think lightning thoughts! Think lightning thoughts!" I muttered, a frantic mantra.

Vincent's grin widened as I closed in. My fist swung toward his neck, but he caught it effortlessly, his palm closing around my hand like a vice. Pain shot through me as he twisted my wrist back, the sound of bones popping.

"Gahaaahaaha!" I screamed, the agony blinding.

"Good job," Vincent said, "At least you didn't cower in a corner. But it's clear you've never thrown a punch in your life."

I glared at him, my teeth clenched, trying to focus on my breathing to dull the pain. The crowd roared, their cheers drowning out my thoughts. They were loving this—my struggle, my humiliation.

"No, this won't do at all," Vincent muttered, almost to himself. His fist slammed into my gut, and I stumbled back, blood spilling from my mouth. My vision blurred, tears mixing with the moisture on my face.

Before I could recover, his knee drove into my stomach, forcing me to double over and retch. I staggered toward the chain-link fence, clutching it for support, but my arms were weak, trembling. Vincent followed, his voice cutting through the noise.

"You metas always get it wrong," he said, his tone calm, almost instructional. "Adrenaline's a tool. You can use it to fight or to flee. But here's the thing—there's nowhere to run."

I spat blood in his face, the only defiance I could muster. His expression darkened, his jaw tightening. "Pissing me off now?" he growled.

His shin collided with my face, sending me crashing into the fence. My knees buckled, and I collapsed onto the mat. The cage spun around me, the crowd's frenzy growing louder. Blood pooled in my mouth, choking me as I gasped for air.

"Can... we do... a time out?" I croaked, my voice barely audible.

Vincent loomed over me, his shadow swallowing what little strength I had left. "I've got a control problem," he said, his voice cold. "And an anger problem. I don't take kindly to people testing my patience."

Suddenly, Vincent staggered forward, slamming into the fence. Cookie stood behind him, her cuffs raised, her eyes wild with fury. She struck him again and again, her movements sharp and relentless. Vincent swung his elbow back, but Cookie blocked it with her forearms, the force pushing her away. She stepped back, her gaze locked on him.

"At least one of you has fight in ya," Vincent said, his grin returning.

Cookie glanced at me, her voice sharp. "Get up, idiot. He's only human."

Vincent lunged, but instead of targeting her, his boot slammed into my side. Pain exploded through me as he kicked again and again, each blow driving me closer to the edge of unconsciousness.

"That's why I'm here," Vincent spat, his voice rising. "Babysitting you weak-ass pansies! Malcolm thinks he can kill me with this gauntlet of nobodies. All because I killed someone important to his trade. Over what? A jar of dirt! A fucking jar of dirt!"

His kicks didn't stop, each one punctuating his rant. My ribs screamed with pain, my breaths shallow and ragged. I couldn't feel anything anymore, just the dull ache of inevitability.

Meanwhile, Ego's words rang through the arena: "WOOOAH, I wished we could've bet on Vincent's major breakdown. What a sight to behold!" Ego exclaimed. "This fight looks like it's wrapping up for our meta guest, as Cookie watches on from afar!"

I was on the ground wondering why this wasn't over yet. In a lot of ways, I did deserve this. Thinking back now, I realized I'd done nothing with my life, just sat around and played video games. It didn't matter if I had parents, not one bit. I could have done better when these abilities started showing. All I'd wanted to do was hide them away, the way I'd hidden away for most of my life.

My vision blurred, my eyes stinging as if doused with salt. Blood filled my mouth, and I couldn't stop coughing it up. Vincent grabbed me by the hair, lifting me off the ground like I weighed nothing. "Looks like our fun's over," he sneered, his free hand snapping my index finger with a sickening crack. Pain shot through me, and I let out a short, broken scream.

I hated myself in that moment—hated my weakness, my helplessness. Why did I even bother existing? They'd boxed me in, degraded me, just like before.

Then, a spark. It flickered across my face, faint but unmistakable. Vincent leaned closer, his grin widening. "Ooh, I spy with my little eye... an EYE!"

"I guess it can't... be helped," I muttered, my voice hollow. "I've always hated guys like you. And I've hated myself for not being like you." My words came out in ragged gasps, interrupted by a cough that sprayed blood.

Vincent drove his knee into my stomach, cutting me off. "You sure talk a lot for a pile of meat."

"SHUT UP!" The words tore from me as my right eye erupted in a blaze of blue light, bathing the cage in its glow. My fist swung toward Vincent, driven by something primal, something automatic. Pain shot through my arm as it connected with his cheek, but he barely flinched.

"That's it?" he scoffed. "All that light, and this is what you've got?"

I hit him again, harder this time, but his expression only darkened. He shoved me against the cage, his boot slamming into my solar plexus. The air left my lungs in a rush, and the edges of my vision darkened. The sparks from my eye flickered and dimmed as my body sagged, limp and useless. The arena fell silent, the crowd holding its breath.

Vincent released me, his grip loosening. But as he did, my hand shot out, wrapping around his ankle with a strength I didn't know I had. Lightning surged through me, crackling down my arm and into my hand. The energy was wild, electric, and unstoppable.

"Let go—of me!" Vincent shouted, struggling against my grip.

The surge of power coursing through me was overwhelming, fueled by a wave of anger I'd buried for too long. Without thinking, I yanked his leg, whipping his body into the cage wall with a force that rattled the entire structure. Before he could recover, I swung him again, slamming him into the mat like a ragdoll. The impact was brutal, and Vincent crumpled to the ground, motionless.

Silence. Deafening silence. My body trembled, every nerve alight with energy. Blood dripped from my mouth, and my breaths came in ragged gasps. I felt like I was falling apart, but it was exhilarating—visceral, and terrifyingly real.

People rushed into the ring, circling Vincent's lifeless form. They kept their distance from me, their voices muffled by the ringing in my ears. I glanced around, catching sight of Cookie being dragged away by guards. The crowd erupted, some tearing up tickets in frustration, others celebrating like they'd won the lottery.

Guards flooded the cage, their eyes locked on me. They shouted, motioning toward my feet. I followed their gaze and froze. I was standing in a pool of blood. My stomach turned as I looked back at Vincent. One of his legs was gone, severed below the knee. Blood trailed from the stump to the puddle beneath me.

Then I saw it. In my hand, I was still holding his leg. The realization hit me like a freight train, and a chill ran through my entire body. The guards' voices finally broke through the haze.

"Put the leg down! Let it go!" they screamed.

I wanted to drop the leg, but my body wouldn't let me. I shook it, trying to get it off, but all that did was spray blood on the stage crew and guards. I could sense the fear and disgust of those inside the cage. Finally, I used my other hand to pull the leg from my grasp, but it was too late. Darts were sticking out of my chest. The last thing I heard before dropping was the announcer:

"With unexpected results, our winner!—Wh-what was this guy's name again?!"

Chapter Six

A voice echoed and faded, *"Our subject is waking, sir."* A bright light stirred the lids of my eyes. Everything remained a blur as vague, disjointed memories began to cycle through my head. I could still feel my hand holding something. The brief ambiance of the crowd charging the back of my head. One massive sneeze broke the barrier of my dull awareness and catapulted me into my current hell. Wait? Leg? Cage?!

And then like a shock to the system, I could recall what had happened before being knocked out. My eyes locked open and I tried pulling away, tried to stand up, but it wasn't happening. My arms were restrained... Again. This time in a strange contraption. My limbs were shackled as my body sprawled out on a circular steel ring. I was elevated off the ground leaning at a thirty-degree angle facing up. Under me were four legs that touched the ground with wheels attached.

A bunch of white coats with ID tags ran around. They walked with a sense of urgency, checking screens and recording information. This wasn't like the hallway I'd started in. I was in a giant room with consoles surrounding me. Some wires ran from those machines and pierced me in my forearm. My fingertips braced the sides of the thin parts of the steel ring to scrape their edges. Extravagant visions of me freeing myself slowly degraded into sequential movements to find comfort. As I did, subtle whispers plumed into my ear. The voices felt like they were right next to me, but sounded like they were in the next room. These whispers weren't legible, they only sounded erratic, excited, and perhaps boastful. As I looked around for the source, a vague scent of rum drifted through the air.

A woman in an open white lab coat walked up to me with a great big smile. The first thing I noticed was that one of her front teeth had a gold filling. Not a typical trait for someone wearing slacks and a tie. Her hair was pulled back in a ponytail that looked bushy and wild behind her head. She leaned in close and used the tips of her fingers to force my eye open.

"Oh, my goodness! You don't know how exciting it has been for me in the past twenty minutes! Not often do we get a meta to survive the arena, much less display their latent abilities! So, how do you feel? I am sure the painkillers I gave you have been helping, hmmm?" She leaned in much closer and blinked her eyes profusely.

My head waded from side to side. No longer slumbering, but not yet fully awake. "Wh-what's going on? I won... right? Let me go!" I strained my body explosively, causing the doctor to step back.

For a moment, the lady just looked at me in a weird, indescribable way and laughed aloud. Literally out loud.

"Ooh, Charlie? Was it Charlie?" She looked down at my chart, "Yes! Charlie—Do you really think we would go through so much trouble patching you up, only to let you back out in the wild like some Discovery Channel special? Don't answer that, because of course not! Since the arena, you have accumulated actual *value!* It's very exciting."

"Actual value... What do you mean by that?"

"Your body holds a substantial amount of electricity. Enough to drive, enhance, and power almost anything! There's really no telling what you can do with that ability. If you get too stressed or focused..." She clapped her hands together, "Boom! It kicks in like a light switch. Your system is very self-contained, almost like your skin is acting like a non-conductible film. We have been trying to draw out your electricity with our equipment, but the best I've been able to do is keep it at bay." She snorted. "With the usual inhibitors of course. I would love to test your abilities for like... Another week," she said with a smile eyeing the ceiling romantically, "But *you,* like other projects, have a deadline."

I was so confused at this point. The painkillers weren't helping either.

"Lady, I don't have some *weird* deadline. You can't hold me here forever, it's illegal!"

She pronounced her hand on her waist and shared a squinting eye, "What part of forcing you to fight to the death and selling you to the highest bidder makes you think we're in the business of *legality?*" She pinched my cheek.

"Sell me?! Ohh no, no no no," I devolved into whispers. "This wasn't supposed to happen. If only I didn't go with that stupid, Haitian asshole!"

"Well, life just isn't fair, is it?" She mocked me with a subtle whine.

I might have been content in a holding cell by the police. That didn't sound much better; there's not an easy answer to any of this, I thought.

"Sit tight, Charlie, you're not alone in this endeavor. Many metas are getting new homes too... Maybe. I just wish I could study you longer." I took another look around the room and found several other people strapped to harnesses like myself. Some looked sickly, or even close to death. Out in the distance, I noticed the elderly man from before the arena and the woman I'd been thrown in the arena with... I think they called her Cookie. I know she was cuffed at the time, but we could have worked together taking that merc down. I don't see why none of the metas here are shaking this place to its foundation.

My blood started pumping. "This isn't some pet adoption clinic you're running; these are people's lives here! I'm sure if any one of them wanted to, they'd turn your body inside out!"

"Oh, Charlie, you're so cute. Now relax, because I'm going to give you another dose to calm you down." Her voice was syrupy, almost mocking, as she pulled a large vial from the drawer beside me. Her index finger tapped the glass rhythmically, a sound that echoed in my ears like distant drums. She locked the vial into the tube connected to the IV bag, and I watched as the blue liquid seeped into the saline solution, its color twisting and curling like smoke in water.

My thoughts grew hazy, the edges of my mind softening as the euphoric wave spread through my veins. My body felt heavy, sinking into the chair, but my eyes refused to close. I stared at the walls, where shadows danced like restless spirits. The whitecoats moved around me, their forms distorted by the flickering light. Medical equipment loomed in the corner, its metallic surfaces gleaming.

The hum of whispers began, faint at first, like the rustle of leaves in the wind. It grew louder, more insistent, emanating from the ring of equipment surrounding me. The shadows on the walls flickered erratically, their movements jerky and unnatural. My vision darkened at the edges, and the shadows began to shift, their forms twisting into something grotesque. My heart pounded in my chest, each beat echoing like the strike of a hammer on steel.

And then, amidst the chaos, a figure emerged—a towering silhouette, its form outlined in flames. The shadows dissolved, their forms scattering like ash in the wind. The whispers faded, replaced by the rhythmic pounding of my heart. My body felt lighter, the weight of the blue liquid lifting.

I blinked, and the room came back into focus. The whitecoats moved frantically. The equipment hummed softly, but its presence lingered.

Just then, a man walked into the room on his cell phone. Despite the drugs, I paid attention to this strange individual; there was something odd about him, something that stood out. He looked to be older with shoulder-length brown hair and sported a chocolate brown blazer and slacks. He was also wearing a yellow button-up shirt with sleek loafers. He looked incredibly stressed and flailed his hands above his head. It was hard not to witness.

"Yes, I know it's a masterpiece thus-myself-purchasing-said-painting!" He leaned against the wall neatly propped and waved his hand in front of him in a rhythmic motion. Each fling of his hand constituted another syllable of his words.

"It's not ruined, okay! I just gave your piece more... Utility!" He listened for a moment. "If you don't like it, there's nothing I can do. It's too late, I'm reassembling it now." He waited, silently listening to the guy on the other end. Jittering his leg as he waited for the person to stop talking.

For a moment, the hallway lights behind him shut off, temporarily leaving himself in darkness. The individual flinched, looking around the space in odd speculation. "My Puzzler is fantastic at his job; you would think it's an improvement after he's done." The speaker started getting indiscriminately louder. "You know what?! If you're going to give me *that* attitude, then I think we should sever ties and I'll find another artist to buy from. They're practically growing like weeds. Like they always say, *buy local!*" He disconnected the call and dropped his phone inside his blazer pocket just as the lights turned back on.

He took time to rub his temples and said something that sounded like a mantra, but it was too quiet for me to understand his words. He turned toward the lab and fixed his shirt collar. The lights flickered over him, causing him to look up at the ceiling inquisitively. Then he looked as us captive metas and shouted,

"Line up the exports, Dr. Beverly Branson, because the crowd will be hungry tomorrow! I need them on the truck and on the way, now! We haven't been this popular since the first quarter."

"Right away, sir!" said the doctor.

A few people were unplugged from the monitors and rolled out to the far side of the room in front of a connecting corridor. The older man I'd spoken with earlier was chosen. The second was a guy in a tattered, dirty gray suit, and the last was me.

The man with the chocolate brown suit took a clipboard from one of the researchers and skimmed over it. He tapped a connected pen to the metal of the board rigidly.

"What a gleeful lot," he muttered. "But you, Jacob! *You* should make our investors a bit antsy." He directed his attention to the elderly man shackled in the very front. "We've had you in our hands for a while now, and you could've been living well if you'd only agreed to my terms."

Jacob squinted at the man with a bitter look. "I'd rather burn in hell than help crooks like you, Malcolm!"

The name echoed to the forefront of my mind; my eyes widened. So that's Malcolm!? He didn't look like much, just some guy in a loud suit.

Malcolm strolled closer to Jacob. "Well, maybe you'll be more reasonable for the next guy," he said with a sharp grin.

"Fuck you!" Jacob replied.

"Glad to see your spirits are high!" Malcolm retorted. "Goodbye, and let's never see each other again." And without further delay, Jacob was carted off into the nearby hallway.

Malcolm approached the next restrained meta, the man with the tattered gray suit. He looked at the clipboard attached to his enclosure, then looked at the meta, then back at the clipboard. "Wholesale this one," he ordered simply. The guy didn't respond and was quickly carted away.

Malcolm snatched the clipboard hanging off the steel ring I was fastened to and scanned me from head to toe. After peeking at my clipboard, he broke a slight smile.

"Vincent kicked the shit out of you, and then you took his leg?" He laughed. I was too groggy to say anything; the medication had kicked in. "So, Beverly, what can we make of this one? He's some sort of generator for electricity?"

"Umm, close—His metabolic state is regenerative. And the source of his meta-anomaly is in his solar plexus: Generating a massive amount of heat when under stress. This results in a strength increase with an outburst of electricity when activated. I do, however, feel like something is missing in our data... If we could conduct more tests, we would have a better idea—"

"Not that interested, Doc. We can't pull from his power source. Let's wholesale this one too." Dr. Beverly's jaw hung loose until finally she swallowed the lump in her throat and walked away.

Malcolm was going to do the same but had stopped when reading more of my report. His hands shook. "Turned in by Isaiah Auguste, the 'Haitian Wick'?!" He balled the report and tossed it to the side, then screamed out to Dr. Beverly, "We didn't let this 'Wick' in, did we?"

The doctor blinked and then rounded her eyes to the ceiling. "If they brought a package, we usually set a meeting with you."

Malcolm checked his phone. "I... Don't see anything about a Mr. Auguste... Why does that seem so familiar?" He pocketed his phone. "Let me go talk to Bill at the front. I was catching a breach in the building at one point." Malcolm swiveled his head to the ceiling as the lighting flickered once more.

"Well, the building has been needing maintenance for weeks," said Dr. Beverly.

"I know, Bev, but it hasn't been *that* bad. I still have orders coming in from the Sahara. Remember to check shipping when your done here. "

The doctor tucked her lip, and then finally gritted her teeth. "I still don't know what you plan to find with all these buckets of sand you keep bringing in. I know you like your art collecting but... Dirt, granite, sediment? These shipments are eating us alive."

Malcolm slammed his hand into the wall. "Don't worry about my money. It's going exactly where it needs to go."

A voice erupted nearby: "Just like you, not knowing the value of something that's right in front of your nose. Pathetic..." Cookie shouted.

Malcolm turned towards her in astonishment, then turned back to Dr. Beverly. "What the hell is she still doing here?! I thought we dumped her in the pits."

"We... did, sir. She keeps winning her matches," Dr. Beverly stated.

Malcolm's face turned red. He pitched the bridge of his nose and meandered off toward the defiant woman. "I've never seen such a stubborn piece of street meat. Why keep fighting us like this? If you just show us what you got, we could move you out of here and with caring *new* parents." Cookie's eyes shrank thin and her expression was one for not being amused.

"Be thankful your fighters are such pussies, otherwise I'd have to resort to collapsing the west wing of your shitty warehouse. You want to see what i can do, unshackle from this thing, i'll give you a personal demonstration." She jilted forward, spittle flying from her mouth.

Malcolm removed an napkin from his pocket, and proceeded to pat his face, "Beverly, do we not have anyone on our roster who can handle a powerless little girl?"

The good doctor approached a console and proceeded to skim for an answer. "Well, sir, in house we only have... the Feral left."

Malcolm's eyes grew wide. "Certainly we can find something less... expensive?" His voice dropped an octave. "I can't purchase another cage for the arena. I mean, that can't be all we have... What about Id, he's working tonight?"

Beverly flattened her eyebrows. "If you want to disturb him during his 'Play Time', be my guest."

Malcolm's shoulders shuddered while he stared off into space. "I didn't realize he'd found someone to his interest."

Beverly spoke. "He's been at it with this one for four days now." Malcolm's eyes widened as he stood silently. "She's... a full-on regenerator." she said.

"You're kidding!" Malcolm flushed air through his teeth then rubbed the back of his neck. "You know what? Fine! Get the Feral in the cage, unshackle the little twat, and give the crowd a show."

Beverly stumbled with her words and looked empathetically at the raging girl. "If that's what you want, will make it happen... Honestly, sir, if we could get another opponent for our wary lightning rod here, I would have more data, which could lend more value!" Beverly's eyes lit up. Her clenched fist bounced in place in front of her with anticipation.

"No, no. I'm not wasting more man-hours on this one, just sell it like the rest."

A steady, hammering noise pulsed in my ears—a sound that echoed like distant war drums. Even in my state, I scanned the darkness, searching for its source. Nothing obvious emerged, until two familiar guards stumbled in from the connecting corridor. Barnaby and Chet appeared rattled; their faces were pale, and Barnaby's hands trembled visibly as he hurriedly closed the door behind them, as if sealing out a relentless pursuer.

"We have a small emergency in shipping!" Chet shouted, his radio a jumble of incoherent chatter. I could barely catch a word as Malcolm strode over and slapped the man across the face.

"Breathe, you fool—what are you even saying?!" Malcolm barked.

Before anyone could respond, a pounding erupted at the door Barnaby was desperately holding shut. The noise grew louder, and an odd heat seeped into the room. Grabbing a radio from Chet, Malcolm spoke, "Everyone in the west wing—watch the lab, safeties off." Tossing the radio back, he strode to the door. "Move it!"

Barnaby stepped aside. Malcolm flung open the door, and flames licked his ankles. Through the fiery haze in the hallway, a tall figure emerged from the lab's glow—Apex's head honcho, Trailblazer. My heart sank as I strained against the wheel that confined me; the brutal reality was dawning.

Trailblazer stepped forward, his presence chilling as the flames danced around him. He faced Malcolm, who stood his ground despite the heat. "Why are you here?

You're supposed to be out surveying for 'meta-activity',"
air-quoting as if dismissing the meta.

I caught a glimpse behind Trailblazer's opaque visor—a look of recognition. I knew he remembered me from that field outside Bernt Hollow, the moment I'd slipped away. For a long, painful moment, the two men stood locked in silent challenge. Then Trailblazer moved aggressively; Malcolm's attempt to restrain him was met with the sting of armored plates.

In the next heartbeat, Trailblazer turned his attention to me, my restrained form trembling in the glare. "This one is mine. Put him in a box—he's coming with me."

Malcolm lunged forward. "Wait—this one is my property! Eugene and I have an agreement—what's mine is mine, and what's yours can fuck off."

"You don't understand," Trailblazer continued. "Charles Conway has been skirting under the radar for days—he isn't for sale."

"So this is the 'speedster' in the news? The one who got away?" Malcolm inquiered.

Dr. Beverly interjected, her tone pricking the tension. "Technically, he's not a speedster, sir—he moves fast sometimes, but it's just a byproduct of... something else."

Trailblazer shrugged. "Look, it doesn't matter what he is—he just has to pay. If I don't make a spectacle of this guy, the public will lose interest in Apex protection, and I'll lose my sponsorships!" Trailblazer's voice seethed as heat began to radiate from his boots.

"Yeah, you're a real peacock," Malcolm retorted. "But how'd you know he was here anyway?"

With a swift motion, Trailblazer pulled out a phone and played a grainy video—a brief clip of me fighting Vincent in the arena. After a few seconds, he pocketed the device.

"As I said, hand him over—right now!" Trailblazer demanded.

Malcolm hesitated, then fished out a nickel-plated Glock from under his blazer—a silenced snub nose. "I don't like your tone. It's all wrong," he snarled as he leveled the gun at Trailblazer's helmet.

"What are you gonna do with that peashooter? I'll wreck your whole lab before you get a shot off," Trailblazer shot back. In a swift change, Malcolm pointed the weapon at my head. I froze as the cold barrel came within a foot of my face, my heart pounding in a rhythm of sheer hopelessness.

"Well, the public will never know what happened to dear ol' Charlie," Malcolm taunted. "Maybe he's still out there—just because Chicago's finest couldn't hold his salt." His tone was icy, even as other guards swarmed into the room, weapons raised. Malcolm silenced them with a single raised hand.

Slowly, the flames around Trailblazer dimmed. He dipped his head and said, "I need proof he didn't slip out under our noses."

Malcolm circled my steel enclosure, contemplating. Dr. Beverly cut in once more, her eyes alight with opportunistic glee. "Let's toss him back in the arena—let him fight the

Feral. I'll get more data, and Mr. Blazer, you'll have a fine show with Charlie's demise. There's profit in reviving a meta champion!"

Malcolm scoffed thoughtfully as he lifted his chin under the harsh lights. "That's a nice thought." He counted on his fingers, then grinned. "He did win his last fight with one of my best mercs... Fine. Throw him back in the cage—let the crowd feast on it."

Groggy and burning with indignation, I couldn't stand to listen as they bartered my death like a cheap commodity. With a surge of unnatural defiance, I managed to choke out, "Look here—I don't give a damn about your payday or your pride. If I ever get out, you'll all pay! I can't help being a meta, and neither can these people. We have fundamental rights—"

Before I could finish, Malcolm shoved a handkerchief into my mouth, muting my protest.

Trailblazer turned to leave the way he'd come, pausing in the doorway. "When you kill him, keep the remains. I'll be back after the fight."

Malcolm snapped, "Don't care what you do with him once he's meat. Everyone, get out of my face so I can think," Striding away in the opposite direction.

In that moment, as hopeless stakes were drawn and my very life became a bargaining chip, I felt the crushing certainty that escape was nothing more than a cruel illusion.

Chapter Seven

Dr. Beverly Branson clapped her hands, then made two of her assistants stand in a line in front of her. They were draped with white masks and hairnets, and one of them had vague droplets of red streaking across their apron. She pointed at me with the tip of her index finger jaunting to a tune. A rhythmic hum followed that strangely sounded like 'In the hall of the mountain king'. The white-clad assistants nodded to a silent understanding of the circumstances. They approached me and started pushing my enclosure. It had wheels, so others could move it like a shopping cart. They took me through the same hallway as Malcolm. He leaned with one leg propped against the wall smoking a cigar. Ample exhaust poured out of his mouth and lingered in the air.

We went through a few rooms, in each of which the lighting seemed to get progressively dimmer. It got so dark to the point of only seeing the exit signs that hung over each entry point. We entered a space with nine individual cages. A blast of dull light lapped over the moving shadows alive inside each cage. The ground seemed to be covered in a layer of sand. On further observation, across the entire floor from one side of the wall to the other lay mounds of glittering sand. Rolling past the first cage was a number of people who were cuffed by their hands and looking miserable.

We stopped at a cage on the outside corner. They slapped the inhibitor handcuffs on me again and released me from my round enclosure. I was tossed into a barred cell with a few others. I struggled some, but the drugs were still in me. They slammed the door behind me and disappeared out of the room. Even with the others surrounding me, it was deathly quiet in the cage. I looked around the cell for anything I could use, maybe a possible means of escaping. The two others sharing my cell kept to themselves and said nothing. The bars were unyielding as I pulled against them. I sat down right after kicking the bars in frustration. No one cared to look; frustration must be the norm. For some reason, the scent of rum filled the air once more and distant strikes of metal caught my attention. Yet the sounds and smells vanished before I could locate the source.

I leaned back and tried not to think about dying. It was going to happen and there was nothing I could do about it. Just because I was a meta in the wrong place and time. It's strange—A mere week ago I'd never thought much of what happened to them. I didn't have to interact or cross paths with them. I was so scared to even go outside just from the possibility of meeting one. I looked around once more and realized these people needed more consideration as human beings. After becoming one myself, it hadn't changed me really. I didn't have this sudden need to kill or take from others. I'm not a monster.

My thoughts were interrupted, however, as someone new was carted in. I saw the two guards from before pushing a circular enclosure toward my holding cell. On closer inspection, I could see it was Cookie! Chet and Barnaby pushed her into my cell and tossed her in the cage alongside me. She jumped to her feet and sneered at Barnaby and reached through the bars while raising a middle finger in his face. Again, he took exception to her emotional display and snapped his teeth at her digits.

"You'll get yours, Tot! You and pretty-boy there." Barnaby walked away alongside Chet.

I considered walking over to Cookie to check on her, but I was still sour from the beating I'd gotten, so instead I leaned against the cage and thought about this 'Feral' they intended us to fight. How I could have deserved all of this? Before, I'd only ever seen the outcome of these Ferals on TV; never had I actually seen one in person, much less heard their side of things. I remembered watching a news story of an entire three-story building having been thrashed and burned to the ground because one had acted out. I had seen postmortem images after an Apex strike team had to take one down. Not enough of a corpse left to tell if it was an actual person or something else. In any case, I knew I was a dead man walking—Ferals were the reason why society was so up in arms about metas roaming the streets in the first place.

I'd gotten lucky with Vincent... As I thought about the mercenary, I studied my hand. Now that I was free to move, I took note of the scar tissue in my palm. It was faint but still visible from when I'd held his leg. The memory made me shudder. I'd taken him down almost subconsciously, pure survival reflex. I was just so angry at the time.

I heard some rattling metal and I saw Cookie fiddling with the locked door. A fluttering tension rose in my lungs, and I flung myself authoritatively at Cookie.

"What are you doing?! You're going to make it worse than it already is," I said.

"What do you mean worse? I'm set to die with your dumb ass in this coming match. Going out by Feral is *NOT* the way." Cookie glared.

"You're just going to get yourself in further trouble. You're not even going to make it to the cage at this rate," I complained.

"I'll take my chances with the doofus twins, then be confined with whatever they have in the back... Or with you for that matter."

I scoffed. "You're throwing shade at *me*?! After I saved us both from that lunatic?"

Cookie continued to work with the lock. "You got lucky. Vincent was a live wire, and he was running a gauntlet in that cage. You only managed to pick him off when he was weak and distracted." The lock popped loose. "There's no such luck with ferals." Cookie turned to me. "Now you can either sit here with your hands in a knot, or you can help me with these cuffs."

I looked down and saw Cookie holding a key. I paused for just a moment before nodding to her proposal. "Do mine first, and then I'll get yours."

Cookie also paused. "Fine," she said, then started using the key on my shackles. She tinkered and then it clicked! The steel loosened around my wrist and slid off onto the cold ground. It made a pinging noise that echoed through the cells, attracting minimal attention. I was startled by the sound and Cookie gave me a deathly look. The kind of look that said, 'Do not do that again!' Cookie hoisted the key.

"Do mine, quickly," she whispered.

I fumbled with the keys, almost dropping them. Nervously, I engaged the lock, but quickly freed Cookie from her restraints. "So, how did you win your last arena match? Are you some trained assassin? Or do you just wait for others to finish the job for you?" I said with mild disdain.

"Nothing personal, buddy. Our opponent was already tiring; my best option was to wait it out after Vincent had taken care of you, then give it my best shot."

"No love for your fellow man, I see..."

"Oh, you mean the love that gets people killed? No thanks. I don't know you from anyone. Me, waiting for Vincent to finish you was the best course of action."

"That's cold..." I said.

Cookie slowly pried the cell door open, gaining the attention of the other incarcerated metas. Before stepping outside the cage, Cookie looked at me. "Are you coming or not?!" she said in a demanding whisper.

I looked at the open cell door and glanced around to see who was watching. Many eyes met mine in the darkness. Some had a shimmer and glow to them, something abstainly not human. For some reason, I had frozen in place. My hands shook franticly, and I was unable to choose. She was right: Taking the chance to escape would almost surely be the better option, but for some unknown reason I felt weirdly inclined to... stay.

A sudden flash of a dark place with plywood surrounds me, like a shed. It's completely dark other than the sunlight seeping through the cracks. I'm... sitting on the ground, dirt ground, and a voice from the outside is speaking to me...

"It's safe to come now," the voice said.

I came back when Cookie clocked me in the shoulder with a right hand. "What was that? I don't have time for this, Space Cadet. This is real life—My life, your life! Spacing out when choices have to be made is how you become another statistic."

I'd never had weird visions crop up like that before... A memory maybe? But the scary lady was right, I can't just wait around to die. I looked up at her and nodded confidently.

"Great! Now you go first!" she said.

She pushed me out of the cell. I don't know why I guarded myself when she did, like I was half-expecting alarms to sound, and lasers to penetrate my body. After a small bit of frantic terror, I opened my eyes and concluded that everything was fine. It didn't stop me from turning toward Cookie and flipping her the bird.

"See! Nothing to worry about, we just need to make our way out this labyrinth."

"Do you know a way out? I'm guessing you've spent a lot of time here, you must know the layout, right?"

Cookie hunched her eyebrows and said, "Sure... I'm such a regular here, I even check the mail." I stood silently, not knowing what to say, and blinked twice at her tone. "Of course, I don't know where to go, you've been everywhere I've been at this point. Any more stupid questions?" she whispered.

I looked up and around, noticing the distant red glow of an exit sign, and pointed to it. "How about that way?"

Cookie looked and garnered my intent. She half-shrugged and clicked her tongue. "I don't know, doesn't it seem too easy to go that way?"

"For god's sake, let's just take the easy answer and hope for the best. What else are we going to do?" I said in frustration.

"Yeah, but it's an exit sign in a room full of prisoners. If anyone wanted to escape, I would have something misleading like an exit sign to steer them in the wrong direction."

I was going to rebut her and say how paranoid she sounded, but for some reason, I second-guessed it and thought to myself, 'That *is* something I'd probably do...'

"Okay! Fine, it does seem... a little too easy. What would you suggest?" I whispered as we crept between the cages.

"Let's find a way out that is not a door; we have a little bit of time before they check our status. Moving a feral from one place to another isn't easy."

"Like a vent? A hole in the wall? Things that only work in the movies?" I said.

We started gathering the attention of the others. They wouldn't say much of anything, though, only stared at us with piercing, troubled eyes. It made my throat tighten up. So many eyes on us. One meta slammed against the cage next to us. His cheeks were sunken in and his eyes looked scared. "Let me out, if you're getting out I want in!" In the distance came the faint sound of other metas stirring.

"Do you have a key?"

"Get these cuffs off of me!"

"We can help!"

"I don't want to die here!"

The noise mounted greatly. Cookie and I glanced at each other with wide eyes and a shade lighter in our faces. It was too much to take in all at once. The cries for help grew louder. Even if we did release every desolate creature in this place, the risk of death would be great. Their safety would be on us as well.

"The time isn't right!" Cookie yelled. "It's too dangerous to release everyone now. We'll have to wait!" But the cries for help only grew louder. Cookie grabbed me by my shirt collar. "We have to go now! There's nothing we can do. It will only get us killed."

I nodded hesitantly; I knew she was right, but something about it just didn't sit right with me. "It's just, we have the power now to help these people. Why wouldn't we? It could help us out in the long run."

"*Or* all the chaos will get these folks gunned down. Powers or not, not everyone's battle-ready or strong enough to tackle a bullet."

-RUN-

The exit door creaked open, and a hulking shadow filled the frame, blotting out the light from the hallway beyond. The room fell into an oppressive silence as the figure stepped inside, each footfall landing with a heavy, deliberate thud. Cookie and I instinctively ducked behind a cluster of cages, our breaths shallow as we tried to disappear into the shadows.

Under the dim, flickering light, the man emerged—a grotesque silhouette of brute strength. His massive shoulders hunched forward, his thick arms hanging unnaturally low, giving him the appearance of some primordial beast. Suspenders strained against his checkered shirt, and his frame seemed too large, too wrong, to belong to anything human. My stomach churned as I caught sight of the dark stains smeared across his clothes. Was this a feral meta?

"He's covered in blood," Cookie whispered, her voice trembling. Around us, the others shuffled back as quietly as they could, their fear palpable. The man's gaze swept the room, his eyes sharp and predatory, lingering on the rusty bars of the cages. He moved with a slow, deliberate menace.

Without a word, he strode to the center of the room, stepping into the weak glow of the overhead light. The bulb flickered, casting his shadow in jagged, shifting shapes across the walls. For a moment, he stood there, silent, his head tilted slightly as if listening to something only he could hear.

"You all..." His voice rumbled, low and guttural, like the growl of a distant storm. "...are disrupting my work. Why?"

No one answered. The only sound was the ragged breathing of a woman somewhere in the room, her panic breaking through the silence. The man's head snapped toward the noise, his eyes narrowing with a predatory gleam. He moved toward her, his steps slow but unrelenting, like a predator closing in on its prey.

When he reached her cage, he opened the door with a creak that seemed to echo. The woman screamed as his massive hand wrapped around her mid-section, lifting her effortlessly. Her cries filled the room, as the others shrank back in terror.

"Hi, darling," he said, his voice so deep it seemed to rattle my bones. "Tell good ol' Eddy what the ruckus is, hmm?" His tone was almost gentle.

"No, please," she sobbed. "I wasn't saying anything, I swear. Please..."

"It's okay, love," Eddy murmured, his lips curling into a smile that didn't reach his eyes. "Just tell me what I need to know, and I'll... let you go."

The woman's breathing hitched, her words caught in her throat. Eddy's grip tightened, and a sickening pop carried through the room. Her scream tore through the air.

"Yesss," Eddy hissed, his voice slipping into a growl. "Just one of Malcolm's for Eddy. Just one, yes Malcolm, just this one!" Another crack, louder this time, sent a wave of nausea through me.

I clenched my fists, sparks flickering faintly from my hand. Cookie grabbed me, her eyes wide with fear as she shook her head. "We can't help her," she whispered urgently.

"But we could—"

"No, we can't," she snapped, her voice barely audible. "That thing is worse than anything in this building. There's nothing we can do."

Her words cut through my anger. I tried to look, but Cookie forced my head down, her grip firm. The woman's screams turned into a wet, choking gurgle, and the sound of tearing flesh and snapping bones filled the room. It was the most horrifying noise I'd ever heard—sloppy, wet, and unrelenting. My knees buckled, and my hands trembled as the reality of it all sank in.

"I just wanted it to be over," Cookie whispered, her face pale and stricken. The sounds of ripping and chewing continued, each one worse than the last.

"Don't look," she said, squeezing my hand as we began to move. We kept low, sneaking along the wall toward the exit. The other doors were too risky—opening one would draw attention. As we passed each cage, hands reached out, desperate and pleading, but Cookie didn't stop. I followed her lead, forcing myself to ignore the cries for help.

When we reached the exit, Cookie hesitated, her eyes darting toward Eddy, who was still consumed by his grisly work. Then, with a whisper, she said, "Now."

We slipped through the open door, the light swallowing us as we left the nightmare behind.

Barefoot, we shuffled down the dim hallway, the cold floor biting at our soles. The screams from the room behind us echoed faintly. The anguish radiating from the darkness wasn't the unknown—it was the certainty of what lurked there. I knew exactly what was in that room, and the knowledge made my chest tighten.

Cookie tugged my arm, urging me forward. We didn't know where we were headed, but at least we were out of holding. The hallway stretched endlessly, its silence oppressive, broken only by the faint hum of fluorescent lights overhead.

"If we run into anyone, be ready to take them down," Cookie whispered.

I hesitated, my throat dry. "What do you mean, take them down?"

She stopped abruptly, turning to face me. Her eyes burned with frustration. "Like you did with Vincent. Use your powers."

"I... I don't know how to fight," I admitted, my voice barely audible. Her expression hardened, disbelief flashing across her face.

"Of course you do! I saw you—direct all your anger and throw it at him. Just do that again."

"That wasn't me," I stammered. "I mean, it just happened. I was scared for my life. Something... took over."

Cookie's lips curled into a bitter smirk. "Oh, I get it. You've got some demon inside you, huh? Harness its power when you get all emo? You're a real catch, Charlie."

"Shut up," I snapped, heat rising in my cheeks. "I know an edgy hard-ass when I see one. Tomboy? Brothers? You've got the emotional threshold of sandpaper. If anyone bites, you bite back harder, right?"

Her face darkened, "The hell with what you think you know about me. If it wasn't for me, we'd still be in that cage waiting for death."

"And if it wasn't for me, we'd never have made it out of the arena alive!" I shot back.

"Then shut up and take these clowns down!" She pointed ahead.

Two men in suits stepped into the hallway from a side door, their movements stiff as they spotted us. Their eyes widened, and one raised an assault rifle. "Wait, is that the stock?!"

Cookie raised her hands slowly, her expression calm. "We give up," she said, kicking me in the calf to follow suit. Reluctantly, I raised my hands, placing them behind my head. The guards whispered to each other, their voices too low to catch. One lifted a radio, muttering into it as they closed the gap between us.

A hand wrenched my arm behind my back. "Oww, easy there!" I hissed, but the guard didn't loosen his grip.

The other guard fiddled with the radio, static crackling as he adjusted the frequency. Before he could react, Cookie lunged, grabbing the radio and slamming it against the guard's temple. The static settled, and a burst of sound erupted from the device. The guard's head imploded with a sickening crunch, splattering the white walls with blood.

My hearing muffled, I stared in horror at the mess Cookie had made, my stomach twisting violently. Before the second guard could react, a spark ignited in my eye. Instinct took over. I grabbed his arm, twisting free, and slammed his body against the opposite wall. He crumpled to the ground, unconscious.

Cookie turned to me, her face calm, almost smug. "See? Easy as pie."

"You killed him," I stammered. "With his own radio! How did you do that? Why did you do that?!"

She shrugged, her tone flat. "Same way you slammed that guard into the wall. Now let's keep moving."

"No," I said, my voice rising. "That's not the same thing. I didn't know we were killing our way out of here!" My eyes darted to the blood dripping down the wall, the metallic smell making my stomach churn. I turned away, bile rising in my throat. My body convulsed as I vomited, the sound echoing in the silent hallway.

Then, a deep, guttural voice cut through the air, freezing us in place. It came from behind, each word dripping with menace.

"If not killing, then you're dying. That radio trick isn't something Eddy's seen."

I whipped around. Emerging from the sleek white hallway was a hulking figure, blood dripping in a macabre trail down his stained clothes. He nearly filled the corridor—each heavy step punctuated by steaming breath and eyes that glowed with the fresh thrill of a kill. In that moment, Cookie and I knew there was no time to hesitate.

"Run!" Cookie hissed, and we bolted. Our hearts pounded as we raced down the hall, every decision made in adrenaline-fueled instinct. Behind us, Eddy's gaping mouth and thundering steps closed in. We darted into another identical corridor; my mind raced with possibilities of escape routes as we weighed our options in a flash.

I spied an armed guard turning toward us. In a split second, I lunged and pressed my hand to his chest, channeling a jolt of raw energy that sent a shock coursing through him. The pain was blinding—but I directed the guard's trigger toward our pursuer. It was desperate. Eddy tore through the man as if he were paper.

We sprinted until a dead-end halted our progress. The only thing there was a massive wall-mounted loudspeaker protruding near the ceiling. "Run to that speaker!" Cookie barked. "You're faster than me!"

"What?!" I shouted, but there was no time for protest. With every ounce of my fading energy, I dashed to the wall and wrenched the speaker free from the drywall, its cords tangling momentarily before it came loose. Cookie intercepted it with practiced ease and, without hesitation, levelled it at Eddy.

"Eat this!" she roared.

Her words combusted into a sonic wave that shattered the fragile silence—cracking floor tiles and rippling through the hall. The force blasted Eddy back; his skin screamed under the onslaught, and he crumpled and cupped his ears. The crash of the collapsing hallway and the deafening soundwave left my ears ringing as I stared in shock at the carnage we'd wrought.

The ceiling was falling in around us, and Cookie was taking another breath for a second volley. I ran to her with electrical bolts arching from my heels, and before she could speak I cupped my hand around her mouth. This didn't stop the flooring from cracking beneath us as it gave way to our combined weight and together we fell into the yawning chasm below; Cookie used me to break her fall as I fell wedged between more ceramic and an able-bodied human being. We were both okay aside from being a little dazed and suffering a few scratches. Eddy fell through and landed hard on his neck. We heard a pop when he landed but he didn't go limp. He struggled to reach us from the ground but collapsed soon after.

"You alright?" I spoke. She lifted her arm with the wall speaker still clenched in her hand. It was falling apart at this point, so she flung it a few feet away.

"...Yeah—" She coughed. "I didn't think that was going to work at first."

"Yeah, heh. It worked..." I said.

We both looked on at the still body of Eddy. Voices gathered faintly from the floor above us. Malcolm's security team had gathered at ground zero and was making a plan to come down. I pulled Cookie from the wreckage and checked our surroundings. It was dark, and there were individual metal doors that ran down the hall on both sides. Each door had a barred window you could look through. Granted, it was too dark to make out anything inside them. There was a lone light that hung from a wire in the hallway that provided minimal visibility.

We pressed on, hearts hammering, when a voice suddenly erupted from one of the cell doors. "Who's there! Come here!" the voice demanded harshly.

Curiosity and survival instinct warred within me; as Cookie urged caution, I edged closer and peered through the peephole. In the dim glow of a solitary overhead light, I saw a woman sitting cross-legged in the center of a cramped cell. Her figure wavered, almost like a mirage, as she swatted at something unseen. Then she stood and approached the door, pausing just at the edge of the window.

"You two don't look like security. What is this?" she demanded in an accent that felt familiar.

"None of your business, lady!" Cookie snapped, glancing over her shoulder. "We don't have time—Charlie, they'll be onto us soon."

But something in the woman's eyes—a faint, eerie golden glow—stopped me in my tracks. A sudden flash of memory stabbed through: the Haitian who'd whispered his quest to me before this madness.

"Are you... Kalia, the preistess?" I murmured, voice trembling with awe.

Her eyes widened in unmistakable recognition. Stepping flush with the cell door, she answered, "I am who you speak of—But a priestess?" She sneered, "It's only what they want to call me." A low hiss followed that seemed to echo in the hollow cell.

In that charged moment, I realized that the thing I'd been told to go search for had found me. Even though I wasn't looking, here it was.

Chapter Eight

I laughed as I peered into the cell, feeling like I'd found the lost ark. I didn't know why I felt this way. Maybe it was like winning an intense game of 'Where's Waldo'. Nonetheless, I found her. I'd been given a task, even if it was one I didn't want and I'd followed through. The sheer luck of falling through the floor to find this woman. Memories of Wick flooded back to my forebrain. With a slight glance and a nod, I noticed she was the same: A Haitian priestess.

"Heh," I chuckled.

The priestess looked on and shifted uncomfortably in the dark. "Well, are you going to keep staring?"

Cookie grabbed my attention by punching the sole of my back, "Dude, we do not have time for any of this."

"Now hold on a minute…" I raised my hand. "There's this guy, that brought me here, and it was to find her."

"Who gives a damn! We have problems, Charlie!" She chopped her palm and pulled me from the door. "Do you see this?!" She pointed towards Eddy. "We are public enemy number one right now, and taking baggage isn't aiding our escape!"

"I am not luggage, you Petrie sod. Just because I am in a cage does not mean I need to be carried," Kalia growled, then turned to walk gruffly toward the back of her enclosure.

I tossed my hands in the air. "Look, Cookie… This?" I pointed towards the cell door. "I have no words for the odds I would actually find this chick—"

"I am not a chick!" Kalia power-walked toward her steel exit. "Look! I don't know who sent you, but *you..* Very rude."

"Hey, it's not like I wanted to be here. But while I'm here—" I shrugged. "Why not? Wick may be an asshole for tricking me, but that's no reason to ignore saving you."

Kalia shifted her glance and sneered at the sound of the name. "Wick you say?"

I nodded.

Here eyes shifted frantically, "Such a dumbass, coming all this way to take me back." She disappeared back into the dark and laughed quietly to herself. "Such a fool."

A light shone from one corner of the hallway. Footsteps echoed with haste and our attentions shifted to the coming guards. The voice of a man sounded out, "This way! Surrender quietly."

Cookie nervously pointed toward the source and said, "Look! They're here! I hope you're happy!"

I electric-charged my fingertips and grabbed the bars that ran through the peephole. With a flourishing spark in my eye, I squeezed the metal together to better fit my grip, "What's it going to be, princess? It's now or never."

Her eyes fixated on the use of my abilities. "You can bend metal?"

"...I guess so?" I said, equally as surprised.

Her eye's locked with mine, "First thing! I am not bound to anyone under the circumstance of freedom, know this to be true!" she said.

"You do whatever you want after this door opens," I answered.

Cookie screamed, "Charlie!!" as the strobing flashlights came closer.

It was only a matter of time before the guards ran us down; I Ignored it and kept my eyes locked on Kalia. She hesitated for just a moment, then she stood in front of the door and languorously stretched her body, placing her hands over her head. I noticed she was shackled with cuffs when she did. Finally, she said, "Clear thee way."

With a strength formerly unbeknownst to me, I pulled against the door, as electrical strands discharged from my body and grounded out through the floor. The door didn't budge at first, but eventually the rusted hinges fractured, allowing me to pluck the door away from the wall. Kalia's cell remained enveloped in shadows. She walked out in normal–looking handcuffs. Her dress was a textured or-ange and brown, which was dirty from her prolonged imprisonment. As my gaze traveled to her neck, what I saw pushed me against the wall to gain distance. I froze in place and fully bewildered from the protrusions coming out of her scalp.

Snakes, lots of them! Slithering along her shoulders and down her back, they hissed and flicked their tongues out as they curiously stretched out. They were brown with maroon patterns on their backs and bellies. All of them protruded out of her scalp.

"Geez'us!! You could of warned me, lady!" I eked out while attempting to be one with the concrete wall at my back.

Cookie forgot about the guards for half a second and was fully enamored by Kalia's scaled headdress. She smiled for a moment, a quick moment. Then the flashlights from the yelling guards became too much to ignore. Before long, bullets started whizzing past our heads. I used the prison door as cover, while Cookie ran into the open doorway of Kalia's cell.

The snake lady looked long toward our enemies and continued to stand there, never moving an inch. "Their aim is off…" she observed. "Old weapons. Bent muzzles, maybe."

I yelled out, "Is your ability being bulletproof? Because if not, I'm really regretting my decisions right now!"

Kalia shot me a look. I tried to break eye contact, but I was too scared and weirded out at the same time. She said, "All that strength and you don't even see your advantage? It's right under your nose."

"What advantage do I have against guns?" As my thoughts fermented, bullets violently ricocheted off my cover.

"…Oh!" I sighed.

I hoisted the metal door and positioned it in front of me. Using my abilities, the electrical surge numbed my fingertips as the charge grounded through the metal. With ease, I grabbed the bars from the peephole and welded the door as a pseudo-shield.

Kalia looked idly by. "Well, Lightbulb, I'm in distress. What are you going to do about it?" She mocked me.

"You don't look in distress..." I said.

Cookie intervened, "And you both look like assholes, could we *do* something already?!"

"Why don't you do something?" Kalia shot back.

Cookie answered, "I need tools, or I need to be in spitting distance."

With a heavy sigh, Kalia rolled her eyes. "Boy wonder, get in front and we'll walk behind you." She gestured toward me.

I did what she said and jumped in the center of the corridor between Kalia and the guards. I held the door steady enough to move toward the gunfire if needed. I kept a distance from the Snake Lady as one of her serpents stretched out to touch me. A bullet in my teeth seemed like a more pleasant option.

Kalia turned to Cookie. "You! What is your meta power?"

Cookie stood in the cell looking pent up with her arms crossed. "I have the power to create a deaf community."

Two other guards joined the two in the hallway ahead of us and the volley of bullets increased. It made it difficult to hear. Kalia leaned toward Cookie to better understand.

"... A death or deaf community?" Kalia reiterated.

Cookie simply said, "Yes."

"Now that we've all had a hasty meet-and-greet, can we get the hell out of here!" I said, clearly running out of patience.

Kalia sternly spelled it out. "I know not, Lightbulb. How do you propose we leave this basement?"

"Just throw the stupid door at them!" Cookie yelled.

"No!" Kalia said.

But it was already too late, I had already made the decision. I swung the steel door horizontally over my head. Kalia ran into the cell with Cookie. Then I did a short hop and skip before I launched the thing with my left arm. Blue sparks floated off the frame as it left my hand.

A scramble of words and obscenities could be heard before the door clashed with the armed men. The Door bounced once and then reverberated as it settled.

"Damn it!" Kalia yelled as she sped past me toward the opposition. She was fast, bolting in like a jaguar. I looked on as the meta disappeared into the darkness. The gunfire may have dissipated, but the screams of injured guards did not. I couldn't see what she was doing to those men, but I was getting flashbacks of Eddy. They pleaded for life yet, one by one, every person was silenced.

Out from the darkness approached the Gorgon. She held four pairs of shoes by the laces. She was faintly smeared with blood from snake to toe. Her golden eyes appeared - Different, more engaged, and focused. Like she was staring right through me. Cookie walked out into the hallway and paused with caution as Kalia closed in. I noticed Cookie held her fingers in a snapping position. From what I'd seen from her so far, she wasn't about to break out in song 'n dance.

Kalia stopped short of me as I hopped on my back foot. She tossed the shoes on the ground in front of us and stared intently. She said, "Do not ever, EVER throw away the only leverage you have. That was dumb."

"Okay. Fine." I held my hands defensively. "Not the best idea I've ever had."

"Good!" Kalia said sharply. "Now find something that fits. There will be more coming." Kalia stared at the unconscious Eddy. Her eyes grew wide and looked quickly between us and the motionless meta. "Hurry!" she rushed.

I looked down and noticed the subtle stir of Eddy as he came back to life. He rolled on his back and inhaled deeply. I froze in place, thinking he was going to pounce, but he was still nodding off. I dove towards the shoes and forced my heel into each one. Cookie, meanwhile, picked up a flat hunk of concrete so heavy that she struggled to heave it over her head. She approached Eddy with malicious intent, but Kalia pushed the slab out of her grasp.

Cookie stepped up to Kalia with red in her eyes and sneered. "Let me end him, he'll only follow us."

"Yes, but you are only going to anger him further." Kalia picked up a pair of boots and shoved them into Cookie's chest. "Don't bleed on the floor, the scent will linger." As Kalia turned away, Cookie stuck out her tongue.

"Where do we go to get out? Do you know?" I asked, hopping to fit the second shoe.

"There's no easy way," Kalia replied, pointing toward the area where the dead guards lay. "I remember a lift that could take us up, but it's probably monitored."

Cookie cut in, "Everything is monitored, since we don't have the element of surprise anymore, we just have to run for it and hope we are a step ahead."

Kalia and I nodded in unison. We didn't waste time. The faint sound of alarms echoed in the distance as we sprinted past the bodies. My stomach churned at the sight—their throats were gashed and twisted unnaturally. Kalia had done quick work, even with handcuffs on.

"Boy, are you there?" Kalia asked sharply.

"...Charlie's the name," I corrected.

"Did Isaiah bring you here? Did he come inside?" she pressed.

"Isaiah?" I was lost for a moment, "Ohh! Wick...He did. After he traded me, he walked in too. Then I was knocked out." I frowned, the realization hitting me. "That's been happening a lot lately."

Cookie chimed in, her tone biting. "Wait, so Ms. Thang's boyfriend turns you in, then gets the red–carpet treatment? That's shady as hell."

Kalia's eyes narrowed, her snakes hissing in Cookie's direction. "Malcolm and Wick have history. I have no love for that bastard of a warden."

Cookie smirked. "You looked pretty cozy locked away in that dark room..."

"Only when I have proper company—I have a thing for Thai food," Kalia retorted, baring her fangs.

"I'm Cambodian, you dollar-store Medusa!" Cookie shot back.

"Both of you! Please! Which way do we go?" I yelled, cutting through their bickering.

The hallway split into two identical corridors, both brightly lit. Before we could decide, guards spilled into the left hallway, their weapons raised.

"Right it is!" Kalia shouted, and we bolted.

Gunshots rang out behind us, but we kept moving. I stayed at the back of the group, adrenaline pumping as we turned a corner—only to find more guards blocking our path. Cookie spotted a stairwell and shoved the door open. We raced up several flights, but every door was locked except the one at ground level. I pushed it open, hesitating as Cookie and Kalia stopped behind me.

"Something doesn't feel right," Cookie muttered.

"Agreed," Kalia added.

The sound of guards rattling down the stairs grew louder, both from above and below. We were trapped. Through the window embedded in the door, I saw a hallway that widened into a large shutter door covered by a curtain. The space was dimly lit, with faint murmurs of people coming from behind the curtain. Before I could say anything, the guards closed in, bullets flying. We shoved through the door into the expanded hallway.

The space was cluttered with pallets of cardboard boxes and steel planks stacked along the walls. A large wooden scoreboard leaned against the wall near a set of double doors. I grabbed one of the planks, using my abilities to wedge it against the stairwell door. The effort burned through me, but I managed to secure it just as the guards arrived. They fired at the glass, but the shots ricocheted, causing chaos among them.

"Good job," Kalia said.

"Yeah, congrats on being slightly useful," Cookie added with a smirk.

I ignored her, sticking my fingers in my mouth to soothe the burns. We moved toward the curtain, listening to the muffled voices on the other side. The atmosphere felt eerily familiar, like a baseball game I'd once attended with Grace. My thoughts were interrupted by a foul stench that filled the air. Kalia tracked it to a dumpster-sized container.

"Plenty of dead in here," she said grimly.

"It's the arena," Cookie blurted out. "We're right under the ring."

Kalia and I shot her a sharp look, silencing her. Just then, a guttural shriek pierced the air, silencing the crowd beyond the curtain. Cookie and I exchanged wide-eyed glances. Even without seeing it, I knew—the feral was waiting.

"This way!" Kalia pointed to the double doors near the scoreboard.

Cookie reached them first, but the door swung open from the other side. A group entered, led by the woman who'd announced my match with the mercenary. She wore a plaid blazer and tie with a black mini skirt, her eyes glowing faintly. Beside her stood a tall Latin man in a black beanie and yellow button-up shirt, his tattoos visible through the open top buttons. Two guards stepped beside them, their assault rifles aimed at us.

Cookie raised her hand to snap her fingers, but the man grabbed her wrist, twisting it until she dropped to her knees.

"Hey!" I shouted, rushing forward, but Kalia stopped me with her arm. The guards leveled their weapons at me.

"Don't even think about it," one warned.

The announcer stepped forward, her hips swaying with unsettling confidence. Her gaze locked onto mine as she spoke.

"Stand and do nothing." Ego said

"No! Charlie! Don't make eye contact!" Kalia shouted, but it was too late.

Her voice echoed in my head, freezing me in place. A chilling sensation spread through my body, locking my muscles. I couldn't move.

"I—I can't... do anything," I stammered, struggling to speak.

The announcer Ego had just implanted some sort of suggestion on me. I looked into her eyes and whatever she said, i was compelled to do. A meta that can compel others with just a sentence. No wonder she was the announcing agent for the arena.

Kalia crouched low, her serpents coiling and preparing to strike. The guards opened fire, their automatic rounds blistering through the air. Kalia darted behind me, using me as a shield. Bullets barely missed me as they whizzed past my standing.

"Ahh–ahh–ah! Assholes!" I gasped, still unable to move. Ego's spell stayed firm!

Kalia sprinted to the scoreboard, shoving it toward the opposition. The guards scrambled to stop it, but it toppled over, pinning one guard and the announcer. Cookie was caught too, but the man in yellow shielded her briefly. Dust erupted as the board hit the ground, and Kalia slipped past them, jumping over the wreckage and through the double doors.

The announcer screamed for help as the man in yellow tapped the scoreboard gently. It splintered and shattered under his touch, bending unnaturally. I realized then—we were all metas here. This guy was able to break the scoreboard with simple taps to the surface of the scoreboard, could he do that to anything?

Slowly, I felt my fingers and toes regain movement. The announcer's hold on me was fading. She coughed as the man helped her up.

"You alright, Ego?" he asked.

"I'm fine, Jonas," she replied, brushing herself off. "That reptilian skank... I'll be glad when Malcolm gets rid of her."

Cookie struggled against Jonas, biting his hand and kicking furiously, but he held firm. From behind the curtain, footsteps approached. Jonas and Ego straightened as someone entered the room. As they approached me from behind, they stretched an arm draping along my shoulders.

"The show must go on," Malcolm said, his voice adorned with leisure.

The feral shrieked again, silencing the arena. Cookie stopped struggling, her face pale with realization. As our eyes met, the pit in my stomach swelled. There was nowhere left to run. It was time to face the music.

Chapter Nine

How could I resist? I haplessly pulled my little sister in line for one of the carnival rides. The festival was alive—music floated through the air, mingling with the scent of caramel apples and fried dough. Bits of the sun's rays melted into orange hues, and purple bled into the sky like watercolor. It was Saturday night, and half the town was gathered on Brook's End, a little field of padded wheat grass that surrounded a dead-end road.

Uncle Larry lent the land every year for the Bernt Hollow Spring Festival. He wasn't really our uncle, but we considered him family nonetheless because of my grandmother. The dogwood trees were in full bloom, their white flowers cascading like snowflakes down rows of trees in the nice neighborhoods. Streetlamps flickered to life as we walked toward the festival, their glow blending with the twinkling lights of the Ferris wheel towering over the treetops. I held my little sister's hand tightly, her protests drowned out by the hum of excitement around us.

"Charly!" she whined.

"Grace, you're big enough to ride this one," I said, grinning. "Don't you want to be aliens?"

"No! Aliens are scary, and I don't wanna die" she cried, stomping her feet.

I laughed, ruffling her hair. "You're not going to die, silly. I'm here to protect you."

The Starship 3000, a giant disk where you stand against the wall inside a giant spinning cylinder. As it spins faster, the centrifugal force pins you to the wall. This one looked like a giant space ship about to crash into the ground. I wanted to ride it so bad because this year was the first year Gracie was tall enough to ride.

Her pout deepened, but I didn't let go. The wind picked up, carrying the sound of laughter and the creak of carnival rides. For a moment, everything felt perfect.

Then, the voice came.

"Dream it, Don't let go of Cookie until you're inside the ring."

The words slithered into my mind, venomous and commanding. My muscles stiffened, my grip on Grace's hand tightening involuntarily. The warmth of the festival faded, replaced by a chilling dread. I saw the steel cage ahead, its doors yawning open like the maw of a beast. Workers reinforced the sides with heavy plating, their faces grim.

Grace—Cookie—screamed, her voice piercing through the haze. "Charlie! Snap out of it!"

I couldn't. The command echoed in my head, overriding every thought, every instinct. My body moved on its own, dragging her closer to the cage. She fought me, her small hands clawing at mine, her cries growing desperate.

"You stupid bastard!" she yelled, snapping her fingers near my ear. The sound was deafening, amplified by her abilities, but it couldn't break the hold. Intermittent shocks wavered from my arm to hers, each one a cruel reminder of my betrayal.

"Dream it, Don't let go of Cookie until you're inside the ring."

But what if I didn't want to let go!? What if I didn't want to go inside the ring!? Even trying to compel myself out of the command, there was nothing I could do. The guards stood by the door, their weapons gleaming under the harsh lights. They didn't stop us. They didn't even flinch.

"Ah, look who's back!" Chet smirked, leaning lazily against the doorframe. "Didn't think you'd survive the first round, mate. Guess miracles do happen."

Barnaby snorted, flicking ash from his cigarette. "Miracles? More like dumb luck. I lost a week's wages betting against you, you know."

Chet shot him a glare. "A week's wages? Try my mother's birthday present! She got a fruit basket instead of that fancy blender she wanted. Thanks for that, genius."

Cookie, despite the dire situation, couldn't resist. "There's no gift you can give that would stop your mom's disappointment every time she looks at you."

Barnaby barked a laugh, but quickly masked it with a cough. "She's got a mouth on her, doesn't she?"

"Yeah, and I've got nails too," Cookie snapped, lunging just enough to rake her fingers across Barnaby's cheek.

He yelped, stumbling back and clutching his face. Cookie pulled something off his belt and hidden it away before they could see.

"You little—!" Barnaby fumbled for his weapon, but Chet stepped in, holding him back with a firm hand on his shoulder.

"Let it go, mate. Her ticket's punched. No use crying over a scratch," Chet said, though his smirk.

Barnaby grumbled, adjusting his belt and glaring at Cookie. "See you in hell, Tot. And don't think I'll forget this in the next life."

Cookie rolled her eyes.

With a huff, Barnaby slammed the door shut, the sound echoing ominously. Chet followed, wrapping the chain around the door with a practiced ease.

Like the last time, the ring had to be lifted up to the second floor. The final touches were made with the re-inforced structure, and the area was cleared. With a half-stumble on the rubber mat, I was able to move on my own again. Like a light switch had been flicked, allowing my mind and body to return to me. I shook it off, leaving the back of my head sore. I realized what I had done to Cookie and turned to face her.

"I'm sorr—" I attempted to apologize.

She smacked me before I could finish. Her hand connected with the bruised side of my face which made it sting so much worse.

"You had to look in her eye again! Stupid boy! It doesn't matter if she's trying to kill us, right? As long as she throws her tits in your face, everything's fine..."

I nursed the side of my face, "I'm... not going to argue with that."

Cookie lifted her hands, and shook her head in bewilderment "We're fucking dead!" She circled and gestured to the hunger crowd. "I'm happy one of us made it out. As if taking pity on some stuck-up snake bitch was going to solve our problems!" Cookie walked away with her fist still clenched. "Unbelievable!"

The bars shifted as the harness cables lifted us in the air. The whole thing swung slightly as it rose, throwing me off balance. The Feral was nowhere in sight; I'm sure they had to make a big presentation about it. Presentation was everything in these sort of events. I looked around the cage at the patch work job of the grafted metal plates that further insulated the ring. There could be a weak spot, something the crew hadn't checked. I circle the parameter while the cage rose to our final designation. Cookie sat cross-legged in the middle of the ring.

"Don't bother. If you could hear the vibration coursing through the bars, you'd know—"

I grabbed the bars before she could finish, and the jolt sent me flying backward. Pain shot through my hands as little puffs of smoke curled from my palms. The cage was electrically charged, and I wasn't immune to it. I rolled onto my side, shaking my hands to cool the burning sensation.

"Ha! Doesn't feel so great, does it?" Cookie raised her arm, revealing the angry burn marks circling her wrist like a brand.

I sighed deeply, the weight of my failure pressing down on me. "Cookie, I'm sorry. I'm so sorry."

She didn't snap back this time. Instead, she turned away, her shoulders slumping as if the fight had finally drained out of her. "It doesn't matter anymore," she said quietly, her voice hollow. "I've been in this place too long. I'm ready to go."

She tilted her head down, staring at her lap. "I've known for a while there was no way out of here. I don't even know why I kept trying so hard." Her fist hit the mat with a dull thud. "I hate them, Charlie. I hate them so much. At some point I wanted to piss them off, so I could finally end this—this so called life."

I stayed silent, watching her as she spoke.

"It wasn't enough that I had to leave my family," she continued, her voice trembling. "Wasn't enough to see my mother cry as I walked away, knowing they'd be punished if they kept me. But now? Now I know it was all for nothing. All of it. All metas will die—for nothing—"

The cage was getting close to the top, the crowd's roar growing louder with every inch.

"And it's because they're scared, Charlie," she said, her voice rising. "Scared of me. Scared of you. They cling to their so-called betters, begging to make everything the way it was before. But it won't be. It can't be."

She dragged her forearms across her face, wiping away tears she didn't want to show. Then she turned her head just enough to glance over her shoulder at me. "This world? It'll never be the same again."

My eyes widened, my mouth slightly open, but no words came. The lights flooded in, blinding and harsh, as the crowd's cheers reached a deafening pitch.

Cookie sat cross-legged in the middle of the ring, her back to me, her silhouette defiant even in resignation. I didn't look at the crowd. I didn't soak in the lights. Instead, I walked over and sat down behind her, my back against hers.

We waited in silence, the tension in my spine slowly melting away. It was the kind of release you feel when you leave a sealed letter on your boss's desk, knowing you've said everything you needed to say. There's nothing else to do now but wait.

The familiar demoness walked out from a black curtain, pushing through to traverse the hanging walkway to the ring. She struck a pose to garner the audience's attention and lifted the microphone to her lips.

"Welcome everyone to our last match of the night!! It's me, Ego!" The crowd roared in approval as Ego took the stage. She walked seductively around the catwalk that surrounded the cage. "We have a very *different* fight for you all here. It's not *everyday* we let animals duke it out in the steeled circle, but we in the back thought you *all* deserved something special."

"I love you, Ego!!" A fan yelled from the stands.

"And I you, sir." She winked. "But! Tonight, and tonight only, a *feral* will grace the ring to hash it out with our returning competitor, the leg ripper himself, T—h—e Baaattery!" She gestured to the crowd as minimal applause sprung from the stands. My eyes shifted… Is that what they're calling me? The Battery? Ego continued. "After his shocking win against our mild-mannered merc, it's only right that we throw him back in for another go at glory! And since they worked so well together last time, we tossed our resident brat, Cookie, in as well. Can they take down the insidious beast? And remember! The cut-off time for betting happens when the bell rings, so hurry and put it *all* on the line, because it's a no-brainer."

Ego raised her free hand and gestured toward the rafters, where a dangling metal crate could be seen suspended above the ring, large enough to hold a person and reinforced with fixtures planted on the corners. It swayed subtly with slight jerking motions, then lowered as an opening receded from the top of our enclosure. The hole that opened from the cage left enough space to allow the box to fit through with minimal fuss. There were stagehands on top near the cage with pole arms. As the crate lowered, a low growl could be heard from the thing. I nudged Cookie to move out of the way. She shrugged me off and said, "I don't care, let the box take me." Her arms spread open, and she held them wide. It was a bit dramatic, like she was waiting for a truck to hit her. There was no way I was letting this happen.

"It's just like you said," I murmured, gripping Cookie's shirt and jostling her by the back of her neck. "Death by Feral isn't the way to go," I hissed. In the distance, a staff member swung a long pole arm to release the straps holding the crate. With a harsh clank, the industrial steel box began its slide—its descent slow yet filled with an unspoken promise of terror.

I lunged, hauling Cookie away from the direct path of the falling crate until she tumbled toward the edge of the cage.

Then the crate crashed onto the mat, tipping over in a shuddering collapse. I stepped back, my eyes locked onto the steel container—a military-grade construct that pulsed with an almost sentient. My heart hammered as I watched the hinges begin to pop off, one by one, clattering like brittle bones dropped in a haunted silence.

Moving next to Cookie as she regained her footing, I felt the weight of the moment. The unknown lurking within that opening was a promise of abject terror—a secret too profound to fathom. In that charged, fragile instant, I silently vowed to protect her from whatever nightmare was waiting in that box.

Ego smiled at me, the kind of smile that said 'gotcha' in the pettiest way possible, "Ladies, gentlemen, and non-binaries, let's get this bloodbath started!! Ring that bell!"

Ding!

The crowd erupted with anticipation; concessions were getting thrown into the ring. The arena mat was getting littered with junk food and personal items.

Ego prompted feedback from her microphone to silence the crowd: "...You know the rules, slugs! No pictures and no interference or you'll find yourself with—No way out! GOT IT?!" She said with serious undertones. The crowd settled in and took the threat seriously. I could only imagine how real the repercussions were here.

The Feral moved with a twisted, labored gait, grumbling and wheezing like an elephant fighting through a bitter cold. The crate trembled and then collapsed, revealing a horrid figure rising from its wreckage. Nearly seven feet tall, its skin was a ghostly pallor, marred by deep purple lesions that pulsed almost as if alive. The flesh looked as though it barely clung to its skeletal structure—as if the body were a fragile remnant barely held together. Long, spindly fingers protruded in nails as sharp and glinting as shattered glass, contrasting with the ragged, patchwork clothing stained with dried blood. Beneath a chaotic cascade of unkempt gray hair, its face bore a sallow, reddish hue, dominated by soulless blue eyes that offered nothing but a void.

Unaware of our presence, the creature shuffled slowly toward the scattered debris of the crate, each step heavy. I longed to press myself against the cage, but i knew that wouldn't end well.

A hushed murmur ran through the crowd. Ferals were anomalies—testaments to a cursed transformation that affected only those metas unable to control their powers. In the end, the very abilities meant to empower them would, in a cruel twist, lead to their undoing. The process was as unique as the individual, yet the outcome was invariably the same: a living, breathing horror, stripped of all that made them human.

Ego spoke into the mic once more. "Behold—a meta who pushed his gift to the breaking point. Once, he fought against muscular dystrophy, a disease that left little hope. But then, during The Outbreak, everything changed. He awakened with the power of elasticity."

In that moment, a camera flash cut through the tension. The Feral's gaze snapped toward the light. Without warning, he stretched a hand toward the bars. His arm extended with a speed that made the metal barely a barrier, sending sparks dancing as they struck the cage. The creature recoiled, a pained shudder running through his grotesque form.

Ego lowered her microphone sharply. "Find him in the crowd. Now!" she commanded a nearby guard.

She then resumed, her voice measured and grim, "His abilities are astonishing—capable of ripping apart bone and stretching cartilage and muscle beyond their limits. But the power that saved him also damned him. While his muscles overextended and regenerated, his skin could not follow. It shriveled and tore as his body stretched relentlessly. The constant agony eventually shattered his mind. The price for his transformation was far higher than any of us could imagine. This is what remains of the man he once was."

The Feral wavered in place, its body trembling with uncontrolled, twitching movements. The crowd pressed against the barricade, desperate to get a closer look at the creature. Armed guards kept everyone at bay, their eyes fixed on the monster as it thrashed against the metal cage—each jolt of electricity sending sparks flying. We were lucky it hadn't noticed us in the chaos; its limited peripheral vision left us almost invisible.

Then, in a low, urgent whisper, Cookie grabbed my collar, "Charlie, we can't just stand here. Let's hit it by surprise."

My eyes widened in protest. "I'm not touching that thing!"

She pressed forward, voice edged with desperation and determination, "Listen, it's only a matter of time before it sees us. We have to do something—now!"

My gaze darted around until I caught sight of broken pieces from the fallen crate scattered on the floor, "Alright... I see something."

I slid quietly toward the center of the ring, careful not to draw attention. Now only ten feet away from the Feral, I charged just enough energy to lift one of the jagged panels of the crate—a makeshift weapon waiting to be re-purposed.

Before we could act further, Ego's voice rang out from the microphone, oozing sardonic amusement. "Watch closely, ladies and gentlemen—our champions are turning even the wreckage to their ad-van-tage!"

Even as her words cut through the tense air, Cookie and I exchanged a look of steely resolve.

The Feral didn't budge; instead, it took the opportunity to elongate its neck. The neck made a wet, popping sound as its head rose to the measure of ten feet. It pulsated and twisted as the exterior skin gave way and tore under the muscular pressure. It was nasty; I could barely watch the metamorphosis. The head flattened out and leaned forward in Ego's direction, attempting to fit itself through the bars. Ego trembled and waved in security to give her some cover.

I took a chance and lifted one of the side panels as silently as possible. Just one piece of the metal panel had to be a hundred and fifty pounds. I struggled to do this quietly and backed away to shield myself as I inched toward Cookie. My partner stood by with unease in her eyes as the crowd got rowdy. She tried to shush them, but the crowd only got louder in return. I was almost back to Cookie and the weight of this thing made my arms strain as I leaned it on my shoulder. I might have used too little of my ability to do this.

A foam cup of soda smacked the side of my face, the cold liquid spilling down my neck. I hadn't even seen it coming. The shock broke my concentration, and the metal panel slipped from my grasp, crashing onto the other panels with a deafening clang. The noise silenced the crowd, their collective gasp hanging in the air like a held breath. My stomach dropped. The Feral froze mid-motion, its grotesque head twisting toward me with an unnatural, jerking movement.

Its gaze locked onto mine like a puppet brought to life by some malevolent force. The creature's jaw unhinged, stretching impossibly wide, and it let out a piercing shriek—a wet, guttural sound that clawed at my ears. I hunched over, hands clamped to the sides of my head, as the scream reverberated through my skull. Then, with a sickening twist of its torso, the Feral lunged.

Its elongated arm shot toward me, the claws at the end of its spindly fingers gleaming like razors. I barely had time to react before it struck, its claws tearing into my chest and shoulder. The force lifted me off my feet and slammed me into the steel bars of the cage. Pain exploded through my body as the electricity coursed through me, burning my skin and searing my nerves. I jerked and screamed, the acrid smell of singed hair filling my nostrils.

Cookie dove out of the way, scrambling to avoid the Feral's reach. Through the haze of pain, I managed to grab its outstretched arm, channeling a surge of electricity back into the creature. It recoiled, its body convulsing as the current ripped through it, but its grip on me didn't falter. With a guttural growl, it hoisted me into the air, slamming me into the ceiling before letting me drop like a rag doll. The crowd erupted in cheers, their bloodlust visible.

Cookie rushed to my side, her hands trembling as she pulled at my shirt collar to inspect the damage.
"Damn it, Charlie! He got you bad. Don't look at it—just focus on staying upright!"

"I think my bladder's done for," I muttered weakly, my voice barely audible.

She slapped my face lightly, her desperation bleeding through every motion.

"Don't you dare pass out on me! Stay with me, Charlie!"

"I—I'm up," I stammered, forcing myself to stand with her help. My legs wobbled, my vision blurred, but I managed to stay upright.

The Feral took another step toward us, its body twitching and contorting unnaturally. It whipped its shoulder in our direction, and I instinctively stepped in front of Cookie. The claws raked across my back, tearing through flesh. I gritted my teeth against the pain as the crowd roared, their cheers feeding the chaos.

Cookie struggled to keep me steady.

"Charlie!! Look at me! Don't let this thing kill you!"

I leaned on her, my knees buckling, my breath shallow. Blood dripped from my lips as I tried to speak.

"Don't tell Grandma I tried to stay with Gracie," I rasped. "She'd be so mad if I tried to leave her."

Cookie's eyes widened, her mouth opening in shock. "Shut up, dummy! Just breathe!"

The Feral, undeterred by its own coughing fits, stretched its arm toward us. Its clawed fingers wrapped around my leg, yanking me away from Cookie. She grabbed my arm, pulling with all her strength, but the creature's grip tightened, its fingers coiling around my midsection like a serpent. With a violent snap, it wrenched me free, sending Cookie sprawling to the ground.

The Feral began to roll me like a yo-yo, its elastic limbs wrapping tighter around my body. My hands, neck, and chest were constricted, my breaths reduced to desperate gasps. The world blurred as the injuries and the creature's sickness seeped into me, a vile infection spreading through my veins.

Cookie slammed her fist into the ground, unleashing a scream that rippled through the arena like a shock-wave. The sound vibrated through the air, knocking concessions from hands and scattering personal items from the front row. Even the Feral staggered, its form swaying as it struggled to regain balance. The crowd gasped as they witnessed the sheer force of her ability.

She reached into her pocket. The Feral's soulless blue eyes locked onto her, and a twisted smile crept across its face, as if it anticipated her next move. But Cookie wasn't backing down. She pulled out a hand radio, flicked it on, and pressed it against the Feral's pale, pulsing abdomen.

The radio emitted a burst of feedback—an amplified sound that tore through the creature's elongated core. The Feral's body ballooned grotesquely, its skin stretching and tearing under the pressure. Blood sprayed across the cage, speckling the metal bars as the creature let out a guttural scream of pain. The force of the attack sent me flying backward, crashing onto the mat. I groaned, my body aching, as Cookie stood firm.

Ego froze, her jaw slack with disbelief. She turned to her staff, her voice demanding.
"Who let her have a radio!? Did anyone know she could do that!?"

Her gaze shifted upward to the private balcony, confusion etched across her face. Following her eyeline, I squinted and saw Malcolm standing there, clapping slowly, a smug grin plastered across his face. With what little strength I had left, I managed a weak, unpleasant hand gesture in his direction before refocusing my thoughts in the cage.

The Feral whipped its stretched arms wildly, its limbs flailing in reaction to Cookie's attack. The sheer randomness of its movements forced Cookie to duck and weave to avoid the lashing appendages. I watched in stunned silence, the magnitude of Cookie's power sinking in. She had amplified the sound from the walkie-talkie to such a degree that it nearly turned the Feral inside out.

That thought reignited a spark within me. Bleeding and battered, I hiked my knee up, forcing myself to rise. I pounded the mat with my fist, each strike rhythmic and consistent.

Bam. Bam. Bam. Bam.

The crowds attention shifted to me. Slowly, the back bleachers began to stomp their feet in sync with my drumming, the sound growing louder as more joined in. The energy was contagious, and I felt it coursing through me. With clenched teeth and a surge of electricity radiating from my fingertips, I stood.

I ducked low, narrowly avoiding the Feral's incoming stab. Grabbing a piece of metal plating, I blocked its second attack, the sharp edge of the plate sparking against its claws. Meanwhile, Cookie darted forward, extending her arm with the radio in hand. She switched to a security channel, and the amplified sound blasted the Feral off its feet. Its limbs recoiled, suctioning inward to break its fall.

Feeling the adrenaline surge, I rushed toward the creature, gripping the metallic plate tightly. With a sharp wind-up, I aimed for its neck, twisting my body as static crackled from my eye. The edge of the plate struck true, slicing into the Feral's macabre neck. As I did, its face spasmed and eyes popped out comically. It struggled for a moment before finally going still.

The crowd fell silent, their breath held as they watched the creature collapse. Its limbs lay partially elongated, like strands of rope unraveling from a broken spool. Cookie approached cautiously, the hand radio still raised, while I whispered under my breath, "Please let it be over."

Even Ego leaned in, her curiosity overcoming her composure. The seconds ticked by. Finally, Cookie and I exchanged a nod, the unspoken relief washing over us.

Soon, distant voices from under the ring sounded out. "That stupid tot stole my radio!" Barnaby pouted.

With that gesture, I nodded with a slight smile as my knees continued to wobble from my injuries.

Ego hesitantly raised the microphone, her voice trembling as she announced, "It is with great... pleasure that we honor our winners! And still—" Before she could finish, the Feral roared back to life. With a violent snap of its elastic limbs, it shoved us aside. Rising again with a cruel, predatory grace, the creature peered into my eyes and expelled an eardrum-shattering shriek that shattered the arena's uneasy silence.

"It freakin' played dead!?" I yelled in disbelief. The entire crowd clutched their ears—except for Cookie. Planting her feet firmly, she lifted the radio as if it were a weapon. In a flash, she switched channels and blasted the creature with a shotgun-like burst of sound. The feedback ripped into the Feral, its gristly body convulsing as if caught in an electric vice.

I leaped to join the offensive, launching a charged metal plate in a desperate shot put toss. But the Feral's elastic might turned the plate against me—it rebounded with brutal force and slammed the plate into my face. My nose crumpled with a sickening crunch, and as numbness spread through my senses, I crumpled onto the mat. The creature wasn't finished yet; it sent a volley of the other metal plates tumbling through the air, They connected with my frame.

Undeterred, Cookie fired back again with that same radio to blast the creature—the sound spurts once and then the device disassembled itself, falling to pieces. Just as Cookie once obliterated a shabby hallway speaker, this followed the same fate.

Cookie was stunned, "Shit."

She backed against the cage wall as the Feral staggered closer. I could only watch in mounting dread as the crea-ture, gathering its remaining anger, raised an sharp elon-gating hand to strike her down. Instinctively, she thrust her hand up as a defense.

Then the impossible happened.

The Feral's head ballooned violently and suddenly exploded! In a spray of blood and viscera that rained over the ring. In that surreal, gruesome instant, its body froze—its elongated limbs twitching like loose, broken rope—before collapsing in a heap. The arena, moments before a cacophony of chaos, fell into stunned silence.

Cookie's eyes said it all—a mix of shock and dread as she stood drenched in the Feral's remains. The arena lay in a stunned hush, broken only by the solitary clap of an unknown figure high. I strained my eyes upward through the settling darkness, trying to discern its source. Before I could focus, Ego's voice crackled over the microphone in a tone laced with condescension:

"As I was saying—our winners, still alive: the Battery and Cookie!"

A torrent of boos erupted from the bleachers. To the bloodthirsty audience, this wasn't a victory—it was a game they'd lost. Every dollar spent on this cruel spectacle had been taken by one man: Malcolm. Concessions flew into the cage, mingling with the grim remnants of the Feral, and Cookie shivered in place. I knew her terror all too well; she was desperate to escape that moment, yet there was nowhere to run. Fresh Feral blood clung to her like a curse.

"Get this thing off of me!" I bellowed, my voice cracking with exhaustion and disbelief. Two jagged steel plates pinned me to the mat. With every ounce of strength, I strained to lift them, while Cookie rushed over, her knuckles whitening as she tugged at the debris.

"Can't you do the thunder thing?" she coughed, blood dripping from her nose.

"I'm trying... It's not working," I gasped.

"On the count of three!" she mouthed silently for a beat before shouting, "Three!" We grunted in unison, managing to heave one of the plates upward as Cookie tipped it over.

The cage jerked; one of its welded pieces chipped off as it descended. The crowd roared in dismay as popcorn and beer cans cascaded onto the lowering cage. The lights dimmed ominously, and Ego's voice returned through the microphone—now a garbled backdrop to my turmoil. I couldn't tell what she was saying; I only knew that the creature lay still, its remnant jerks lingering. Its head was scattered across the mat, while the elasticity of its body retracted back to a feeble normalcy.

"What a way to go," I whispered. Cookie, haunted by the explosion of the monster in her face—a sight too gruesome to forget—simply stared blankly outside the cage. As I staggered free, the cage thudded onto the platform below. I reached out for Cookie's hand.

"Cookie," I said, voice low and desperate, "I promise—we'll get out of this hell."

She avoided my gaze at first, then slowly met my eyes. Her brows sloped, her large pupils shimmering with pain, and her mouth drooped in a silent plea.

Outside, chaos continued to unfold. Four figures and a scattering of armed personnel rushed to surround the ring. One guy in a yellow shirt and beanie lit a cigarette, inhaling deeply before exhaling a cloud of carcinogens against the chain-linked fence. Then, the heavy drag of footsteps creaked from behind him, and a large, box-like figure emerged from the darkness. With a gravelly wheeze, he announced:

"Let me take one, Jonas. Just one for Eddy."

"Naw," Jonas barked, shaking his head and pointing at a nearby guard. "We're not under orders to dispose. Get the hose—we need to prep them for the good Doctor."

Even as the crowd's anger and disappointment simmered, the truth was undeniable: Malcolm had rigged the match and profited from every agonizing moment. We might have survived the carnage in the ring, but the cost was etched in our minds. In Malcolm's twisted game, he was the ultimate victor.

Chapter Ten

Chapter Eleven

L ooking ourselves over, we were covered head to toe in various fluids, mostly dried blood.

"You think this is funny? I've been through hell since the moment I set foot in this place and guess what?" I pulled at my lower lip to reveal my teeth and the absence of a beacon. "They found it and pried it out of my mouth immediately."

The lab shook as Eddy tossed Trailblazer towards us. Wick spotted it and slammed the door. A second later, the impact of the Apex meta loosened dust from the hallway ceiling, nearly caving the door in. I took the opportunity to go through the keyring once more to get the inhibitor off my wrist.

"It's de one with the green strip on it, looks like a flash drive. Dat one!" said Wick.

I found the key of which Wick had spoken and used it to unshackle my cuffs. They dropped to the floor and rolled away. Wick smiled at me.

"See, got what you were looking for."

"Shut up…"

Just then, the door that Wick was wedged against shifted as another blow to the frame shook the surroundings.

"Eddy and Trailblazer, yeah?" Wick noted.

I ran to hold the door with Wick as the frame bent once more to the impact of the other metas. The impacts became more frequent as the wall cracked.

"Have ya found her?" Wick screamed.

"Wha–at?" I asked, the surrounding noises louder than his voice.

"Kalia!! Di'ja find her?"

"I did, she's around here somewhere, out of her cell, she knows you're looking for her!!"

Wick's eyes widened and a smile flashed across his face. "Then I'm not too late?"

I stared, "Given the life expectancy of anyone in this dump, I'd hold your horses on assuming that."

Moments later, the wall collapsed, and debris tumbled into the hallway. We were hurled onto opposite sides of the doorway—Dr. Beverly lay slumped, unconscious, on the floor. Through the raging, flaming opening moved the scorched Silverback, Eddy, his form half-devoured by shadows. I scanned the lab, Trailblazer had vanished—leaving only a monster freshly wounded from battle.

Before I could gather my thoughts, Wick bellowed, "I told you I'd get you out, yeah?" He rifled through a knapsack and produced a stick of dynamite.

"Wha—what are you doing?" I shouted, bewildered.

"The door behind you! That's your way out!" Wick ordered. He raised his gun and fired at Eddy to draw his attention.

"Run!" he commanded.

His words hammered in my ears as the distant, rhythmic clanging of a hammer filtered through the chaos. I stared at the exit—the one door that promised freedom—and then caught sight of Wick at the threshold. He struck a flame on the dynamite with deliberate calm; though silent, his eyes mouthed the single word: *GO*. My legs trembled as the prospect of escape pulsed through me. I bolted to the door, unleashing my abilities to flash through the gapping door and slammed it shut behind me just as the dynamite exploded in a final, searing blast. For one heart-stopping second, I hesitated—should I turn back to help? Wick did give me the opportunity to fee, but I'm not sure that explosion is enough to kill Eddy. I pondered my dilemma at the door, stuck between two actions.

It would a waist if I didn't take the opportunity when it arose, just like Wick using me as his opportunity to enter this building.

On the other side, a vast warehouse unfolded before me—a truck bay lined with shuttered doors and shelving units labeled A through F, each stacked with meticulously packaged goods. Two shutter doors swung open, offering a view of trailers being loaded with large wooden crates. Nearby, two guards armed with AR assault rifles were making their final adjustments. I ducked into the shadows and listened:

"Get everything out now! I don't care if there's anything left—we take what we have to auction immediately!"

"That explosion back there was awfully close..."

"You can check it out if you want."

"No—let's just leave. Malcolm and Jonas scrambled out in a hurry; I'm not investigating."

After a brief exchange, one guard slammed a shutter door as the truck's engine roared to life and drove off, while the other, clipboard in hand, inspected the second truck.

"Hey! Let me bum a smoke—I ran out after the arena finished."

"Yeah, sure. But you can't smoke here—something about combustible freight tanks."

With a nod, the guard stowed a pack, then moved to shelving unit F. He unlocked a set of double doors using a keycard and propped the door open with a rock. That was my exit—a narrow chance to vanish from this nightmare. Just two men barred my way.

I dropped low and crept along the hall, melting into the shadows behind towering shelves. The clipboard-wielding guy remained inside the truck, and the other guard drifted idly by. Freedom was within reach. Yet, as I inched past the shelving areas, a disquieting sound reached my ears—a chorus of voices coming from the back of a trailer. Then I heard it clearly: a woman's desperate cry.

A cold dread curled in my stomach. I knew I couldn't help them all. I continued toward the next aisle, passing shelves labeled D then E. At the very end of section E, my foot nudged a stray screwdriver. It rolled noisily across the concrete floor, drawing the attention of an armed guard.

He spun around, eyes scanning the freight. I dove behind a solid pallet, pressing myself against its rough surface as I stifled my breath.

"Is there anyone there?" the guard demanded.

He was on one side of the shelves while I crouched in silence on the other. The exit door stood just fifteen feet away. I calculated my chance: a quick burst and I'd be out before he could react. But my racing pulse betrayed me. I pressed both hands over my mouth, forcing my breathing to quiet as the guard ambled past toward shelf D. Seizing the fleeting moment, I dashed toward shelf F and skirted around to the cracked doorway.

As I crossed the open space between the shelf and the door, I locked eyes with the man emerging from the truck. He recoiled in shock, his clipboard clattering to the floor as he shouted, "Hey you! No one's authorized to be here!"

In that instant, static seemed to snap from my foot to the ground as I hurtled for the door. I gripped the doorknob but it swung away from me. The nearby guard jumped up, weapon drawn—and I was faster. I lunged and seized the muzzle before he could fire. Almost simultaneously, the guard hidden near the shelves opened fire. A surge of panic electrified my body. I wrestled the AR from his hands and, ducked away. I saw the guard at the door take two fatal slugs to the chest from friendly fire. Regaining my balance, I leveled the weapon at the aggressor and, with a vice-like grip, squeezed the trigger twice. The sound of the shots was muffled by my deafening heartbeat, and the guard slumped, motionless.

In the sudden, heavy silence that followed, the gruesome reality crashed down on me. Blood—literal and guilt-ridden—stained my hands. I hadn't fully registered what I'd done until it was too late. The overseer of the trucks had already bolted into a distant corner, leaving me alone with the echo of dying curses. "Ohhh! Bastard…" the guard at the door groaned, his face draining of color as he fumbled for his radio. His ragged breath spiked into a desperate cry, "Code Red in shipping! Code Red!"

I struck him again with the butt of the AR until he slumped, the sound of my own heartbeat booming in my ears. The weight of those moments—of each shot fired—sank into me.

I forced myself through the open doors. Outside, a rush of cool air enveloped my face, and I moved forward mechanically. Step by step, I trekked through the parking lot toward a dark alley where I could vanish. Freedom beckoned, and yet every nerve in my body screamed in protest.

Then, a muffled voice shattered the momentary calm: "Please help us!"

It came from somewhere behind me—a fragile, desperate plea that halted my steps. I heard it again, echoing in a way that was achingly familiar.
"Don't leave me."

In that moment, again I was caught between two choices: run to secure my own survival or risk everything to help those in need. I knew what I'd done—the guards, the chaos—and the weight of that carnage made it nearly unbearable to move. Blurry with tears, I stood frozen, my soul wracked with remorse and indecision.

Tears streamed down as I choked out, "I'm so sorry, Gracie. I'm so very sorry."

Fragments of memory surfaced—a car door slamming shut, a brown sedan, a bald man in a pleated jacket. Gracie was there, her pigtails bouncing as she laughed. And then she wasn't. The bald man reached for me next. I bit his hand, but his boot struck my face, sending me sprawling onto the roadside. He pulled out a gun, aimed it at me. I ran. I hid. They didn't find me for a few days—a mile from the blue house.

'You were so very young.'

"I was a coward," I whispered.

I stayed in that shed for hours, trembling, waiting for them to find me. Waiting to be next. When they finally called for me—Mom's voice breaking through the dawn—they searched for Grace for weeks. And when they found her... she wasn't the same.

'Mom cried a lot. She drank.'

Another memory struck like a shard of glass: a beer bottle, a broken lamp, blood staining the carpet. Her voice echoed, sharp and cruel:

"Go ahead and run, you little shit! Run like you always do."

"And I'd run away," I murmured.

'It's okay, big brother. I'm okay now,' Gracie's adolescent voice whispered, a fragment of comfort from a time long gone.

My throat tightened, a wheezing sound escaping as I shuffled my feet and rubbed my arm. The memories came faster now, disjointed and raw. The police came. Mom and Dad fought again. I hid in the closet. Gracie left with our aunt.

Rapid flashes: the closet, Grandma's white porch swing.

"And then... nothing."

'Grandma loved you all the same,' Gracie's voice echoed.

Another memory unfolded—Grandma walking into the room, finding me pacing, tears streaming down my face. She pulled me close, her arms wrapping around me as she swayed gently.

"Don't worry about it, Charlie. There's nothing you can do, so it doesn't make no sense to cry."

Another time, I stood in the front room, ceramic angels staring at me from the counter. I nursed my cheek with ice wrapped in a paper towel. Grandma inspected me, her thumb pressing against my jawline.

"Charlie... just walk away next time."

Back in the present, I stood in the parking lot, one hundred feet from the shutter door. A flash of light illuminated the sky, and thunder rolled in from the east.

"I smell rain," I said.

"You should have left it alone, Charlie. Why put yourself through all that?" Grandma's voice echoed as she poured coffee.

"Your eye is still healing from the operation."

RUN.

Another memory clawed its way forward—standing in the living room, porcelain angels lined up on the counter. Mom hugged me tightly, sobbing. Grandma watched from nearby.

"I'm your mother, Charlie! Me!" she cried.

"Then why do you always run from me?!" I whispered in the parking lot.

I had lived with Grandma for months then, I accidently called her mom in front of her. She couldn't handle it. She flicked a cigarette into the yard, then sat beside me on the swing, her arm draped over my shoulders.

"I'll always love you, Charlie."

Back in the present, a jolt of electricity surged through my body, pain detonating in every nerve. It scattered across the concrete, locking my muscles as my bones cracked and my hair singed. Blood dripped from my nose, and I screamed into the sky. The sound echoed, carried by the wind, until it was met by a distant hammering, a metallic *clang.*

The night held its breath. *Clang.*

I inhaled deeply, the air heavy with smoke and rain. *Clang.*

I turned around.

The low-lit complex loomed ahead, its exterior unassuming, almost abandoned. Thunder rolled in the distance, a guttural growl from the heavens. My body trembled. *Clang.*

Facing intentions I'd never dared to confront.

"Just do it already," I whispered, the words barely audible.

The double doors ahead were ajar, wedged open by the foot of a fallen guard. Light spilled out, cutting through the darkness. I stepped forward, one foot, then the other. Each step felt like sinking deeper into an ocean's crushing depths, but I kept moving.

At the threshold, a shadow blocked the light. The doors swung wide, and the figure lumbered down three steps into the parking lot. He adjusted his suspenders with a snap, licking his lips as a grin spread across his face. He stopped just short of the concrete barricades, his massive frame dominating the space.

I kept walking.

The figure cracked his knuckles, it echoed across the lot. He rolled his shoulders, his neck popping audibly. "What's the matter? Did your balls drop?"

I didn't answer. My right eye sparked faintly, a hum of energy building with each step. My teeth chattered uncontrollably.

Clack, clack, clack.

"Good boy," he sneered. "It's just one more for Eddy."

He stepped over the barricade, his boots thudding heavily against the concrete. His hand stretched toward me, massive fingers curling as his shadow engulfed me. At that moment, nothing else mattered.

RUN.

The word flashed in my mind. The electricity grounded through my feet, propelling me forward. I seized two of his fingers and wrenched them back with a loud crack.

Eddy roared, swinging his other arm in a wide arc. I stepped back, letting the punch follow through, leaving him off balance. He stumbled forward, his face now level with mine.

I stepped in with my right foot, driving my left fist forward. *Crack!* My knuckles collided with his jaw, unyielding. My arm followed through, my elbow smashing into his cheek. A flash of light accompanied the hit, illuminating the monstrous figure as he staggered. He was covered in blood and ash, his clothing nearly rags

Eddy was strong—monstrous, cannibalistic, and utterly unhinged. But this was it for him. His eyes rolled into the back of his head, his jaw slacked loose. He collapsed to the ground, motionless.

I stood over him, waiting, my breath ragged. I clinched my fist, thinking he was going to stand, thinking he was going to smile, thinking that this would be the moment he would kill me. He didn't move.

Thunder rumbled closer this time, a deep, resonant growl. A breeze swept through the lot, carrying the faint scent of rain, heavier than before. A small knot of leaves tumbled against my ankle, caught in the wind.

-FIGHT-

A bolt of lightning struck close to the building. A cool numbness spread in waves through my body. The back door was heard striking against the guard's foot from the uptick of wind and over that came the little murmurs of meta-humans trapped in the trailer. They pleaded with a measure of powerlessness I was long since familiar with. Pushing the doors open, I kicked the guard's foot inside. With one last peek behind me towards that dark alley, my forearm aided to dry the moisture on my face.

To the truck trailer. Once inside its dark cavern, my abilities took cadence as each wooden lid was ripped off. One by one, metas ran out of the confined clutter of boxes, allowing me to continue down the line to free each one. They gave thanks and praise because their freedom extended to where mine sat—Just at the edge of the backdoor.

Each one had cuffs latched to their wrist and stood by, longing to be free. The freedom I could readily give. Ten meta-humans walked out of that box; none were Cookie.

Three didn't take any chances and ran out the back door just like I had. If they could have just waited a bit longer, the key in my pocket could have saved them some heartache. Seven waited outside the truck, looking on at the two dead men who'd been dispatched in my escape. I avoided looking. No matter how necessary it had been, even the thought of what I'd done tightened my stomach.

Looking over the trailer once more, there was still one person inside the trailer among the broken boxes. He looked on, clutching his arms as he sat in the remnants of his plywood prison.

"There's not much in the warehouse that can hurt us at the moment, but we need to act quickly," I told him. "Let's go! I can get those cuffs off for you."

The young man shook his head vigorously.

"What... What's the matter?" I asked.

The young man raised his head. "I want to go to the auction, take my chances elsewhere. It's enough to be out of this hellhole."

"You can't be serious; you can walk out whenever you want right now! Why would you not take that?"

He stared up at me with familiar tears. "Because there's nothing for me to go back to. They're all gone because of me, and maybe this is my penance."

I looked closer at the person and noticed he was clutching a link of beads, a necklace of sorts with a cross that dangled on the end of it. He rubbed it between his forefinger and thumb, muttering words I could not quite distinguish. A prayer, maybe. Straightening my body out as

I breathed deeply through my nose, I exhaled slowly and nodded at the weary stranger.

Walking out of the box with the key revealed in my palm, each meta gathered. It took two minutes to release everyone willing. As the cuffs hit the ground, the motivation of each one took over. Three more ran out the back door, singing phrases and shouting. The other four searched the bodies of the fallen and grabbed the assault weapons that lay idle on the concrete floor. They left soon afterwards. I happened to grab a hand radio from the floor.

My feet itched when looking at the doorway outside. Was this enough? I thought. Could I leave now? But I was pulled back. A magnetic connection I didn't understand wanted to lure me back into this place. Cookie had gone to auction; I'd seen it on a clipboard the overseer was holding before he ran off. He was probably the driver of the truck. I couldn't just leave her behind as well. There had to be someone in this place who could tell me where the auction was being held. Malcolm had to have left something around.

I could leave her behind like i left...

I needed to go see my grandma... She was in the hospital and I didn't even know her condition. I punched a metal sheet next to me to keep the intrusive thoughts at bay. More people needed help, I thought; I can do that. I can do that much.

"I'll come visit, Grandma, but your baby boy has shit to do," I said aloud. As if God would carry my message to where it needed to go.

With a single step, I made my decision. My shoulders hunched, but my mind was quiet. It was enough. The barrier had been re-breached, and the facility closed in around me as my walk turned to a march.

The dials and lights on the hand radio sprang to life as I listened in through the channels.

Around the corner in the hall, a guard hurried. As his sights centered on me, his body sprang into action like he'd just gotten hit with a cold shower. The cock of the gun was all I needed to hear before sparks flew. I grounded out through the floor for half a second before pinning the guy to the wall with my hand barred against his neck.

"Where's the auction being held? Tell me!" I said as my hand squeezed tighter.

"I... don't know!!" He attempted re-angling the weapon, but I pulled it from his grasp.

"I'll ask it again! Auction! Metas! Where!? Now!!!" I pulled his neck away from the wall and reintroduced him to it with force.

"I don't know!! I don't know. They never tell us, it would be a security breach," he whimpered.

"Where is meta holding?"

The guard gingerly pointed. "Take two lefts and a right. You'll find it." I knew he had nothing else to offer. For good measure, I shocked him. Just enough to knock him out.

With static streaming around me, I bolted to the location as per the guard's instruction. In through the double doors where Cookie and I had attempted to escape from the first time. Inside, the lights were bright and there wasn't a meta in sight. The cages were empty, and the only things left behind were the fine impressions of blood left on the floor. Even the blankets were gone. Did they all go to the auction? I thought. Two truckloads full, maybe.

"You're still here?" A sudden whisper caught me by surprise.

At the other door was the Gorgon and following behind her was Wick. They entered the room together.

"So bright in here," Wick commented.

"I see you finally found her," I said with a stern voice and a sharp eye.

"Thanks to you, Charlie." Wick nodded.

"Only by the skin of my teeth. I nearly died in here."

"But you didn't. As I see it, you got what ya wanted." Wick pointed toward my hands.

I looked down at my hand gently interlocking around the wrist. Looking up, static flickered from the cornea of my right eye. "I guess you found what you wanted." Wick nodded.

Kalia mentioned, "As promised, I will not be going back to the temple, right?! No more parading in front of them as their lesser deity" An amalgam of serpents leaned out toward Wick as Kalia side-eyed.

"Correct. Where you go from here, I go."

"So, neither one of you is going back?" I asked.

I approached them in quiet strides as I perched myself against one of the cages. Looking upon them, I could tell that they'd been busy. Fresh blood stains matted both their outfits.

"How necessary was all this bloodshed?" I asked.

Wick replied, "Every drop... Dey dare to face us. Dey will face the wrath of iron and fire." His eyes lit up as he grabbed an iron chain around his neck.

Kalia cut in, "What happened here?" She looked around the room.

"A lot—These metas are gone to the auction. Cookie was taken with them."

"So... You want to get your girlfriend back?" The Gorgon smiled.

"Ha, it's not like that," I remarked.

The Gorgon stared intently into my eyes, neither blinking nor shifting her gaze. "Of course not," she said, stepping closer. Her eyes never left mine and the urge to look away mounted. My eyes darted away, but Kalia grabbed the tip of my chin to bring my focus back on her. "It's not enough, Charlie. Some burdens we learn to carry a lifetime. This is one of them."

"I may know where de auction is," Wick said as he fiddled with a blade from his belt.

Kalia shifted her gaze. "Ohh, since when have you started doing charity?"

"The kid wants to help; who am I to stand in de way of that?"

"Where is it?" I asked. An evasive energy struck me as I stepped toward Wick. The static traced around the corners of my eyes.

"Okay, wait!" Kalia said. "You can't just send Lightbulb off to die."

"Oh yeah?" I inquired, "You surely left us back at the arena," I said.

The Gorgon's eyebrows hunched. "There was no other way out of that situation. I had to leave."

"Anything could have happened" I inserted.

"And you're still standing now! Never mind, look! If it will help, we'll accompany you," Kalia said.

"We will?" Wick said, perking his eyes up as he put away his knife.

"Well, it is your fault that he's in here in the first place. I would say it was your lack of resolve that you couldn't find me yourself," Kalia teased with a belittling smile.

"Why would you help me do this?" I lifted myself off the bars. "You can easily take off and leave this place behind."

Kalia explained, "I have a 'being sold to the highest bidder' issue, and after seeking the slug that brought me here, I know now that Malcolm has left for the auction as wel l.".

"I'm surprised he would just readily abandon this place while metas are running loose," I said.

"Everything of value he's already taken: The money, the stock..." She trailed off with a distant crease above her nostrils.

Wick stepped in. "You are a measure different from when I first stopped you. Something happened, I can tell." Wick stared for a moment longer, then cracked a smile with a guttural laugh. "And all I planned to do was to save one; I'd never thought it would cascade into som'in bigga!"

"The Shadows of Iron and Fire can breathe mercy into us, even today." said Kalia. "If that's your thing, of course." She clutched at her own necklace with a silver cross.

"Fine den, let's free those held against their will, and punish those who've stumbled into the darkness," Wick exclaims.

Chapter Twelve

T he heat grazed my ankles and shoulders as I sat idle for the first time in days. The subtle sways of the seat and low volume of the radio playing was enough to put my mind at ease. No memories, nor a single thought of the future. The only thing that mattered was these cloth seats and the heavy lids over my eyes. Wick and Kalia occupied the front seats, the latter thumbing through a travel brochure of Paris and speaking fondly of pumpkin soup, butters, and breads. Wick chuckled and seemed plenty relaxed while he drove. It was as if we were on a day trip in the city. As for myself, I couldn't help but daydream. I did not feel at all like we were traveling to crash an auction, either. I couldn't explain the feeling, but I didn't care much for questioning it. For now, I'm just along for the ride.

We turned onto East Chestnut Street. The fringe of cold air rattled my teeth as we approached a giant, steel-locked building going as high as the eyes could see. Almost a crisscross pattern of steel all the way to the top. There was a circular garage attachment with a toll booth guarding its entry point. In front of the tollway was a stretch of vehicles lined up to pass the tollway.

Wick spoke as we passed near the building and headed a block down the street. "That was it, Malcolm will sell his product dere. The most reliable auction house for international trade in this part of America. Dere's only one way in."

"Through the toll?" Kalia asked.

"Yes. dere will be armed guards crawling all over tha place. Many important people will be here to purchase. From what I was able to gath'a, Malcolm isn't the only one selling."

"How do you know all this?" I asked.

"Let's just say I didn't waste time in Malcolm's Warehouse," Wick answered, "You can't simply walk in without a clearance badge."

"Do we have one?" I asked?

"No, we don't." Wick pulled into a parking garage one block away from the skyscraper on Chestnut Street. "Just know, attempting to free dese people will take guts."

"You mean bat-shit crazy," Kalia answered.

"Once we are in, there's no going back. In some ways, resigning these poor souls to their faith would be the easiest solution. Are you sure you want to do this?" Wick traded eye contact with both Kalia and myself.

Without hesitation, Kalia said, "I'll be damned if I let slave traders abuse me and walk free afterwards. Let's liberate." They both turned to me in the back seat and expected an answer.

To be honest, I was scared. I had no idea what to expect in this place. I just knew Cookie needed out. I may not have been able to help my family when they needed me back then, but I can change that now. I raised my hand and stared into my palm. A trickle of sparks zapped from my fingers. With a clenched fist, I looked at them both.

"Let's do it."

Just then, a truck and trailer drove past. Nothing special about it, just that it was oddly similar to the others. I whispered to Wick, "That truck, let's see where it's going."

Wick backed the car onto the street and crept behind the truck at a distance. We didn't have to follow long before it turned into a below-ground receiving dock. Luck would have it that the freight had pulled right onto the property of the giant, steel-racked skyscraper. But it only pulled in front of the receiving door and hadn't gone in yet.

"Park this thing and get to the back of that truck!" Kalia directed sternly.

Wick pulled into a nearby parking garage, letting Kalia and myself out of the car to approach the trailer. The Gorgon pulled out a cloth and used it to wrap her snakes in a bun.

"How much practice have you with your powers, Lightbulb?"

"Enough to do simple actions on command. It still hurts, but not like it used to."

Kalia finished binding off the wrap around her head. "Show me,"

Successfully, we avoided security as we walked down the incline. As we went under, we were able to disappear from street level. Now to get inside this truck. As we approached the back, Kalia's eyes widened, and she raced to the lock on the trailer door. She fiddled with it for half a second.

"Do it!" Kalia whispered.

I popped my knuckles and right before I could grab the lock, she pulled me to the side.

"From here on out, we don't use names; we are unknown forces in enemy territory. NO. Identifying. Names!" Her stare pierced mine and it was difficult to look her in the eye, "Got it?"

"Then... What should I call you?"

"It doesn't matter, just get the lock open."

My shoulders dropped from the lack of code words exchanged in the moment. With a handle on the lock and a jolt. One flick of the wrist and the padlock snapped off its latch. With quick hands, Kalia slid the door up. Her eyes widened and mouth hung to reveal two benches full of shackled meta children. Looking at the equipment, they didn't seem to be of Apex's origin. The metas inside were of varied nationalities, and some anthropomorphic. They huddled as we stood there and some cried. These were not Malcolm's. Someone else here had skin in the game and they worked a particular niche of meta trade.

Wick approached quickly from behind and slowed with each step. He had to be seeing the same thing we were.

"Do you know who would be behind this?" I asked.

Wick answered, "...No. We need to pile in."

"No." Kalia turned sharply toward Wick. "We need to free them now."

"We have no one to look after them, we need to keep moving." Wick announced.

"You would abandon these children!?"

"If we do this correctly, they can all be saved."

Just then, a small door swung open next to the shutter entrance at the front of the semi truck. Two individuals conversed as they approached. We all looked at each other and jumped into the back of the trailer in unison. Wick closed the trailer door as silently as possible. They rounded the corner the moment the latch clicked into place. My chest thumped waiting for any signs of being caught. They might have noticed the lock wasn't on the door, they could have heard the door slam. My thoughts spiraled through the possibilities. Kalia placed a hand on my shoulder and signaled for me to breathe by mouthing the word to me. Wick imposed a finger to his lip, attempting to settle the children down.

"Everything is in order, courtesy of Mr. Baumer," the driver spoke.

"Twelve miscreants... Any signs of injury, disease, trauma, or other behaviors our guest would find repellent?" the coordinator asked.

"No more than the usual, these kittens haven't been smudged since acquired. Our standards are high, as you know."

"Get them in and we'll prep them for the stage." Two loud thumps hit the side of the trailer wall.

"One last thing," said the driver. "Sign off on these papers and we'll be out of your hair."

A moment of silence transpired and a shift in the trailer swayed us as the whole thing started to move. We all gave each other approving nods and waited quietly with our ears to the walls. We didn't traverse far before the vehicle settled to a stop. That was good. It didn't seem like there were a lot of people around. More than a few for sure, but not enough to feel cornered. Someone approached the back trailer. We sat down on the bench in front of the other captives. The door rolled and revealed two guards, one of them armed with an assault rifle. The un-armed guard climbed into the trailer.

"They didn't say we had a mix of older ones in here," he exclaimed, referring to us.

"Who cares? Pull 'em out and prep them like the others."

The guard first approached Kalia as she hid her face. Her hair was in a wrap, so her reptilian nest wasn't apparent. The guy reached for her chin and lifted her head to make eye contact. I'm sure he didn't know It was going to be the last thing he ever saw. Kalia jumped from the bench and slammed the guy into the trailer wall. During the struggle, Wick pushed his way to the armed guard outside the truck door. The kids erupted in hysteria as it was all taking place.

The Gorgon managed to pin the guy's arm behind his back. A second later, I heard his neck snap. Wick pounced, knocking the other guard down. He snatched the gun away from him, but not before he got a shot off.

"Damn it! Too slow," Wick berated himself.

He jumped up from his fresh kill and looked around. I was nearly in a panic just watching.

"That shot was loud!" I whispered.

"I know," said Wick.

"We got to leave!!" I continued as I stepped out of the truck.

"I know!!" Wick said, agitated.

"Well, they can mark 'trauma' off that list they have for these kids." I continued.

"Please! Shut up!" Wick yelled.

Kalia intervened, "Both of you!" She tapped her index finger on the center of her lips.

Wick set his eyes on a nearby storeroom closet—I knew what he was thinking. Kalia pushed the guard onto the concrete off the trailer. I helped carry the guy with the broken neck, and they carried the other guy. We managed to push the bodies in the closet and shut the door in less time than I'd suspected. It took three seconds for us to slip into a stairwell as a crowd approached the semi truck.

"They got to the kids anyway. We should have taken care of the driver outside and led them to safety." Kalia ranted.

"We would of never got inside, we took the only chance we had." Wick argued.

"Both of you shut up, we're in now and nothing has happened to the kids. Let's just be thankful we didn't get caught," I spoke.

Kalia's eyes grew wide, and she approached me like she wanted to cause great bodily harm to me. I started to cover myself before she stopped short. She said, "You're lucky you're right, or else you would be going in that closet as well." I swallowed hard and started following them up the stairwell.

After three flights of stairs, the Haitians hovered around the 3rd floor doorway. Looking through the window, we saw the service sector. A kitchen with tons of people moving about. Waiters, cooks, and managers filtered in front of the door. Food was being carried out to the left. A central hallway ran straight down from where we looked. On the right was the kitchen.

"Wherever they'd be going is de dining hall. Everyone invited will assemble dere and start the auction afterwards," said Wick.

"Do you think meta holding is close?" I asked.

"Not a chance. 'Prep' can get loud if the enslaved haven't been broken yet," Kalia answered.

Wick turned the doorknob slowly. I caught it and asked, "What are you doing?" He ignored me. "That hallway is full, there's no way we can walk out there."

The moment I said it, Wick cracked the door and lunged his arm out into the hallway.

"Woah!! Wait!" I yelled.

A waiter got pulled into the stairwell and Wick quickly cupped his mouth. The guy panicked and attempted to scream.

"Stop! I am not going to kill you." Wick attempted to quiet him.

His voice fell on deaf ears as he continued to struggle. Wick chopped a spot on his neck and the server collapsed.

After a moment of silence, Kalia kicked the guy's foot, sig-naling that he'd been knocked out cold. I was dumbfounded because I'd only ever seen that move done in the movies and hadn't even considered it was something you could do in real life. Wick looked toward me.

"This one is you."

"What do you mean 'this one is you'?" I said mockingly.

"Put his clothes on, we're going to blend in," Kalia said.

My arms fell in front of me with my palms open wide. "...There's no way this is going to work."

"You got a better idea ?" Wick retorts. He proceeded to open the door again to drag another waiter into the stairwell.

"We're really doing this..." I started taking off my shoes. "You're all nuts. Completely bonkers."

Kalia smiled as she folded her arms. "Have a little faith."

Wick pulled in another server. This one tried to shield himself with a serving tray, but Wick shoved it repeatedly into his forehead. "And have a little fun, don't cha."

We managed to change into clothes to 'blend in'. We all wore the same attire: Black slacks with a charcoal vest and bowtie. Lucky for Wick and Kalia, they'd managed to get shoes that fit. I was stuck wearing my dirty tennis shoes. All three personnel were stripped and left uncon-scious a floor above.

"We all go in, act cool, gather any info that can lead us to meta holding," Kalia said.

Wick followed up, "If anyone identifies you, get the hell outta dere."

"And go where!? Where can we possibly go?" I asked.

"Move!" Kalia pushed me out into the hallway. My eyes grew wide and the urge to panic settled into my spine. Someone flew by me holding a food tray, and then another. A woman yelled out to me:

"Hey dingus! We need runners to the tables, get in here!!"

I turned to make eye contact, and to my surprise, her skin was bright orange with black shapes populating her face. She had scales that blended down to her lips and fins that poked out the sides of her head.

"A fish?!" I blurted out.

"Yes, we have flounder backed up on the line. Get a tray and GO!" she yelled.

I turned to the right to enter the kitchen. On passing, I looked to the stairwell exit and I could see Wick snickering through the window. I answered with a sneaky hand gesture before pushing through the double doors.

The line in the kitchen was full of people. Some of these people were metas in the visible sense. One of the chefs was a man with horns protruding out of his head and dark skin. Another had a third eye! He was chopping a radish and flashed me a disapproving look when I stared too long. It was a mix of metas and normal-looking people. They all could be metas for all I knew. My legs froze in place, and I couldn't stop staring. How could this be possible?

Then I looked closer. These metas all had something fastened around their wrist. So the ones who didn't have that bracelet I could assume were human.

"Meta inhibitors," I mouthed quietly to myself.

The Human Expeditor shouted and pounded his fist against the table. "I don't have time for gawkers! Get these orders out of here now!!" He screamed at me. My feet started to move, but didn't know what direction to go in. Clumsily, I walked over and picked up a tray full of rigatoni pasta, two side salads, a bowl of tomato bisque, and salmon on a bed of rice. With it balanced on my shoulder, I ran out of the kitchen while clutching the ticket that was on top of it.

Table 23...

Back in the hallway, I glanced once more at the stairwell door and peeked through its small window—there was nothing unusual beyond it. A short-tempered server waited impatiently behind me, eager to enter the dining hall. I continued through the doorway and found myself in the fanciest auditorium I'd ever seen. The space was massive, filled with candlelit tabletops and softly dimmed lights. Almost no one could be recognized in the darkness. The walls were lined with gold and draped in intricate Turkish tapestries, while a colossal chandelier—its dangling crystals nearly eclipsing the ceiling—reflected the minimal light into a dance of star-like sparks. All the spectators were fixated on the stage, barely aware of their surroundings. I considered myself lucky, as I could move between the tables unnoticed; it didn't hurt that I could pass as human.

As I moved deeper into the hall, my ears caught the delicate strains of a piano, each note fluttering harmoniously across the venue. My eyes were irresistibly drawn to a giant glass box positioned on stage—a striking contrast as the atmospheric lighting dimmed further. Inside the box, the brightened fog slowly drifted along the ground. Adjusting to this shifting luminosity, I saw her: a woman clad in a white kimono adorned with embroidered blue flowers. She sat gracefully at the foot of a jet-black piano. Her hair was styled into a neat bun, accented by a long, spiked accessory, and her porcelain skin was highlighted by cherry red lipstick.

As her fingers glided over the keys, stark specks of light began to flicker and twirl inside the glass box. Then, as if by magic, it started snowing—fine flakes gathering atop the piano, dancing briefly upon the ivory keys before settling. For a few moments, I lost track of why I'd come here. The mesmerizing visual overture captivated me, compelling me to forget everything else as the black piano and its snowy veil slowly faded into the background.

"Ouch!"

A sudden surge of electricity leapt from my fingertips onto a nearby tray of food, and I lost my balance for a split second. Unfortunately, that brief lapse was enough to draw the attention of a nearby guest—one who, to my surprise, was wearing a mask. Scanning the crowd, I noted that every guest sported a uniquely designed mask. The woman who had caught my gaze tilted her head inquisitively. Mortified, I drifted toward the back of the dining hall, desperate to escape her curious stare.

After a few minutes, the pianist concluded her piece with a final, resonant stroke of the keys—and as abruptly as it had begun, the snow stopped. Rising from her seat, the woman approached a glass wall facing the audience and bowed slowly. A hush fell over the venue. Then, one person clapped, and another, until soon the entire audience was on its feet. The lights gradually returned, and the crowd erupted in roaring approval before eventually settling into a hushed chatter.

From the left side of the stage emerged a meta I had long come to detest. Ego herself approached the podium near the glass box, surveying the crowd with a self-assured smile. She was clad in a shimmering white ball gown paired with matching high heels. "Ladies and gentlemen, no introduction is needed for this display of artistry," she declared after a brief throat-clear. "Let's begin the bidding at three-hundred thousand." Grinning, she stepped back as a platoon of guests sprang from their seats. Numbers flew through the air, each bid higher than the last.

"Five-hundred and fifty thousand! Do I have six?" she announced in a delicate accent.

As the bidding numbers began to fade, my eyes returned to the mysterious meta within the glass box—her hands clasped before her, her pointed chin pressed into her collarbone, obscuring her features. In the ambience, streams of silver glints cascaded—a mesmerizing yet unnerving spectacle.

"Hey! Sir! Sir!!"

A man approached me, dressed in an outfit similar to mine. "I understand the stage can be distracting, but table twenty-three needs their food!" he called, gesturing toward a round table near the center of the dining hall. I glanced over and saw two men and two women, completely absorbed by their wine.

I moved slowly toward the table. One woman was dressed in a burgundy gown while another wore a low-cut almond dress. Sitting between two female guests was a man in a black suit and tie, his hair tied back in a gray ponytail, and his outfit accented by a black cloth strap with a touch of Zorro-esque flair in frilly cuffs and a sombrero-style detail. On the far side of the table, another guest in an off-white suit and tie wore a rhinestone-decorated mask, its design forming an hourglass on his forehead; his brown hair fell in shoulder-length waves. As I began calling out entrees, they all politely raised their hands, and soon, conversation turned to the performance on stage.

"Can you believe the talent among this lot? There's some real competition out there, Sands. You'd do well to follow up strong," remarked the man reminiscent of a masked avenger.

"Ehh…" The other gentleman interjected, "It's all well and good—but it's a bit too much like American Idol for my taste. Let's get some judges, score each performance, and then start the bidding." His tone was unamused.

"You're only jealous because you didn't have money on that one," came a teasing retort as I handed him a bowl of soup.

"I'm not here to entertain, I'm here with the product. Go on—rattle off the specs, and let's move on with our lives. Now I have to dance for pennies?" he continued, knocking back a crystal glass of wine.

"Not every buyer is looking for death match survivors," someone remarked dryly.

Hourglass scoffed, "What are my choices, really? My team barely puts in any effort anymore—let alone what you bring to the table. Does your front man really have to maim two out of four prospects before I see them? Honestly, death by cage match is a mercy at that point."

"Even still, you can't keep a lid on your operation."

"Our operation," Hourglass corrected sharply.

The man with the ponytail sipped his soup as he added, "How often does Eddy cut into profits?" I handed him two salads, which he promptly placed in front of his guest. For a moment, Hourglass remained silent.

Then Ego's melodramatic announcement rang out: "Going once! Going twice! Sold to the gentlemen in the Ronald Reagan mask for eight-hundred and twenty-five thousand!!"

The crowd responded with hoots and applause. As the curtain drew, a lone spotlight shone on the buyer. I heard the sharp clank of a wine bottle hitting the table—Hourglass had taken his second glass since I'd arrived.

In that moment, our eyes met. My mind stuttered as a spark danced across the silverware I was setting down.

It was Malcolm.

Chapter Thirteen

"Charlie?" Malcolm's voice cut through. He rose slowly from his seat. My heart sank. Without hesitation, I tucked my food tray under my arm and turned away, walking as fast as I could toward the back of the dining hall. My pulse quickened as I noticed Malcolm following me.

The auction was at its peak, and most guests were too engrossed to notice anything amiss. I weaved between tables, dodging guests and nearly knocking over a waiter in my haste.

"Thank you for a spectacle of an evening!" Ego's voice rang out from the stage.

I glanced up and froze. She was staring directly at me, her eyes burning with frustration. Her teeth clenched as she paused mid-announcement. A tense silence rippled through the dining hall, and a few guests began to notice the urgency of my exit.

Nearly at the door, I snatched a cloth napkin from a woman's lap and pushed into the gallery space. The walls were lined with paintings, each flaunting an exorbitant price tag. Oddly, some of the works were styled to look like jigsaw puzzles... I paused at one label, barely registering the words in my haste: "Portrait of a Young Man" by Raphael. Strangely, a single puzzle piece was missing—right where the heart would have been.

My eyes darted to a server near the center of the room, holding a bottle of wine. He looked eerily similar to me—same height, same hair color. An idea struck.

I approached him quickly, flagging him down. "Here, take this," I whispered, grabbing the wine bottle and tucking the napkin into his palm. "A special someone is looking for this. Make it visible enough so they can see." Before he could respond, I mussed his hair slightly and darted toward the next room.

Before moving on, I glanced back. Malcolm had caught up and grabbed the server's wrist, snapping a bracelet onto him. I couldn't help but smirk before slipping into an open ballroom.

The ballroom was alive with energy. A live blues band played as swarms of masked men and women danced under the low lighting. Fairy lights strung across the ceiling created the illusion of stars floating in the darkened space. One side of the room featured banquet tables laden with alcohol on ice and a Mediterranean spread.

A man in a feathered white cockatoo mask approached me.

"Hey there, lad, top me off."

"What did you say?" I leaned closer, feigning confusion.

"I'm parched, dear boy," he said, raising an empty glass and motioning toward the wine bottle in my hand.

I hesitated but poured the wine, letting a few drops spill onto his jacket sleeve.

"Sorry, sir. It's difficult keeping my head on tonight. Such a big event."

"You're lucky you only hassled me and not someone more important. There are dangerous important people here tonight. Any one of them could end your career for the slightest imperfection," he said, removing his jacket.

His words made my stomach drop. I scanned the room, realizing that every guest was masked. These weren't just attendees—they were powerful, untouchable figures.

"I see," I said, trying to keep my voice steady. "They're all here for the auction, I take it?"

"Not everyone," he replied, licking his lips. "Personally, I couldn't care less about procuring Inhumans. Though, under the right circumstances, they can be... entertaining." His hand grazed my chest, lingering uncomfortably.

I turned away, coughing into my armpit to mask my unease. Composing myself, I said, "The piano recital was extraordinary. A performance like I've never seen before."

"Ah, yes. Magnificent artistry," he said, leaning in conspiratorially. "Our far-east traders have really upped their game. Their meta–to–population ratio far exceeds anywhere in the States. Japan alone has twice as many meta–related incidents. Lucky for us."

He rambled on, making uncomfortable eye contact. I realized he was an executive, deeply entrenched in this operation.

"Well, still doesn't beat what we have in-house tonight," I said, brushing my hair back.

He rolled his eyes. "It's... not terrible. But most of what we have is local and nearly picked clean."

"Can't be all bad. Could we take a look?" I asked casually.

He hesitated, then tapped his earpiece. "I'll be off the floor for a little while. I'll need cover in the ballroom."

He gestured toward a hallway guarded by two massive men. I had a lead, but I needed to shake this guy first.

As I stepped toward the hallway, sharp, stabbing pains erupted in my chest. I stumbled, dropping the wine bottle.

"Are you alright? Let me help you," the man said, placing a hand on my back.

Before I could respond, another hand clasped his wrist. I turned to see Malcolm, his hourglass mask glinting in the dim light.

"Apologies, Assistant Director, but this meta isn't on the staffing list," Malcolm said coldly.

"Meta?" The man looked me over. "Where's your inhibitor, then?"

The three of us stood frozen as the music shifted. Rapid drums thundered, and a stammering saxophone wove through the melody. The dancers around us switched partners, oblivious to the tension.

"I don't know how you made it out here, but you're going back," Malcolm said, his voice low and threatening.

"Take it easy, boy," the Assistant Director said. "It doesn't have to get ugly."

"Looking at this soiree, it's way too late for that," I snarled.

The Assistant Director pressed his earpiece, calling for security.

I bolted, shoving my way through the crowd. Malcolm and the Assistant Director followed, but I managed to stay ahead. The two guards from the hallway joined the chase.

A circle formed on the dance floor as a couple took center stage. The music paused, and two bronze-skinned dancers posed dramatically. One wore a devil's mask, the other a geisha's. The music resumed, and their routine began—a mix of primal energy and intimate movements.

My pursuers closed in, forcing me into the circle. The woman in the devil mask grabbed my arm, spinning me into their routine. Her partner blocked the guards, giving me a momentary reprieve.

The devil pulled me close, placing my hands on her waist. I stumbled, tripping over my feet as she guided me. Our eyes locked, and a memory surfaced—bright yellow eyes behind a locked iron door.

"Just follow my lead, Lightbulb," she whispered.

"Kalia?!" I said. "You two are attracting too much attention."

"The best way to hide is under their snobby noses. Did you find your friend, who is a girl?"

I felt flustered. "She's not my... you know what, never mind." She took my hand and spun me out, then pulled me back in to continue the dance. "Malcolm's onto me. A few others are chasing as well."

She looked towards Wick as he pulled a young woman from the crowd to dance. In doing so, he blocked the others who were chasing me. "How did you get found by the worst possible assholes?" she said.

I shrugged. "On the bright side, I know where to go. The rest are through there—" I grabbed her hand and directed her in a marching fashion towards the now-vacant hallway where the guards once stood.

Kalia nodded. "Let me take you there."

She spun me toward the edge of the circle and into the crowd. Wick followed, spinning his partner into the throng as well. I pushed through the sea of elaborate outfits, my eyes locked on the maintenance hallway. Before slipping away, I glanced back at the dancers. Kalia, in her devil's mask, caught my gaze. Her eyes fluttered as she pulled Wick toward my side of the circle, their routine seamlessly continuing.

I plunged into the crowd, darting through the hallway and out of the ballroom. Turning back, I saw no sign of pursuit. Maybe they hadn't noticed me leave. The lights and chaos of the event worked in my favor. Slowing my pace to avoid suspicion, I walked briskly down the hall, hoping the wait staff wouldn't seem out of place here.

The hallway split into a T-junction. I paused, scanning left and right for any clues, but it was just a maintenance area with numbered doors. From the right, two men in yellow "Stage Crew" shirts approached. They barely glanced at me as I passed, though one lingered with a brief, curious look. I quickened my pace.

Rounding a corner, I found myself backstage at the auction. The ceiling soared high to accommodate stage lighting, with walkways crisscrossing the rafters. Props and wires lined the walls, and dangling ropes connected to three red curtains that divided the staging area. The front curtain was drawn, shielding the audience's view as the crew prepared the next metas for display.

Three metas were restrained in Apex inhibitors, their bodies suspended off the ground in a circular steal ring bound by their wrist and ankles. Immediately I recognized them: Cookie, gagged and cursing furiously; Jacob, the older man I'd spoken to before the arena; and the figure in the tattered gray coat from the lab.

The backstage crew bustled around, but none were dressed like me. I stuck out like a sore thumb. A few workers stopped what they were doing to stare, their expressions hardening. Some picked up sturdy objects. My pulse quickened as I turned to leave, but before I could, Ego appeared—her face inches from mine.

"Leaving so soon, dear?" she purred, her smile sharp. "We needed one more for our quartet."

Her hands clamped around my head, palms pressing against my temples, forcing me to meet her glowing eyes. **"Now! Walk to—"**

I cut her off with a swift kick to the shin. She stumbled, and I seized the moment, driving my knee into her solar plexus. A sickening pop echoed as her sternum gave way. Her glowing eyes rolled back, and she crumpled to the floor.

Cookie mumbled furiously through her gag, but I couldn't focus on her. The stagehands closed in—five of them, one armed with a gun.

"Let's take it easy now, champ," the armed man said, cocking his weapon. "You did your best, but it's over."

"Over?" I raised my hands, fingers curling. "I think we can play this out."

They advanced as a group. My instincts flared to life—ones I hadn't realized I'd lost until now. The first man threw a metal baseball bat. I spun vertically towards me. I raised my hand, and the bat froze midair, hovering near my fingertips as a string of electricity grounded to the metal. With a flick of my fingers, I spun it a hundred and eight degrees to grab it by the handle. Static crackled along its length as I swung it in front of me.

They charged. Electricity burst from my body, and I felt everything—the grains of dust in the air, the vibrations under my feet, the hairs on my arms standing on end. Time slowed. The gun fired, but the bullet missed by a mile.

I lunged, slamming the bat into one man's ribs. Grabbing his shirt, I hurled him into another, sending the man sprawling. He didn't get back up.

Another gunshot. I ducked, then surged forward, my hands clasping the throats of two stagehands. Electricity coursed through them as they screamed, the smell of burning hair filling the air.

A third shot grazed my side, forcing me to release them. They collapsed, unconscious. Stumbling, I planted one hand on the ground to steady myself. The armed man fumbled with his .38, backing into a wall. I closed the distance in a flash, slamming his head against the hard surface. He seized up as shocks darkened his eyes, then crumpled to the floor.

I stood over the fallen stagehands, their strength fading. Brushing myself off, I raised a triumphant hand—only for something to latch onto my wrist.

A stiff punch to the nose sent me reeling. Jonas had slapped an inhibitor on me and was pummeling my abdomen with thunderous hooks.

"You... should... always... check your... SIX!" he grunted between punches.

I shoved him back with my foot, but he countered with a clothesline that flattened me. Dust billowed as I hit the ground, my vision doubling.

"Come on, Jonas... just let me have my moment!" I groaned, struggling to my hands and knees.

Jonas pressed two fingers to his ear. "Malcolm, we've got him. Call off the guards."

Ego stirred, raising a hand as Jonas helped her to her feet. She approached me, her high heels clicking. One heel tapped the floor beside me; the other struck my ribs.

"All this trouble... Get him in the line up," she ordered, brushing off her hands.

"Do we clean him up first?" Jonas asked.

"No. Let the audience see what a piece of trash he is. Shackle him, gag him, and be done with it."

Chapter Fourteen

Cold, familiar shackles clicked as my limbs were tied down in the circular inhibitor. Blood slipped out of my mouth and trickled down my chest to Ego's delight. She walked up to me, smeared a finger in it, and brought it to her lips. Her eyes closed with nefarious gratification. Then she took the very same finger and dotted the tip of my nose, marking it red. With one breath, I welled the leakage in my mouth and spewed it all over her face and dress. Unamused, she took a step back, calmly removed her glasses, and wiped them clean with the hem of her dress. She appeared to turn away for half a second, but then quickly lunged a heel into my crouch, which was openly exposed due to the inhibitor spreading my legs apart.

A high-pitched squeal shot from my mouth before my larynx swelled to silence me. My body went limp soon after. Jonas rolled me in line with the others. Our inhibitors interlocked on the side so only one person needed to push. There were four of us in total.

"Kid, stay with us now," Jacob said.

Still writhing from the pain, I could only give him a sporadic shake of my head in his direction. He was positioned the farthest to the right of all of us. The next guy to my right was someone I didn't know—I'd seen him in the lineup of metas in the lab, but nothing more. He hung his head and muttered to himself, wearing a tattered, gray suit. It looked like he was crying, and honestly who could blame him? Next in line was myself, and on my left was Cookie. She was the only one out of all of us who had a gag in her mouth. I leaned as far as I could in her direction.

"Hey..." I gulped. "I wanted to get you out of here, but, ya know..."

Cookie wrenched her eyes and shook her head in short motions. She mouthed an arrangement of muffled syllables. They extrapolated sharp and quick. Probably meant to tell me how stupid I was for coming.

"It's going to be okay," I tried to calm her down. "I mean, at least we're not dead."

"'Okay is kind of subjective here," Jacob added.

"Let's have a little faith, man," I followed up.

He gave me a look, the kind of look you give when a grown man says they still believed in the tooth fairy. "Look around, brotha. Faith? It's not here."

I couldn't deny his outlook. Looking around, I saw the moving cogs of a larger machine perpetuated by the exploitation of others. There was no reason for Jacob to have faith. Not when humanity had failed him to this degree.

"Well, let's get this over with, scants," Ego took a few steps back toward the curtain. I looked up into her eyes and noticed her pupils had a subtle glow to them. My resistance melted away as I continued staring. I'm sure the same thing was happening to the rest of us. Ego's voice dropped a tone deeper like there were two people talking:

"You will all say nothing and do nothing until the strike of my gavel."

Her abilities were immense. Even with prior knowledge of what she could do, I was still reeled in by her comforting stare. The power of suggestion was on her side in a big way. No wonder she was working as a public speaker. The glow from her eyes faded and I was left compelled to stay frozen. Paralyzed, like someone had hit the pause button on my nervous system.

Ego then took one last stroll around to inspect us. While doing so, she notified Malcolm on her comms, stating they had 'Charlie' and added him to the lot. The mood had picked up on their side and she disconnected with a glow in her cheeks. With a quick smirk, she called out to Jonas.

"They're prepped and ready, love." She frowned at the mess made to her once-white, now red-streaked gown. "I'm going to clean up. Keep watch until I get back."

Ego left through one of several doors connected to the backstage area. The tall, beanie-wearing boxer strolled closer to us and leaned against Jacob's inhibitor. He sat silently as some of the stagehands were cleaning up the gentlemen I'd flattened before getting caught. It was hard to believe that Jonas was a meta too. The only display of his abilities I'd seen was him knocking on wood, shattering the large scoreboard at the arena. It didn't seem like much of a power, honestly.

The only thing I had use of was my eyes, so I watched attentively. The stagehands were nearly finished cleaning up. They removed two of the men I'd knocked out and managed to revive the other three. I'd kind of made a mess of the area earlier so they reorganized the set. They did so in a pace like their life depended on it. Some seemed a little spooked from the noises creaking above them. I heard them as well but thought paranoia was settling in.

Suddenly, one of the men collapsed to the ground. Another followed suit. They appeared to be out cold. Two men remained standing, and they'd just realized their co-workers were falling unconscious. Jonas had started noticing as well. He removed himself from Jacob's enclosure and ran towards the bodies. He knelt to shake them awake, but nothing helped.

Jonas had caught something strange when investigating one of the crew. A red mark blistering the neck. On closer inspection, he plucked a needle from his neck, then brought it to his nose and smelled it.

"What is that?" one of the crew asked.

"This was inserted in his neck. His vagus nerve, specifically," Jonas said.

Just then, another one of the crew dropped the same as the others. The last of the stage crew started to panic and ran towards one the doors to escape.

"Cover your neck!" Jonas yelled, but it was too late. He fell into the door and was unconscious. Jonas hopped to his feet and quickly looked for the source of this aggression. He covered his neck with his hand and spun himself frantically in a circle.

"Where are you? Show yourself! ouch!" He lifted his hand from his neck and found a needle sticking out of it. It dawned on him to look up. As he did, the flash of an apparition dropped behind him from the rafters, landing silently on the wood flooring. The mask of the dancing devil gleamed under the stage lights as she crept close enough to breathe down his neck.

She lunged her nails to strike, but Jonas side-stepped. He grabbed her wrist and twisted her over his shoulder.

She landed on her feet.

They were facing each other now. Kalia removed her mask and dropped it to the side.

Jonas rolled his sleeves and pocketed his sunglasses.

"Heh," Jonas snickered. "I had planned a city-wide hunt for you. Thanks for saving me the trouble."

"Why?" Kalia asked. Jonas paused to cock his head to the side. "Why do you subjugate your own?"

"Isn't it obvious?" He closed in to throw a right cross, which Kalia dodged with only a slight movement. "There's no pride in being a sheep."

Kalia's expression soured. "There is none in being a heretic, either."

They clashed! Jonas barreled in with heavy hooks and straight shots to her body. Kalia dodged most of the attacks before getting nabbed by a lingering body shot. The Gorgon pulled the scarf from her head, untangling her crown of serpents. Now, every punch Jonas threw was met with a snake bite to the hand. After two successful bites, Jonas jumped back to gain more distance... Kalia didn't allow such reprieve.

She spun her body forward, extending each snake with centrifugal force. He ducked, snagging the loose chain lying on the floor and snapping it like a whip. The Gorgon still managed to dodge it, but her serpents were getting mangled as a few caught the tip of the chain as it popped. It looked painful.

Meanwhile, Kalia readied herself for another snap of the chain. It paid off as she grabbed it, pulling Jonas in. The middleweight looked surprised and let go before he got too close to her. She now had the range advantage as she bombarded the Latino boxer with venomous strikes of iron.

Jonas altered his hand positioning from a fist to extruding his knuckle from his index finger. He prepared for her next attack by changing his fighting stance. As Kalia whipped the chain once more, Jonas connected with a strike at the head of the chain. In an instant, the collision had burst all the links into dust. Iron particles flung towards the vicious snake lady as the shrapnel pierced her skin, causing her red–orange blood to drip onto the ground, staining the wood.

She was injured, but to my surprise her wounds healed quickly as the blood coagulated. I could tell because the exposed blood boiled before it hardened on her skin.

Kalia's breath was short and sweat glistened off her shoulders. She took a single step forward that caused her to lose balance and she dropped to a knee. Jonas was winded as well, though not as badly as Kalia. Likely a perk of being a boxer with the endurance to go multiple rounds. He stood, popping his knuckles.

"Well," Kalia said. "Finish it."

Jonas took a single step and something strange happened. His leg stiffened up and his face twisted in pain. He went to hold his leg, causing him to fall over on his side. Rhythmic breathing followed as his leg contorted unnaturally, then went straight as a board.

The Gorgon laughed. "Like the toxin I slipped you?"

"What did you do, witch?" Jonas gritted. He continued to roll in pain.

Kalia spoke, "The needle?" Jonas checked his hand where he was hit earlier. "It had a coat of alkaloid extract. A few different strands."

"No."

"By itself, I engineered it not to do much... But."

Jonas let out a scream as his knee started to shift out of place.

"When mixed with my blood—" She grinned, "it activates muscular degeneration. Pulling at one's muscle fibers and bones."

Jonas lunged for his other leg as it too started extending out, flattening like a board. One shoulder started pulling back unnaturally as well.

"You didn't bleed on me, snake bitch!"

"Ohh, didn't I?" At closer inspection, I noticed some of the serpents were bleeding from their mouths. Jonas noticed this as well. "You see, even though these beauties don't produce a toxin, they do have strange defenses. One of which is bleeding from the mouth, to 'play dead'."

Now I remembered… Kalia had used her boas to bite Jonas twice.

Kalia begrudgingly stood. "And now, heretic, it is your turn to play dead." She sneered.

Jonas's body twisted and turned. My ears took note of his bones popping. He tried his best to fight against it, but there was no use. He was pretzeling in front of our eyes.

She picked up a nearby monkey wrench and approached him. "I am your destruction, brother… But, let me be your salvation." She struck Jonas in the face. The blow caused his head to bobble back in a daze. He tried to shake it off, but only fell limp in the process.

Dropping the bloodstained wrench, Kalia dragged her feet to our position. We were set a level off the ground with our enclosures hooked onto a rail that led to the stage. Kalia managed to get to us. She seemed a little confused because none of us were speaking, bound as we remained by Ego's spell. The worst part of all was that they'd searched my body and snagged the keys I'd taken off Dr. Beverly. Without those, getting us out would be a tremendous act. She looked around our restraints, the back of the contraption, and any nearby panels, but found nothing that could help.

Just then, Ego walked in sporting a red sequin dress that sparkled under the light. As she did, two guards followed her. At first, she looked around and noticed the arrangement of new bodies.

"Ohh."

Then she saw Jonas flattened on the ground.

"Ohh, no!" she said.

Lastly, she stared at us and Kalia. Her eyes fermented into a 'thousand-yard stare' followed by a single smack of her lips.

"You know... I really tried to make things as perfect as they *can* be," she said as the two guards cocked their weapons and pointed. "But there's always a floundering CUNT taking a *piss* in my menagerie!!" she screamed out with a most rancid tongue.

"Someone has *certainly* lost the plot, haven't they?" Kalia mocked.

Ego clenched her teeth. "Open fire."

A volley of rounds sputtered out of their AR-15s and Kalia darted away from our position to keep us out of harm's way. At least I hoped she did. The Gorgon was slow from her fight before, so she jumped towards a low-hanging rope near the curtain. With the trail of gunfire at her heels, she gripped the rope and pulled a lever next to it, catapulting her into the air near the walkway suspended above us.

"Stop!" A voice carried from afar. "Stop shooting!"

Malcolm came running from the maintenance hallway. He waved his hands in the air to garner attention, which he did. The guards ceased fire and lowered their weapons. He marched with malicious intent. Ego was still seething.

"Sir! Your 'prized' Medusa is getting away!"

"Malcolm's eyebrows shifted high. "Kalia? She's here?!"

"Yes!" She pointed up to the rafters. As everyone's eyes gathered to the sky, the only movement they saw was a swinging head lamp. The guards accompanying Ego added, "She was just here, sir."

"She managed to get away."

Malcolm rubbed the bridge of his nose. "You two, go find her. That damned bodyguard of hers is likely here as well."

"Why on earth would they come here? Didn't they manage to escape?" Ego asked.

"It doesn't matter, just find them! Ego, prepare for the audience. The guests are panicking because *gunshots* can be heard behind the curtain. This is our moment to rake in a nice stipend for the end of the year and my people are fucking it up by ordering a *firing squad* in a white-collar affair! "

"My apologies, sir... But—"

"No buts! Just shutting the hell up, prepping the stock, and doing what your paid to do!" Malcolm fixed his off-white tie. "I need to go out there and dance for some very important people, so they stay for the rest of the auction. Just clean this up and get Jonas some medical attention!" Malcolm put on his mask and grabbed Ego's red neck scarf, then pulled her close. "Don't screw this up!

My reputation is at stake." With that, he pushed her off and walked through the curtain and into the dining hall.

Ego stood beside herself, shifting her weight and trying to compose herself. She looked at the guards. "What the hell are you looking at? Go pull Jonas out of here and report to the other guards that intruders are loose in the building."

Time passed and, before I knew it, we were pushed onto the stage. We sat there in silence for a long time, just staring at the curtain. The murmurs of the crowd were comforting to some extent. But we were all going to be sold to the highest bidder—That much was certain. We would be owned by another human being. Cookie would be subjected to this; Jacob would be further subjected to this, and I would be subjected to this. The world was truly against us.

Suddenly, the red velvet curtains were drawn back to reveal a grand dining hall. Candlelit tables, set in a vintage Persian style with shades of brown, sandy yellow, and deep red, filled the room—but with noticeably fewer guests this time. Overhead, balconies offered a view of silent spectators. As the clack of footsteps approached the podium, it became clear: Ego had arrived.

"Welcome, everyone, to the B-side auction!" she declared, her voice singing as she swept her arm in a confident gesture. "I know each and every one of you has traveled far to be here tonight. We have been working lo-ong and hard to collect the finest meta-humans!"

Her seductive charm and smooth rhetoric captivated the crowd, promising that their wallets would soon be light. I couldn't help but wonder at the lengths she would go using the power of suggestion.

"Without further ado, our first lot!" she announced as the stage lighting intensified on our positions.

Ego began her roll call with calculated drama:

"Item number one is a sensory type," she said, referring to Jacob, "capable of reading intentions through the slightest movement and even delving into minds under high emotional stress."

"Item number two," she continued, "possesses a unique ability to move small objects to an exact spot within a fifty-foot radius—ideal for exchanges, magic tricks, and even casino shenanigans." I mused silently over how easily someone with such a covert talent might slip by unnoticed.

"Our third item," she added with a sly smile, "has proven his mettle in the arena by using electrical pulses to boost his strength. This little battery is as versatile in circuit fights as he is on odd jobs." The implication wasn't lost on me—there were whispers suggesting that I might be the fighter they wanted to sell.

"And for our final item, we have a wave amplifier," she declared, her eyes gleaming. "This meta can generate force from sound waves, transforming and amplifying music from speaker boxes—or even a simple sound from her hands." That announcement drew particular attention, and I could feel the anticipation building among certain masked figures in the crowd. In mere moments, our fates would be sealed.

Her tone grew more authoritative as she laid out the rules: "Remember, when bidding, you're purchasing the entire lot! You cannot choose one over the other. All sales are final, and we are not responsible for the actions of any lot item once the checks are signed!" She paused to build suspense. "Now, let's start the bidding at—"

"Fifty thousand!"

I noticed immediately that they were valuing us lower than the other meta girl which had made it snow.. But soon, the bids began to escalate. Three distinct groups clashed in a fierce bidding war:

At the back, a small group wearing smiling devil masks quietly competed. Three of them raised markers for the bid "Sixty thousand" in unison, though none exchanged a word between each other. In opposition stood a burly man masked in wood with iron borders; someone tugged his arm insistently, and he countered with a resounding "Eighty thousand!" The final group comprised four figures in animal masks—a cow, a chicken, a pig, and a mule made of ceramic. Amid spirited debate, the mule held up a marker "One hundred thousand!"

Random bids punctuated the atmosphere, but these groups dominated the exchange. "One hundred and fifty thousand!" someone shouted, escalating the tension. Typically, the animal group would counter bids from the smiling devils, while the wooden giant reserved his bids for when the room fell too quiet. "One hundred and seventy thousand!" The enchantment of the auction began to wane, and I felt my nerves tremble as my fingers twitched with anticipation. Then came the decisive cry: "Two hundred and twenty thousand!!"

At that moment, the animals clinched the bid. The wooden-masked man fell silent, and the smiling devils showed their frustration—one even discarded his marker onto the walkway.

"Going once?!" Ego roared as the animal group started to rise, signaling the final verdict.

"SOLD to the—"

"Hold on dere, London Bridge." A familiar voice from the crowd shouted out and stood from one of the tables. He was cloaked with a tablecloth made to look like a poncho and adorned with a geisha mask with dreadlocks hanging out the back. He raised his hand and pointed at the auctioneer who stood frustrated from the intrusion. I stared long at Wick and wondered what the hell he was thinking.

"Did you have a bid, sir? Otherwise, I'll have to award this lot to our highest bid thus far."

"I don't have de bid you're looking for, but I'll take the lot nonetheless," said Wick.

"Cheeky bugger. Look, if you're not offering anything of value, then I'll have to remove you. We don't want to subject our guests to such intolerance, so you aren't leaving us with any other choice."

"It's not a matter of whether I can afford the lot, it's more if *you* can afford not giving dem to me."

Ego leaned in over the podium with a glow in her eyes. "I'll adore watching security pummel you into an Irish whip."

"I believe dat course of action has already been compromised."

At that, Wick removed his makeshift poncho, revealing a home-made bomb strapped to his chest. Household items have been fastened together with duct tape and wires. There was even a digital timer. It showed ten minutes and some change. From the device were wires running along his arms and chest with sensors fastened to his skin.

Chapter Fifteen

I mmediately, the crowd removed themselves from Wick's general area. In a fleet of panic they pushed and pulled away from the emanate threat weighting their lives in the balance. There were nearly two hundred people in the hall, and they all scrambled towards the exits. But it seemed they weren't able and screamed out that the doors were bound. Up towards the central exit leading to the art gallery was Kalia, just now placing the final touches to bar the door handles. They were wrapped in chains with a large padlock. Kalia adorned a new mask, one feathered and with speckled wings in a circular arrangement on its face. She twirled a key around her finger. This was revealed to everyone trapped inside.

"No one leaves until we get what we want. Release them on stage, now!" she yelled.

A few of the guests tried to overpower her. They reached for the key, but she hid it out of sight. Two men tried holding her from behind, which proved a poor choice when he realized the snakes on her back were real. He panicked, leaving himself open for Kalia to break his arm in the struggle. and the other guy didn't get back up after she spun her heel into his temple.

"Anyone else?" She re-dangled the keys in front of them. "I am open to new blood." From the other side of the doors, there were many attempting to break in. The double doors buckled under exceptional force but did not budge.

"We have little time!" Kalia yelled at Wick.

"Correction... You have no time," Ego yelled.

"And you have no guards." Wick motioned his hand to the armed men lying on the ground. They lay still and small signs of blood could be noticed from each one. They must have been taken out during the bidding war.

"Everyone down on the ground!" Wick pulled a pistol from his side and fired it into the ceiling. "You're all a long-long way from home. We are taking what we came for. Every meta heya and in the back. All of dem are coming with us!"

"The children too!" Kalia yelled.

Wick approached the stage. "And we are not opposed to opening up an English whore to get it."

"You are truly undignified, Wick. To think, once upon a time, I might have trusted you." Ego stepped out from behind the podium, her voice dripping with disdain. She adjusted her gown with deliberate grace, letting one strap slide off her shoulder. Her eyes glimmered—an unnatural, predatory glow that Wick knew all too well.

Wick's grip tightened on the machete at his side, his jaw clenched. "Cap Haitien was a mistake. You know dat."

Ego smirked, her movements slow, calculated. "Mistakes are your specialty, aren't they?" She tilted her head, her gaze locking onto his. Wick had not faltered, his eyes darting away, just as she had hoped.

In that moment, Ego's hand slipped beneath the folds of her gown. The sharp crack of gunfire shattered the tension. Wick staggered, clutching his thigh as blood seeped through his fingers. He dove behind a table, cursing under his breath.

Ego lowered her weapon, her expression unreadable. "You should've stayed home, Wick. Your just a fish out of water here."

"If I die!" Wick's voice cut through the chaos. He paused, his chest heaving as he fought to steady himself. "If I die, this bomb will take out this room—and the ones next to it. You wanna chance that?!"

Ego's gunfire tore through the air. Kalia unleashed a volley from the semi-auto rifle she'd snatched from a fallen guard. The stage erupted into chaos as bullets ricocheted off walls and shattered glass. The cries of us trapped in silence under restrained and under Ego's spell—muffled, guttural, desperate— It was all so terrifying.

I felt the spell's grip loosening, my body trembling as I clawed at the edges of freewill. My throat strained, a broken murmur escaping—a sound so faint it barely registered amid the storm. Ego ducked low, her gown trailing as she dove behind the podium. At the same time, laser guided dots focused in on the Haitians from behind me. More guards filed in as backup had arrived, leaving Wick and Kalia in a hampering situation.

Wick's eyes burned, his voice slicing through the chaos like a blade. "If I die—then boom!" He mimicked an explosion with his hands. His gaze locked onto Kalia, who advanced with her weapon trained on every guard and masked guest in her path. "If she dies, the same thing happens." Wick's finger dragged slowly across his neck, the gesture chilling in its finality.

"Well, we'll have to make our shots count." Malcolm's voice rang out. He strode onto the stage, his presence commanding as he removed his mask and placed it atop the podium with deliberate care. His gaze swept across the scattered guests, their faces pale with fear, before landing on me.

"Did you—" Malcolm pointed at me, while speaking to the Haitians, "team up with this waste of space to get in here?"

I lunged forward, the inhibitor biting into my skin as I strained against its hold. The air shifted, and then it happened—Malcolm's chest jerked violently as a bullet tore through him. The sound was sharp, final, and the whip of smoke and particles from his suit hung in the air like a ghost. The crowd froze.

Malcolm collapsed, his body hitting the ground with a sickening thud. He clutched at his wound, his fingers trembling as he shielded his face. Ego rushed to his side, her gown pooling around her as she knelt to check on him.

In the seating area behind the overturned table, Kalia stood, her weapon still smoking. Her expression was unreadable, but her resolve was clear. In an instant, every laser sight in the room zeroed in on her, the tension thick enough to choke.

Wick staggered forward, his leg crudely bandaged with a cloth napkin, his voice commanding the room. "Stop! Remember—she dies, dis room goes up in a fireball!" He patted the bomb strapped to his chest.

"Just shoot them already!"

"Kill them both and let's get on with our evening!"

"Hurry!"

The hostages' cries erupted as the tension reached a breaking point. The guards hesitated, their focus splintering between Wick and Kalia, whose vital areas now glowed with the ominous red dots of laser sights. Wick stepped forward, his voice rising above the chaos.

"You know what? Go ahead!" He threw his hand in the air, revealing a wire running from the bomb to his wrist, crudely taped in place. "If my heartbeat stops, you know what happens."

The room froze as Malcolm's voice cut through the noise. "Put your weapons down!"

Heads turned as Malcolm stood unnervingly calm. The bullet holes in his shirt were unmistakable, yet his body bore no signs of injury. The guests whispered in hushed tones, their speculation swirling.

Malcolm raised a trembling finger, his gaze locking onto Kalia. "You get one, Kalia. Just one... Ego?!"

"On it."

Ego's eyes burned brighter than before. Wick shielded his face, while Kalia rolled her eyes, her defiance unwavering.

"Is that all you've got? I expected more." Kalia's voice was mocking. She motioned toward Malcolm. "And do you not bleed?"

Malcolm's expression darkened, his patience fraying. "Alright, too many questions!" He flung his hand in a dismissive gesture. "Clip her wings."

The guards fired in unison, their weapons unleashing a storm of bullets. The Gorgon's eyes marbled. She didn't move—why wasn't she moving? I tried to scream, but only gibberish escaped my throat. Wick lunged, grabbing her arm just as the volley threatened to tear through her. The debris clouded my vision, the chaos swallowing any certainty.

Wick and Ego ducked behind an overturned wooden table, its surface splintering under the relentless barrage but holding firm. The air grew thick with dust, the room dark and suffocating. Coughing and cries echoed among the guests. It wouldn't be a stretch to think some of them had been hit.

Finally, Malcolm raised his hand, his gesture commanding silence. The gunfire ceased, leaving the room in a heavy, oppressive stillness. Dust hung in the air like a shroud. The man in the off-white blazer motioned for two guards to investigate. They moved cautiously, their weapons raised, splitting up to approach each side of the table.

The room held its collective breath as the guards crept closer. They peeked behind the table. "Targets are not moving. Seems clear," one of them reported.

The words barely left his mouth before two knives sliced through the air, embedding themselves in the guards' necks. They dropped their weapons, clawing at their throats as they crumpled to the ground. The room erupted in gasps and muffled cries.

Wick's voice cut through. "I don't think you heard me proper when I said we'd all die if we died."

Malcolm stepped forward, his expression of disdain. "And I think you're bluffing," he said, his tone cold. "Duct tape, some wires, and bottled water? That's not a bomb—it's a joke. The day that passes for a meta uprising is the day I go back to doing my father's work."

Kalia's voice rang out. "Don't worry! We plan to put you into permanent retirement."

Malcolm's tone changed, almost pleading. "You could've had it all, Scales. A peachy life. I had buyers lined up around the block for a crown like yours. You could've been adored by hundreds—thousands!"

Kalia's laugh was bitter. "I'm sure it all comes with a poolside condo and a pretty little collar." The sound of her spitting punctuated her words.

Malcolm's face darkened, his patience snapping. "Have it your way. If none of that is good enough for you, then die with your trash servant."

Kalia moved in a flash, her hand darting forward as she hurled a knife at Malcolm's face. The blade spun through the air, its trajectory deadly. But before it could reach him, Ego's hand shot out, snatching it cleanly by the handle. She adjusted her glasses, her expression calm, almost bored.

"Impeccable aim," Ego said, her voice mocked. "But too slow." She drove the knife into the podium with a deliberate force. The impact made me jump in my restraints, the tension in the room coiling tighter.

From the back of the room, one of the guests ran towards the stage. "Get me out of here!! I didn't sign up for this." His nasal voice overtook our attention. The man ran in a disheveled way in his penny loafers and jet-black suit. He wore a plastic Mr. Magoo mask that was merely fastened with a string. Wick noticed quickly and ran over to the man to cut him off from the stage. The guards started shooting but Malcolm screamed, "Stop! Stop it!" He waved his arms. "You'll hit the old man."

Wick proceeded to drag him over to his overturned table and placed a gun against his temple. "Do you hear me now, slave trader?!" Wick proceeded to cock his pistol. From behind cover, Kalia rose, her semi-automatic rifle gripped tightly in her hands. She swung the weapon wide, the muzzle hovering over the remaining hostages sprawled on the floor.

Her voice erupted "All the metas! Right... now!" Kalia screamed, her fury shaking the air. Her stance daring anyone to defy her. The hostages cowered, their fear feeding the tension that hung heavy in the room.

Malcolm's composure changed and his leg shook. He shoved his bangs out of his face. Ego approached Malcolm to hold him still, whispering, "We can't let them harm the guests or we'll never get business here again."

"I KNOW!!!" Malcolm yelled. His voice carried an echo through the dining hall. He was at his wits' end.

Wick followed up, "Cut your losses. Let us take dese metas, and we'll be on our way. No one else need to get hurt!"

"Cut my-Losses? Ooh, nu nu no." Malcolm pulled out a stainless-steel revolver, one of the biggest I'd ever seen.

The tension in the air was suffocating, a weight pressing down on every breath. Sweat streamed from my hairline, stinging my eyes as I strained against the restraints. Malcolm's footsteps echoed ominously as he strolled toward the first restrained meta on my right. Jacob's entire body trembled, his breath hitching as the cold muzzle of Malcolm's gun pressed against his temple. His lips moved in a silent prayer.

"You wanna play?!" Malcolm's voice cracked, he was becoming unhinged. He cocked his weapon. "We can play!"

Kalia lowered her weapon, her hands trembling. "It will not end well if you keep going like this!" she pleaded.

Malcolm's laugh was bitter, venomous. "You should've thought of that before shitting in my yard." Without hesitation, he pulled the trigger.

The gunshot thundered through the dining hall, a deafening roar that left my ears ringing. Jacob's body jerked violently, and a plume of blood and debris erupted, painting the stage in a grotesque tableau. Gasps and cries rippled through the room. Malcolm had crossed a line.

Ego staggered back, her hand flying to her glasses as she readjusted them. "No, not again!" she lamented. "He was paid for!" Her fists clenched, her face reddening as her glowing eyes flared brighter, vibrating with barely contained rage. She locked eyes with Malcolm, her gaze a searing challenge.

"Stop, right now!" she demanded as the echo of layered voices expelled.

Malcolm hesitated, his expression darkening as he turned to face her. In one swift motion, he closed the distance between them, his face inches from hers. Ego's eyes continued to glow, but she didn't flinch. Malcolm's hand shot out, gripping her neck with a force that made her gasp. He pulled her closer, the barrel of his revolver tracing a cold line along her cheek. She yipped, the sound sharp and involuntary.

"Last time you did that to me, it didn't go well for you... Remember?" Malcolm's voice was low, almost a growl, as he tapped the barrel against her forehead. Then, with a shove, he pushed her away, nearly sending her sprawling. Ego caught herself, straightening her blouse with shaking hands. Her glowing eyes dimmed, replaced by a hard stare. Frustration flickered across her face, visible to everyone.

Without a word, she reached into her blouse, pulling out a rectangular key with a blinking light. She wound up her arm and hurled the key toward the Haitians. Wick caught it mid-air. Ego turned on her heel, marching off into the back her muttered curses sounding out as she disappeared.

As she left the stage, another shot rang out. Specks of red splattered across the right side of my face, warm, sticky. The air caught the fragments like flower petals in the wind, drifting in front of me before settling. Dark matter spread outward, unfurling in slow motion, too surreal to fully register. My spine jerked, but I was frozen, trapped in this moment. The man in the gray suit was gone.

Malcolm stalked forward, weaving around me like a predator inspecting its prey. His voice slithered through the air, laced with cold amusement. "Looks like you didn't come for them, Wick."

Kalia's gaze flickered between him and me, her eyes wide, pleading. Her skin gleamed under the low lights, "Don't do this."

Malcolm let out a slow, breathy laugh, tilting his head, savoring the tension. "Heh. Ha ha." The sound was hollow. "It's too late for that. I knew you were bluffing."

He took his time circling me, deliberate, savoring the spectacle. Then, he strolled to my right side, and I felt it—the scorching heat of the muzzle pressed just close enough for the hairs on my ear to curl. My breath hitched. My body sagged under the inevitability of it. A shallow inhale, far too calming, far too final.

I watched Kalia, her lips moving, words spilling toward Malcolm in desperation. Wick released his hostage to reach the woman he'd traveled across a country for. It was all happening so slowly.

I was alone. I had always been alone.

No abilities, no voice, no muscle. Helpless. Just as I had always been.

A single trickle of warmth traced the path down my chin. I swallowed against the burn, against the regret that curled inside me like a dying ember. I miss you, Grandma.

She had saved me from so much. And I had just left her.

This is what I deserve.

Thunk!

A searing pressure ignited in my chest, and my vision blurred before snapping into sharp focus. The machete's blade quivered in my sternum, a grotesque exclamation point to my agony. Malcolm froze, his face a mask of disbelief.

"You're killing him before I can? I'm not petty enough to care, Wick!" He aimed his revolver toward the Geisha masked combatant. The mercenary shot a guard that was closing in on Kalia. He removed the mask afterwards. As he did so, he revealed a grin as sharp as the blade in my chest.

"Checkmate," Wick said.

The room erupted as tendrils of electricity burst from my chest, crackling like a storm unleashed. Malcolm recoiled, his revolver clattering to the floor as a bolt struck his hand. He cursed, cradling his arm, while the energy spiraled out of control, lashing at walls and splintering the ground beneath me.

Wick's eyes locked onto mine, a flicker of understanding crossing his face. "Clear de room! His cage is about to give way!"

"Dammit!" Malcolm turned towards his guards, "Get that door open to the gallery, Now!" Malcolm snarled, retreating from the chaos. Guards scrambled to the barricaded doors, their panic visible as they tore them open, freeing the hostages. Light flooded in, mingling with the wild arcs of electricity that danced across the room.

Wick unstrapped the bomb from his chest and tossed it behind a table—He couldn't risk a stray bolt of energy striking him. Kalia leaped on stage, guarding herself. Wick followed behind her, keeping low to avoid any bolts lashing out from me. Kalia pulled him on stage, but quickly he guarded her and was stung for his efforts. Kalia held the key and hastily started unlocking Cookie's shackles. One cuff clicked, releasing her left hand and she immediately yanked the gag out of her mouth.

"Help Charlie! I can handle this." Cookie took the key and continued freeing herself.

Kalia and Wick exchanged a glance, their resolve hardening. The energy surged, a relentless tide threatening to consume me. My body convulsed, my hands clawing at the air as the pain twisted me into a grotesque marionette.

Wick breathed in deep and lunged his hand for the machete lodged in my solar plexus. His hand was zapped hard, so he tucked it away. He couldn't touch it. All three pulled back off the stage as the surge got more erratic.

Kalia grabbed a tablecloth, twisting it into a makeshift grip.

"Hold on, Charlie!" she yelled, her voice determined. She whipped the cloth around the machete's handle, bracing herself. With a guttural cry, she yanked it free.

The storm ceased in an instant. Silence fell, heavy and absolute. My body crumpled, the weight of the ordeal dragging me down. Cookie rushed to my side to unlocked my shackles.

"You're such a dumbass." She hoisted me from the contraption. "You didn't think to get a mask to conceal your identity?"

"None of the waiters—" I took a moment to inhale some air, "were wearing them," I said with a withered smirk.

Cookie's face appeared tight-lipped and her eyes squinted. "I'll let you have that, since you risked your life to get here."

"It honestly hasn't stopped since I left my house." My knees buckled, and I stumbled forward. Cookie caught me, steadying my frame as I fought to shake off the tremors. Sparks escaped my lips in a sudden, embarrassing burp. I clamped my hands over my mouth, mortified.

Cookie leaned in, wrapping her arms around me despite the gaping wound in my chest. The pain was sharp, but her embrace didn't help.

"Thanks, Chuck," she whispered, her voice barely audible.

Wick stared blankly, as if watching a movie he didn't care for. Kalia, on the other hand, grinned so wide it made me want to dive through the nearest window.

"Ouch! You're welcome. The chest thing is still... a thing," I muttered.

"This is great, really it is, but it's time for the rest," Kalia began, but Wick cut her off.

"We leave now... Or we be quick with the others," he said, his tone sharp. Wick was only human, and his leg wound needed immediate attention.

Cookie chimed in, her voice steady. "I know where you can find the rest. Through the back and down the utility elevator. It's big enough to fit a four-door Dodge Ram, so we'll all fit easily."

Wick winced, clutching his injured leg. "We need the quickest way out. Let's take it."

"Everyone thinks the bomb will go off if they attack us. Let's use that to our advantage—find the other prisoners," Cookie added.

We nodded in unison, and Cookie darted behind the curtain. I hesitated, my gaze falling on Jacob's lifeless form. Malcolm's bullet had found its mark. My stomach churned as I stared at the execution. It could have been me. If Ego had swapped me differently, I wouldn't be standing here.

"We don't have time for sightseeing! Move it, Lightbulb!" Kalia's voice snapped me out of my thoughts.

We followed her into the staging area, veering left toward the elevator. Cookie reached it first, hammering the button like her life depended on it. The hallway was eerily quiet, but I knew it wouldn't last.

Ding! The stainless-steel doors slid open, and we piled in.

"Second floor! Second floor..." My finger traced the panel until I found the button. The doors closed, and the elevator hummed to life.

Indie rock played softly in the background, a strange comfort against the storm in my head.

Ding!

The doors opened, and the Haitians shoved us against the elevator walls, keeping us out of sight. Cookie peeked cautiously.

"It's clear. Come this way," she whispered.

We slipped out, taking a right and then a left. The hallway opened up, revealing guards stationed in front of an iron-barred double door. Familiar faces from the arena. We ducked behind the corner, straining to catch their conversation.

I told you, Barnaby, easy money here." Chet flicked a cigarette butt on the white linoleum floor. "We just keep watch, they sit still, We get paid in the moarn'in!"

"We tell them what to do, they listen. I could do this every day, mate." Barnaby attempted to spin his assault rifle like they do in those BBC ceremonies.

"I did hear there was some trouble over the comms. Something about the auction being cut short due to... a live wire?" Chet questioned.

"Perhaps a shortage in the system? I mean... It's not our problem."

"They are late getting here to collect the next batch." Chet circled the floor while opening another box of cigarettes.

Sounds of something human, was apparent through the bars behind them. Both Chet and Barnaby spun around, dinging the bars with the stocks of their rifles.

"I told you all to shud'up!!" Barnaby shouted.

"Don't make us come in there! Be a shame if we bruise a few tomatoes, heh." Chet marveled at his handiwork.

We moved silently, shadows slipping through the dim light. Chet and Barnaby stood ahead, oblivious to our presence. Their casual postures betrayed their lack of vigilance—Barnaby leaned against the wall, arms crossed, while Chet took a lazy drag from his cigarette, the ember glowing faintly in the gloom.

Step by step, we closed the distance, careful not to disturb the air around us. The faint hum of the building masked our movements, but every creak of the floor felt like a thunderclap in my ears.

In one swift motion, we struck. Wick and Kalia snatched their weapons with practiced precision, the metallic clink of the Glock and AR-15 barely audible.

"Bloody hell!" Chet exclaimed, spinning around, his cigarette tumbling from his lips. His eyes widened as he took in the sight of all four of us standing before him.

Barnaby froze, his hands shooting up in surrender. "This whole thing... isn't ending well, aye?" his voice trembling.

Chet, ever the defiant one, smirked and stubbed his cigarette out against the wall, sliding the butt back into his carton with deliberate slowness.

A spark flickered from my right eye, a warning of what was to come.

"Oh you know It's gonna hurt," I said.

I lunged forward, my hands clamping down on their necks. Electricity surged through my fingertips, crackling and snapping as their bodies convulsed violently. The frayed edges of their garments smoldered, the acrid scent of burnt fabric filling the air.

I held on longer than necessary, the vindication coursing through me like a drug. The pain in my chest was distant now, replaced by the sharp sting in my hands, my grounding points. When I finally released them, they crumpled to the concrete, unconscious.

Wick and Kalia wasted no time, rifling through their belongings. Wick pocketed the Glock, his movements efficient despite his limp, while Cookie took the AR-15.

We turned to the doors they had been guarding, the heavy iron barriers looming before us. Beyond them were the persons we sought.

Chapter Sixteen

The room was large with high ceilings. Large consoles protruding out of the walls had wires and IVs that fed into each meta as they lay encapsulated in Apex's Mobile Inhibitors. Each one was lined up next to each other flush against the walls, six adult metas and five children, all gathered against their will in this single space. The little ones couldn't possibly fit in large inhibitors so had been placed in the far corner of the room. They all huddled together with shackles latched onto their ankles. In the middle was one man with glasses and a clipboard. As we walked in, he froze in place and his shoulders hunched. Kalia approached the man who shivered with his glasses sliding down to the tip of his nose.

"Is this everyone?" she asked.

"This-this is everyone that hasn't gone on stage, yes."

Kalia took the clipboard from the man and meticulously scanned over the names. "The numbers seem to match with what's on the list. Move them."

One by one, we used the key to unshackle each one. I couldn't explain the amount of energy filling the room with each meta we released. It was breathtaking. Everyone chipped in, getting everyone on their feet. The emotional threads plucked from them all made a rhythm I could sleep at night to. After everyone was released, I felt lighter, somehow sensing more of the world around me and in more vivid color than before. Despite the dire situation, I couldn't manage to hold back a smile.

Kalia snapped her fingers, "Everyone! As we walk down these halls and out of this hell, keep together! Do not use your abilities unless you absolutely have to. If you can't control them, we'll use an inhibitor to suppress them until we are somewhere safe."

One of the adults spoke. "Where are we going to go that's *safe?*"

"Yeah, Apex can find us, no matter where we go. Then we'll be right back here again."

Kalia felt at a loss for words. In reality, they were right. For metas like us, there existed no place that was truly safe. We would always be hunted.

"Don't worry! I know de place to go, just for a bit, anyway," Wick followed up. "It will be good for tonight."

A silence crept over the lot; everyone knew what was coming next. Kalia peeked out the doors and still, no one was around. She motioned for us. Quietly, everyone moved through the hallway until we'd made it to the elevator, which had a large enough interior to hold all of us. The button was pushed and we waited for the elevator to come to our floor.

"Our best bet is the basement," Cookie said. "There will be a few ways out from there, and we won't be cornered so easily."

Ding!

The elevator doors slid open with a metallic hiss. Instinctively, everyone took a step back. I shifted into what could generously be called a defensive stance, bracing myself for what we'd feared most.

Inside the elevator shaft, Malcolm stood at the forefront, flanked by a handful of metas, and a swarm of armed guards. Guns rose on both sides, and I found myself trapped in the middle of the standoff. We lingered in the hallway not making any sudden moves. No words were exchanged, but the tension was high.

Most of us were tough enough to withstand a grazing shot, but I wasn't sure about the other metas. Then, the unexpected happened—one of our rescued captives melted the linoleum beneath us, transforming it into a sticky, tar-like substance that clung to our feet.

"Ughh!!" Cookie groaned, her voice weak.

Before I could react, the one meta we'd rescued turned on us, plunging a knife into Cookie's back. The blade pierced through her waistline, emerging from the front. Blood splattered onto the warped linoleum, pooling around her feet.

"Cookie!!" I shouted, rushing to catch her as she collapsed forward.

Kalia moved swiftly, snatching the knife from the traitor and pressing it to his throat. "May you pass to the other side with regret."

Wick stepped forward, his pistols raised, shielding us from the weapons aimed at him from inside the elevator.

The metas on Malcolm's side began to stir, their abilities manifesting in ominous ways—eyes glowing, hands crackling with energy, bodies shifting colors. The air was thick with the promise of violence.

"I think we should all cut our losses and go our separate ways," Wick said, his tone calm.

"Except this one," Kalia interjected, tightening her grip on the traitor. The blade pressed deeper into his neck, drawing blood. Her crown of serpents coiled around his head, their movements making him visibly tremble.

The hostage stammered, "I did what you asked, Malcolm! Now get me out of this!"

Malcolm's smile didn't waver. "Sometimes, you've got to sacrifice one for the greater profits of others. Something my dad taught me long ago."

"That wasn't part of our deal!!" the traitor screamed, his voice cracking.

As their negotiation unfolded, Cookie tugged me toward the elevator's control panel. I tore off my coat sleeve, pressing it against her wound to staunch the bleeding.

"You're not going to die. Just let me stop the bleeding," I whispered.

"No," she said, her eyes darting to the control panel. "You're like a lightning rod... right?"

"Umm..."

"Can you run your abilities through the elevator wiring?"

"I—I guess?"

"Then do it!"

A shot rang out, aimed at Wick. He dodged, but the bullet struck someone behind him.

"Now!" Cookie screamed.

I slammed my palm onto the elevator's hallway control panel, electricity surging from my right eye and grounding through the wiring. The lights inside the elevator flickered, catching Malcolm's attention.

"Whatever you're doing? Stop—" he said.

Cookie snapped her fingers, and warmth radiated from her hand into mine, an energy that seemed fluid and can travel between bodies. The elevator speakers fizzled, cutting off the music, and then—BOOM!

A deafening eruption of sound waves filled the elevator stall, throwing everyone inside off their feet. As the chaos unfolded, I reached inside the stall, pressing the elevator buttons, starting with eighteen, then dragging my hand up the entire panel.

The doors slid shut just as Malcolm's group began to recover, sealing them inside. They were going to be stuck inside that elevator going floor to floor buying us some time.

Wick looked our way with his mouth hanging and eyes wide. "How did you even?"

"Just a hunch," Cookie said.

"How did I even?!" I shook off the moment and refocused on the task at hand.

"Not a surprise," Kalia said.

I picked Cookie up while she held the bit of cloth to her stomach. I shuffled her on my shoulders to aid her while she walked. My eyes darted from left to right, looking for another way out.

Wicked opened the doors to the stairwell next to the elevator and heard more of Malcolm's goons coming from below. He slammed the door and barred his weight against it.

"Our position is compromised," he said.

"Not yet!" One of the freed metas stepped forward. He had strange hazel eyes with blue flecks that glinted at a certain angle. He stepped forward from the band of escapees and observed the end of a hallway. It was a walled-off dead end with boxes stacked against it. He kept staring at it.

"If we go through that wall, it will lead us outside toward the lake," he said.

"How would you know that?" I asked.

The meta forked his fingers and aimed them toward his eyes before aiming his forked fingers at me. "The same reason I know you're wearing boxer briefs with lips print-ed on them."

Everyone went silent and stared at me. I turned my gaze away from the group and said, "They're 'The Stones', okay?!"

Kalia interrupted, "Good! We have a seer. Can anyone else get us through that wall?"

The elevator lit up once more. The stall was moving down in our direction. Floor eighteen as of now, seven-teen, sixteen... I ran up to the control panel and used my abilities to overload the electrical circuits of the console.

The slat of metal displaying the buttons shorted out with sparks and a puff of smoke. We all looked up at the digital display above the elevator door.

Strangely enough, the numbers stopped just for a moment. But then...

Fifteen...

Fourteen.

I tossed my hands into the air. "Well, I'm all out of ideas."

A child with putrid yellow skin ran up to the Gorgon. "Me! Pick me! Me me me me me."

"Okay! Child! What do you want?" she said, clearly annoyed.

The kid ran up to a wall next to us and slapped the concrete with his bare hand. What followed was an ignition of force that flashed through the hallway before sparking a mini explosion.

BAMMM!!

We all took caution as our instincts and perhaps traumas caused half of us to fly to the ground, covering our heads while smoke dissipated. Then Kalia ran up to the kid and said, "Don't do that again!" She turned to the others. "Does anyone have a *safer* way of breaking down the wall?"

Wick braced his back against the stairway door as a tremendous thud intermittently slammed against him. Groups of Malcolm's goons attempted to force it down while Wick dug his heels into the linoleum floor as best he could.

"Now would be a good time to step up!!" Wick struggled.

Other adult metas and a child ran up to the door to help hold it. Gunshots rattled through the door's glass window, causing panic in the hallway. One of the adult metas was hit. Everyone hugged the wall as more bullets rang from the doorway window. Wick returned fire through the very same window, keeping them on their toes. As I observed the chaos, a certain urgency took hold of me as well. I placed Cookie in the Kalia's hands and let her wrap her arm around the Gorgon's shoulders.

"Wait! Wait!! Ahhh!" Cookie screamed as the serpents took hold on her.

With a jolt from my feet, I picked up the explodey kid, then spun once to gain speed and threw him to the end of the hall.

"Weeeeeee!!" the child yelled. He collided with the dead end and another flash of light blinded us as the foundation of the second floor shook. More smoke flooded the hall-way.

Kalia yelled out with bass in her voice, "You *threw* him?? You really threw him... Are you crazy?!"

This time, it was Cookie who attempted to hold the Gorgon back while she unsheathed a knife from her waist as the other children snickered with each other over it. But then a gust of wind funneled through the hallway, clearing it. As it did, we saw the yellow child running up to me with an excited grin and bouncy nature.

"Again!! Again! Do it again!" he shouted.

I looked up at the massive hole in the wall as the smell of salt hit my nostrils. We saw distant streetlights and trees gently moving. I don't know why, but it all felt different. A wave of chills ran down my spine and newfound energy filled my body—It was finally time to leave. Then, one by one, I saw them: metas running toward the light. The hole of freedom. I looked down and the child was still jumping in front of me, hands raised and smiling. As they reached the hole, they started climbing down from the second story ledge using their various abilities to do so. Wick, Kalia, Cookie and I all stayed behind just a bit longer, allowing the others time to escape. We stared at the elevator as the number kept going down. Wick's strength was giving out, so I ran up to help hold the door.

Five.

Four...

"All of us! Now!! Run!!" the Gorgon screamed.

At her word, Wick abandoned the door and pushed some crates in the way before running towards Kalia. I took Cookie and flopped her whole body over my shoulder as I ran. We all made it to the hole as both the enemies from the stairwell burst through and the elevator let out. Malcolm was the first to look in our direction as they poured into the hallway. The Haitians leaped from the opening first and I followed, but not without extending my middle finger towards Malcolm as I dropped.

I landed on the concrete, tendrils of electricity grounding from me. I put Cookie down and helped steady her balance. She brushed herself off.

"I can manage, hero," she said with an ironic sneer, but behind it I thought I could see her blushing. We all gathered in a tight circle. It was freezing outside.

Wick walked forward and made sure everyone could hear him. "I have a place we can go this moment, but only for de moment. Everyone, *be careful.* We're not out of hell just yet."

"Never has a truer word been spoken!" a voice resounded from above.

We all looked and saw Malcolm and company standing in the second-floor hole we'd just made. Red dots paraded over us. I looked around for a place to go, but there was so much clearing. A field of grass and trees along the coast—It would be suicide to escape through that. Perhaps we could try going around the building, hugging close to it.

"We got the high ground, you jovial pissants. There's nowhere to run!"

A flicker of red lights danced across our line of sight—as if the very sky had split into shards of warning. One flash yielded to another until the entire block was bathed in an unrelenting glow of red fluorescence. Then, slicing through the charged silence, the sirens began to wail, hammering home the arrival of our pursuers.

"The city's meta detection system," I spoke.

Malcolm and the others' demeanors changed. I was sure the Chicago PD would have a time investigating a gaping hole leading to an illegal meta-trading nexus. They gathered above as red dots started disappearing from our position. I couldn't make out what they were saying, but it was obvious that Malcolm was having a fit. They knew their pursuit had reached its end.

"Guns down! Everyone!!" Malcolm barked.

Slowly, they pulled back into the building. I couldn't believe we'd made it this far, but now we had to find a way to make all of us disappear. Wick's silent hand gesture commanded us to stay put. He bolted around the corner while the rest of us sank low behind a cluster of parked cars and a battered bench installation—a motley refuge in a collapsing plan. The feeling of being trapped was all consuming, as if the darkness itself conspired against us.

Kalia sprinted up to me, her eyes wide with the urgency of our dwindling time. "Apex, they'll be here soon. We need proper transport, Wick has run to get it," she hissed, her tone tinged with desperation.

"Can we really wait long enough?" I asked, the hopelessness of our situation anchoring each word.

Before she could answer, a fierce gust of wind heralded an unwelcome arrival. The unmistakable roar of helicopter rotors tore through the night as a spotlight cut across the darkness, systematically searching for us. We were flirting with the edge of that burning beam—just beyond its crimson reach but exposed all the same. Distant sirens strained their chorus as our nightmare closed in. Nevertheless, something had to be done. We needed time for Wick to get back. I pushed myself upright from our hidden formation. My pulse hammered in my ears, the reality of our entrapment sinking deep into my bones.

"We need to distract them," I declared, my voice rising above the anxious murmurs, each syllable heavy with desperation. Even as the darkness pressed around us and fate loomed with stark finality, I knew that a plan—any plan—was better than succumbing to the inevitable.

"Charlie!! Get down!" Cookie yelled.

"They're going to catch us anyway," I countered, electricity thrumming at my fingertips. "We can't just sit here like baby ducks."

Kalia exhaled sharply. "Okay, Charlie. Don't do anything stupid."

I let out a breathless chuckle, my grin sharp, reckless. "Heh... Why? That's the only thing I've ever been good at."

Energy pulsed from my right eye, crackling as it raced down to my feet. One last look at Cookie—a silent farewell—and then I was gone, tearing across the open field, straight into the blinding beams of the helicopter's searchlight. The roar of its engines drowned out the shouts from its loudspeaker, their words garbled, meaningless. I refused to glance back, unwilling to give away the others' position. The only thing that mattered now was keeping the eyes on me.

Another helicopter swept in from the south, its rotors carving through the night like a blade. Police cruisers screeched onto the scene, headlights slicing through the dark. This was it—the moment they would try to box me in. I kicked off the ground, dirt spraying behind me as I threaded my way through a narrow alleyway, my lungs burning, every fiber of my being screaming for speed.

Then it happened.

The second I emerged from the alley, a force slammed into me—something sudden, and brutal. My vision tunneled, zeroing in on an outstretched hand lunging toward me. Every instinct I had should have told me to react—to fight, to dodge—but I froze. A chill coursed through my spine, my fight-or-flight response failing in a catastrophic second of hesitation.

Steel fingers closed around my throat.

Trailblazer.

The searing burn of his grip sank into my skin. My feet left the ground as he kept running, dragging me effortlessly, as if I weighed nothing. The world blurred around me, but all I could process was the raw, suffocating power that had me in its grasp. My gamble had turned into something else entirely.

This wasn't an escape.

This was an execution.

"Want to see what it feels like, speck?!" Trailblazer snarled.

He barreled forward, dragging me along as if I were nothing more than a ragdoll in his grip. My back slammed into a massive tree, the force splitting bark and sending splinters flying. The impact rattled through my bones, my vision blurring as the world lurched. My feet barely skimmed the pavement before he pivoted, steering us onto the road—Lakefront Trail. I recognized it instantly, the distant shimmer of beachside waves and the ghostly silhouettes of trees framing our path.

The pavement stole what remained of my shoes, the relentless grind of burning rubber peeling them away like a grater against my skin. His entire body pulsed with blistering heat, searing into the flesh of my neck. Finally, I managed to claw at his wrist, desperate to trigger my abilities—but focus slipped through my grasp like sand in a storm.

"This is almost too easy," Trailblazer laughed, reveling in my helplessness. "Let's go somewhere private, just you and me."

He started to slow down when we got close to a statue; it was the Signal of Peace Monument, I was certain because the plaque was the last thing I saw before going face-first into it. I don't know how, but my body was weightless in the air. My body joints and tendons begged for relief as it felt like they were being held together with scotch tape. From on high, I could see a strange windmill on the beachfront. It didn't erase the fact that I might have internal bleeding, but it looked nice when the city lights reflected off of it. When I landed, my body was going fast enough to make the world spin as I rolled in the grass.

Trailblazer ran loops around the park, looking like a single red laser whipping through the brush and sand. He ended his display of speed and recklessness to come walking leisurely up to me.

"Not everything went the way I wanted today... But now, I can sit back and take my time burning you to ash." He rolled his shoulders, flexing his fingers into tight fists. Flames flickered along his knuckles like living embers.

I barely had time to brace before his boot drove into my ribs. Pain exploded through me, lifting me just off the ground before I crumpled onto my side, choking, blood flooding my mouth.

"You see, I can't just have some other random meta with abilities like mine—" Another kick, sharp and brutal, sent fire lancing up my spine. The steel rims of his boots made sure I felt every ounce of it. My body jerked, rolling further into the grass.

"I'm the fastest in this city... and it's going to stay that way for a long time." He loomed over me, predatory. "Two speedsters in this town? No, no."

"I'm not... a speed—"

Another kick.

This time, his foot seared hot in the stomach. I yelled out from the sting and continued rolling myself away from him. I had succumbed to light-headedness and my knee trembled as I tried to find my footing. I had to do something, holding back tears wasn't going to cut it. I leveraged my hand on a nearby crabapple tree as I gripped my mid-section.

"I was originally tasked to take you in, process you, throw you in the system. Funny you would end up in Malcolm's rink anyway. Anyhow, I did run a check on that old bag of yours." My heart slammed against my ribs.

"Relax, momma's boy. I wasn't gonna do anything... yet."

Rage ignited something deep in my chest. Energy surged through my arm as I launched forward, slamming my fist into his jaw.

He barely moved.

A sigh hung in the air before he caught my wrist, yanking me forward and flinging me back against the crabapple tree with ease.

"She's in critical health. She's in that hospital bed wasting away from her injuries, injuries that *you* caused her!" He pulled at the rim of his gloves. "You're an abuser, Charlie. You leeched off her until she didn't serve you anymore, and when the time came you ran, like you always run. Just live what purpose you have left and die."

His words struck harder than any punch. My teeth clenched, temples throbbing with the weight of everything—every regret, every mistake, every burden I had ignored. My throat tightened, my breath coming in ragged gasps as a salty stream of tears traced down my cheeks.

I had never hated someone so much.

I had let this happen.

I had let her down...

"You don't know me..." My voice trembled, fists curling into the earth.

"Not a single thing—and I'm not running, anymore!!"

Trailblazer stood before me, his suit flashing with manufactured brilliance—the shimmer of his helmet, the advertisements stitched into his fabric. All of it was a facade, a false idol masking something far uglier beneath.

A murderous intention spread through me like wildfire; my emotional state swallowed me. I'd thought I wasn't enough to handle this; maybe I'd been right to think that, but now, I could feel *it*. The emptiness filling in—something born out of malice, even more out of necessity. A charge in my energetic field acted on its own. For the first time, I stopped doubting.

My electrical field sprung to life, chaotically pouring out of me. Trailblazer took a step back to avoid getting struck by the surge of energy. The weight of my body felt heavy, as if I was a magnet being pulled through the ground. I planted my feet, fighting against the pain Trailblazer poured on me.

Trailblazer trembled, his fingers twitching as he tried to steady himself. He clenched a fist, his arrogance flickering, then shook it off like a weak flame fighting for air.

"You think you're better than me?! I'm the meta who will bring our kind to a new age!" His words were desperate, layered with frustration. "You? You're nothing. Just another speck caught in my wake. Do what you were bred to do—sit, obey, and let me handle it!"

Then he vanished.

A streak of fire erupted in his wake, a molten path scorched across the battlefield. I barely had time to react before a fist slammed into my jaw, knocking me through a tree. I staggered, sparks flying off my body, the world tilting. I didn't fall—but when I looked up, he was gone again.

Silence.

A blistering second later, another blow connected, hotter and sharper than the last. My skin burned where the strike landed, the scalded mark stinging with raw fire. He was getting faster. Faster than I could track.

From another direction—another hit.

The force nearly sent me tumbling out of the park. I let loose a primal scream, static sinews snapping outward, rooting me where the grass met the sand. My breaths came quick, shallow. He was running loops, disappearing into the darkness, leaving me blind to the next strike.

Focus.

I lowered myself to the ground, fingers pressing into the earth. I let my breath slow.

Listen.

Feel.

The trees were burning in his wake, the ground quaking under his heat. He was coming—he was close—

WHAM!

Another fist barreled toward me.

I didn't move.

Trailblazer collided, expecting me to crumble. Instead, he spun out, his balance breaking. His eyes darted to mine, a flicker of something unfamiliar—shock. He scrambled to his feet, and wound up his arms before taking off into a explosive burst of hellfire. His speed doubled, the air distorting from his velocity. Park benches flipped, bushes scattered, trash cans launched into the air. The pressure was immense, the wind screaming as the earth braced for impact.

I closed my eyes. The world sharpened. The wind whispered.

Over the lake—he ran.

NOW!

I pivoted, my stance locking into place, my left hand stretched outward in anticipation. My right eye surged with light, my body reinforcing a singular thought: Don't falter!

KAPOW!

His attack met my grasp—his fist caught clean in my palm. The force dragged me back ten feet, the shockwave shredding through the atmosphere, ripping leaves and debris into a vortex.

POP!

Trailblazer's body jerked violently. His scream tore through the chaos.

I broke his hand.

The fabric of his suit burned away from the sheer energy radiating from our clash. His helmet shattered, fragments lost in the storm.

And then, I saw him—the real him.

Beneath the mask, beneath the bravado, Trailblazer was just a man. Stark white skin. Shaggy red hair. Freckles dotting his cheeks. Dull red eyes, wide with disbelief.

The force of our energy had sunk the earth beneath us, forming a crater. He yanked at his wrist, trying to break free—but there was no escape.

I pulled my right fist back, energy coiling around my arm like a live current. The storm in my chest begged for release.

All this anger...

Thunder clapped and I swung my arm, bringing the hammer down on him. It caused the ground to crack and upheave as The Mighty Flame of Justice plummeted into the earth. Bones cracked and gave way to the pressure. Blood spewed. Then, as quickly as the thunder had come, it vanished. The static atmosphere dissipated, and the flow of wind downgraded to a gentle breeze. Trailblazer didn't move. His arms and legs lay lifeless like a puppet cut from his strings. Residual jolts of electricity grounded from his body.

Did I kill him? I thought.

I jumped as lights layered everything around me in red. Right on cue, the ol' familiar announcement sounded out:

"ALL CITIZENS—PLEASE LEAVE THE RED ZONE—ALL CITIZENS—PLEASE LEAVE THE RED ZONE" I looked on as Apex's leading man was draped in red light, motionless. "ALL CITIZENS—PLEASE LEAVE THE RED ZONE—ALL CITIZENS—PLEASE LEAVE THE RED ZONE."

I looked down at the broken meta once more, almost empathically. As my body grounded out the rest of my energy, my eyes began to feel heavy. Only the creases in my cheeks I felt as I stared off into the clouds. A crooked smile to show whomever was up there—if anyone—that I had done it. I fell to my knees as my world went black.

Chapter Seventeen

L ight filtered through my eyelids, warm but intrusive. As I stir, the faint image of a fallen Trailblazer flickered in my mind, sending a jolt through my chest. My breath stuttered, and before I knew it, I lurched forward, nearly on my feet—until a firm hand pressed against my shoulder.

"Take it easy! You're not dead, and you're not in prison. You can thank Kalia for that," Cookie reassures.

"What? How did I—where are we?"

Cookie watched me quietly, letting my confusion spill into the open. "Safe house. Some old taxi station Wick had in mind."

I blinked, adjusting to my surroundings—a dark, cramped room, a lone mattress sprawled across the floor. A thin curtain covers the window, doing little to block out the daylight seeping through. The floor creaked beneath me, winter's chill creeping up through my soles. I tried to stand, but my body protested—aching shoulders, stiff knees, bruises deep enough to remind me of every second I have been out.

"How long has it been?"

"A day and a half." Cookie moved to the window, pulling back the curtain to let in more light. "The city's on a manhunt for 'the meta that took out Trailblazer.' He was their only line of defense against paranoia—at least, that's what the news says. It's kind of a big deal."

I swallowed hard. "Is he... dead?"

"Hmm, doesn't seem so. Apex announced the dickhead is in recovery."

"And Malcolm?"

Cookie smirked, but there's no humor in it. "No one's heard anything worth mentioning."

She winced, adjusting slightly. I noticed the way she cradles her side.

"How are you?" I asked.

Her expression was unreadable. She stared off for a moment before snapping back to reality. "The bleeding finally stopped... Good thing, too, because we don't do hospitals. The only thing keeping me distracted is Motley Crew and running their little magic school bus."

I slow blinked. "I don't know what's weirder—you babysitting or you knowing who Motley Crew is."

"You're so stupid," she laughed, shaking her head. "They're all brats. If they actually understood what human trafficking meant, they'd be making me breakfast every morning. Instead, they cry about everything—all the time. So annoying."

"Well, it's not like they have anywhere else to go." I paused. "Can we trace their origin?"

"It's not that simple. Some of these kids come from all over the world. Even parents around here could've had kids they were willing to give up. Legal implications and all."

"So, I guess they're stuck here until we figure something out," I said.

I pulled my shirt over my head, wincing as sore muscles protest the motion. Cookie types on her burner phone, her eyes trained on the window.

"What are you gonna do now?" I asked. "You're free, but it doesn't seem like you want to go home."

"I've been talking to Mom since I got out. She's happy to hear from me, but we can't risk a meeting... not yet, anyway." Cookie exhales, a small smile tugging at the corner of her lips. "But it feels good, ya know?"

I hesitate. "I'm happy for you."

She flicked her gaze back to me. "Where are you going? You still need to rest."

"There's something I need to do. I'll be back... Maybe."

"Well, you're gonna do whatever you want anyway. Stay warm."

Cookie tossed me a thick black and gray jacket, fur lining the inside. I pulled it on, zipping it halfway up, feeling grateful for the weight of fresh clothes.

"Thanks."

"Just don't get caught. Patrols are thicker than usual—they're all looking for a guy matching your description."

"Well, I did always want to be the popular kid at school," I joked, laughing despite the tension still clinging to my ribs. "Say, can I borrow your phone for a moment?"

Cookie closed her phone and hands it to me. My head still ached, memories foggy, but I push through, willing my mind to recall numbers I haven't used in far too long. My fingers typed something in.

The phone started to ring.

A familiar voice answered.

"Hello? Can I help you?" Grace said.

"It's me, Sis."

Silence lingered—an air of hesitation, thick enough to cut through.

Then—

"Oh, my gawd... You've been all over the news!"

"...Yeah."

"You jumped the Trailblazer—are you nuts?!" Grace's voice was sharp, filled with disbelief. I opened my mouth to cut in, but she kept going, her words tumbling out in frustration. "I knew there was a chance of you going feral, but not after just a few days!"

"I'm not going feral! Relax. And besides, Apex isn't what you think they are."

"Oh, bro, everyone knows they're crooked. 'Rehabilitating metas'? Please. We would've seen proof of that by now."

"Then why get so defensive over Trailblazer?"

"Because I don't want you to get hurt!"

Her words sat heavy between us, and for a moment, I didn't respond. The concern in her voice was real, but the reality of what had happened made her worry seem misplaced.

"Well, you don't have to worry too much. I'm safe. I have friends."

"...That's reassuring. Is that why you're calling me from an unknown number?"

I sighed, rubbing my forehead. "Sure, Sis. It has nothing to do with media propaganda demonizing me... And Grace—sorry. For everything."

"What do you mean?"

"I mean everything. From when we were kids. I should have been there for you more. Taken initiative. Maybe then... things could have been different."

"Ohh..." Her tone softened, uncertain. "Well, umm. We were kids, Charlie. There's nothing we should think that far back on."

I swallowed hard. "I was scared, Grace. Back then. But it's different now. If it came down to it, I'd never let that man take you again."

Silence stretched between us. I heard something muffled on the other end—a faint voice, something indistinct. When Grace returned, her voice was thick with emotion.

"That's... that's—Charlie, I can't get into this. It's too much. I'm glad you found something you can call change, but... I need to tell you something."

She cleared her throat.

"Grandma isn't doing well."

Everything inside me stilled.

"I was there yesterday," she continued, "and the doctors said she doesn't have much time."

The words sat between us, unspoken grief forming cracks in the conversation. I tried to speak—tried to say anything—but nothing came.

"She's in Saint Joseph's now." She inhaled deeply. "Hospice care. I'm sorry."

I kept quiet.

"I know she meant the world to you, and you're not able to see her now with your... situation. But maybe I can connect with you on video while I'm there. I'm going back tomorrow—bringing flowers, some of those statues she had in her house. The fire department was able to salvage a few. I want her room to feel more like home."

I fiddled with a bit of lint in my pocket, my mind drifting in circles. Cookie sat nearby, watching me without a word, her gaze flickering across the room as if she could sense the weight pressing against me.

Grace's voice came again, breaking through. "Charlie? Don't do that thing you always do. Say something. Anything. Are you angry? Sad? Confused? Say something!"

"I..." I coughed, forcing words through my throat. "I'll go see her."

"What do you mean, go see her?"

"I'll visit her."

"She's on the fourth floor of the hospital. Behind several locked gates. People are scanned in the lobby. You know this."

A shiver crawled across my shoulders, but I forced myself to breathe.

"I can try. I owe her that much."

"Charlie, it's stupid. You're just going to get yourself caught."

I hung up the phone and handed it back to Cookie.

"Good luck," she said simply.

I stepped onto the grated walkway above the garage, the metal groaning under my weight. The space stretched below—a mechanic's relic of a shop, dust-coated tools resting against stalls, Wick's GTO parked neatly beside an engine hoist. A handful of people moved through the space, cleaning the remnants of what had once been a working taxi station.

The air felt thick with energy. I wasn't sure if it was unease or something deeper.

A small figure dashed past me—quick, ghost-like. I jumped slightly, turning to find him, but he had already disappeared. Before I could dwell on it, a hand rested on my shoulder, sending a calm rippling through me.

I turned—and met a pair of slit-pupiled eyes staring dead into mine.

"Woah!" I stepped back, startled.

Kalia stood before me, somber and unreadable. She wore a long black fleece jacket, the hood pulled deep over her head, barely concealing the serpents writhing beneath.

I smiled faintly and stepped forward, wrapping my arms around her. She didn't react, but her serpents coiled over my shoulders, weaving themselves around me like silent witnesses. I pulled away after a moment.

"Get enough rest?" Kalia asked, her voice coated in mist.

"Maybe too much." My breath formed its own cloud.

"You put on quite a show. Don't expect to wake up safely the next time you go crying out for attention."

"Well, it got everyone out, didn't it?"

"...No. It didn't. We lost one during your retrieval."

The words hit harder than expected, sinking into me like stones.

Kalia lowered her head. "The one who could see through walls. The police shot him. We had to leave him behind."

My jaw slackened. I tried to speak, but nothing came out.

"Is... is he dead?"

Kalia held my gaze. "Who's to say? He got shot. That's all I know."

I nodded slowly, my thoughts twisting in on themselves, consuming me.

It was my fault.

So stupid.

I let this happen.

"Charlie! Come back." Kalia smacked me lightly. "It won't help sinking inside yourself. Targeting yourself. Just understand the consequences of your actions and seek to do better next time. What you're doing... It doesn't actually change anything."

I breathed deeply, trying to shake the voices in my mind loose. Kalia placed both hands on my shoulders and pressed her forehead against mine.

Her presence steadied me. I matched her breathing, letting the whispers inside my head dull.

A single image remained—my grandmother, standing in the archway of her house, unmoving.

You have to run, Charlie.

The archway flickered, catching fire—but I didn't pull away.

I stepped forward, wrapping my arms around the fading memory.

"I won't run," I whispered aloud.

The tension inside me cracked, releasing something heavy I hadn't realized I'd been holding. My shoulders straightened, my chest lifted. Kalia watched me, something genuine flickering in her gaze.

"Thank you," I said softly.

She nodded, then passed me on the walkway, murmuring as she left. "Don't be your own worst enemy. If it wasn't for you, more wouldn't have made it."

A quiet relief settled in.

I raised a hand, watching flickers of static dance between my fingertips. I clenched my palm. It felt warm. I slid my other hand along the railing, letting bolts arc into the metal.

Something had changed.

It didn't hurt anymore.

I gazed at the old clock posted above the dispatchers' office on the ground floor. Its steady ticking reminded me that darkness was still hours away. With a determined leap, I vaulted over the rail and landed softly on the cool concrete floor. A few nearby metas started at my sudden appearance—I paused long enough to offer a quiet, sincere apology before moving on.

At the entrance loomed a double door adorned with intricate, wood-carved impressions of twisting vines and clusters of grapes—an echo of times long past. The aged beauty of the door stirred something inside me: a bittersweet reminder of stability amid chaos. Then, a voice bellowed, cutting through my thoughts.

"Take de back door through the alley! We don't need unwanted attention because some asshole checked the mail!"

I turned to see Wick emerging from underneath his GTO, slowly climbing up from the creeper. With half-closed eyes and a knowing wrinkle on his nose, he surveyed me. After a brief pause, he wiped his hands on a nearby rag and said, "When you get back, there's work to be done. We need to check the generator, get the radios working, or find another way out—we can't let things stall here."

I couldn't help but ask, "What makes you think I'm coming back?"

A crooked smile played on his lips. "Heh," he replied. "No one runs off to play tag with the cops like you—playing the distraction—unless they're trying to save something." I shrugged, adding, "Or maybe I just walk out that door, mess it all up, and get caught." His laugh was soft and laced with amusement. "Fifty-fifty chance with you, honestly. But der's a good fight in ya yet."

Reaching into his pocket, Wick pulled out a neatly presented handgun. "Could use some backup, yeah?" he asked. I waved the firearm away with a resigned chuckle. "Naw, I'm good," I insisted, confident in my words despite the lingering uncertainty. "Then be quick with ya business," he urged, settling back down on the creeper. "The lot of them... a bloody hand full."

Before I could fully absorb his words, a sudden crash echoed from afar. When I looked, a ghost-like child—fleeting and ethereal—darted past, disappearing into a thin, lingering mist. That brief vision, fragile yet poignant.

As I turned back toward the door, I caught myself smiling wryly. "Stranger and stranger,"

Chapter Eighteen

There remained just a bit of overcast as the sun flashed an orange brilliance before it snuffed out. Good—It almost felt like home. I approached the hospital from the dark reaches of its property. From what Grace said, she was on the fourth floor somewhere. This place had one massive tower, and people were constantly going in and out of the entrance area. I couldn't walk in through the front. Someone would surely recognize me.

I looked along the building's structure and saw there were divots I could possibly use to climb. My hands and feet were charged, and with one deep breath I zipped to the edge of the building and leaped for an extended part of a ledge to the tower. I caught the edge of the second-floor roof and zipped across to the tower to do the same. Once I'd grabbed the window seal, checking windows wasn't an issue. I swung between each one and for the life of me I thought finding her would be easy. Some of the fourth-floor windows were closed or shaded. Others had to be avoided due to the current company in them. Visiting hours were still in effect. Finally, I came across one window with an angel statue positioned to look out the window. There were a few angelic statues in many windows, but this one was beat up with soot imprinted in the ceramic. It had chipped wings as well.

I paused, listening for any sign of movement inside. The soft murmur of a TV was the only clue. With a measured tug, I eased the window open. The lock gave way with a soft clatter as it rolled onto the floor, and I slipped inside. In my careful passage, my leg knocked over the damaged angel; instinctively, I caught it before it hit the ground and set it back on the windowsill.

Inside the room, the fluorescent glow revealed a single bed cradled in quiet solitude. Grandma lay there, surrounded by an array of pillows and a handmade blanket adorned with yellow squares and floral patterns—a piece once knitted long ago and later brought by Grace. The soft light of the TV traced gentle patterns over her face, deepening the lines that spoke of a long, cherished life.

I didn't want to wake her. Instead, I pulled up a chair next to her bed and sat there quietly. Shadows passed by from the door's view window, but I didn't pay them much mind. It was so dark in the room. The staff would be hard-pressed to see me from the hallway. I let my eyes wander over the muted TV screen—its shifting colors and soft energy a quiet counterpoint to the memories surging within me. I remembered distant afternoons spent together—sharing meals and sweet tea, sneaking hotdogs and candy into movie theaters, tending to her garden on warm summer days, and watching her delight as she plucked the first ripe tomato of the season.

A trembling voice broke through the silence. "I'm sorry..." I said.

Her eyes met mine, and I heard a gentle, fading question: "For what?"

Startled, I looked first toward the door, then back at the woman in the bed. She appeared thinner than I had remembered. Her eyes, deeper and more reflective, held me still; even as her once-bountiful brown hair had thinned, it still framed her face with a quiet dignity. I dragged a hand across my eyes, the unsaid words choking me.

"Nothing, Grandma. I just wish I'd been able to visit sooner."

"Well, you're here now." She struggled to clear her throat.

"Yes... I'm here," I replied softly. "Where have you been all this time?" she pressed, voice barely above a murmur. I hesitated. "I've... honestly, I don't know. So much has happened." A fragile smile traced her lips. "You can handle it. Whatever it is, we've always managed, haven't we?"

"We can still make it—just like before."

The old lady laughed and stuttered as she coughed. She looked at me with eyes wide and she shook as she held eye contact. "I wish I could've done some things different. Hopefully God will see it in another way."

"I'm sure God knows you're human. He'll love you just the same. And... You won't have to worry about me. I promise."

She smiled and shut her eyes as she settled in her bed. I reached for her hand on the bedside. She grasped my fingers and I held on. Her hands felt frail, and I could feel her pulse weakening.

"You can... Watch whatever you want on the TV."

"Anything in particular you want to listen to, Grandma?"

"It's... Whatever you want."

I nodded and then, after a moment, she added hesitantly, "Charlie?" "Yeah?" I replied, my voice barely a whisper. "I love you," she said.

"I love you, too."

In that quiet room, with the muted hum of a television and the tender press of her frail hand in mine, I understood.